OPERATION PARADISE

Sarah Evans

Clan Destine
PRESS

This edition published by Clan Destine Press in 2021
First published by Clan Destine Press in 2014

Clan Destine Press
PO Box 121, Bittern
Victoria, 3918 Australia

National Library of Australia Cataloguing-In-Publication data:

Sarah Evans

Operation Paradise

PB ISBN: 978-0-6450426-6-5
EB ISBN: 978-0-6450426-7-2

Cover artwork by © Willsin Rowe

Design & Typesetting by ClanDestine Press

Clan Destine
PRESS

www.clandestinepress.net

1

THE BLACK MINI SKIRT WAS COOL. THE RED SLUT HEELS WICKED. THE scarlet top would have been tastier cropped, though not on DS Fox. Even the perp would have baulked at the hairy belly button.

'You're looking cute, Foxy,' I said into the transmitter.

Foxy slung a hip over one shapely, spangle-stockinged leg and pouted.

'All the boys are hot,' I added for good measure.

Foxy held up an explicit finger.

'And you should show more respect towards a senior officer,' I said.

Even from this distance I could see his stance freeze, his lips working on a litany of silent curses. Fox then dipped his head and spoke into his cleavage. 'Sorry, boss. I thought you were one of the team.'

'I am. I've just come aboard. DI Eve Rock.'

'Welcome to Paradise, DI Rock,' said Fox.

That could have been a slick one liner but Fox was actually referring to Operation Paradise, a police operation launched to apprehend the person or gang abducting young women from the Paradise Nightclub. I'd been seconded to help head the operation. This was my first day.

'Thanks, Foxy,' I said. 'Good luck and careful you don't snag a stocking.'

'Yeah, right.'

I terminated radio contact and leaned against the wall, gazing down at the street corner where DS Fox was strutting his stuff. I was in one of the top rooms of an office building that was directly opposite the purple-painted Paradise Nightclub. The guys had been camping in this room for a couple of days and it was already a festering tip. Fast food wrappers spilled over from the bins and half-drunk cups of cold, scummy coffee littered every available surface. The air was stale with sweat and old pizza. It made my blood zing, causing my heart to shift up a beat or three. I love surveillance. It's a buzz.

But the ultimate is catching the crooks. That's better than sex. Even better than chocolate, and that's saying something. But right now, a box of Belgian shells would've had the edge. We had nothing to go on and time was ticking on. DI Sodbury was the investigating officer but he'd hit dirt and I'd been seconded from the suburbs to lend a helping hand, much to his disgust. It was a Wednesday before the long weekend's revelry and the Chief didn't want any more girls going missing. Abduction took the shine off holiday jollies.

So far three women had disappeared in a fortnight. Thankfully no bodies had surfaced, though that wasn't to say they wouldn't. I'd read the case reports just that morning. There was, as yet, no common denominator between the women, except they were young. Whoever was abducting them didn't seem to mind if they were fat, thin, blonde or brunette.

I didn't hold out much hope of Fox leading us to the abductor. Neither did Sodbury. It was the one and only thing we'd agreed on since I'd met him at the briefing.

Sodbury was one of those precious dinosaurs who believed a woman's place was in the home, barefoot, pregnant and preferably wearing slinks. He was late fifties with thin sandy hair holding on to a balding scalp for dear life, small, beady eyes that continuously flicked back and forth, a cauliflower nose and slack-lipped mouth. No Mr Universe and not my type by a thousand-fold, but that didn't stop him being a good solid copper.

Sodbury and I were told that Fox was an excellent undercover officer who knew the seedier side of life. The deskbound superiors reckoned it was worth having him on the ground floor, saving them the hassle of having a woman cop in the firing line. I didn't agree. The firing line was why I'd joined the force, but who was I to argue the toss? I'd learned the hard way to keep my mouth shut on these smaller skirmishes. It was the overall war that mattered.

I trained powerful binoculars on Fox. He was getting some grief from the local tarts who thought he was poaching their punters. Some hope. He said something to them and the next minute the women were slapping their bare thighs and laughing loud. Fox turned slightly sideways and I zoomed in on his impressive bosom. It was firm and fruity. He must have borrowed a D-cup bra from a well-upholstered WPC and stuffed it with a lush pair of grapefruit.

'Damn but he makes a tasty chick,' said Burton, one of the surveillance officers. The brown-haired cop, who at a guess was in his mid-thirties, was already running to fat due to the lifestyle of too many stakeouts. 'He beats those old broilers hands down.'

'You interested, Burton?' said Ely, another officer. He was younger, thinner and darker. He grinned. 'I could set you up.'

'Get out of here.' Burton slung a chewed apple core at Ely who ducked effortlessly. They'd obviously done this routine before.

'What's Fox like?' I asked them once the horseplay subsided and Burton had his eyes screwed to the binoculars again.

'Private,' said Ely with a shrug. 'Keeps to himself. Spends most of his time undercover.'

'Trustworthy?'

'Absolutely. He's as squeaky as they come.'

The tarts were soon speeding off in customers' cars and Fox moved back into the shadows. He did the cleavage talk thing again.

'I'm going inside to have a look around.' His voice was crackly and distorted over the wire. 'Don't contact me unless it's an absolute emergency.'

'Ten-four, good buddy,' said Ely sounding like some Yankee truck driver. He'd be wittering on about rubber ducks next.

Half an hour later Fox reappeared on the arm of a burly dark bearded man. The man dwarfed Fox as he steered him towards a sleek silver Rover. The car was one of those sporty types that make me salivate. Burton jotted down the number plate and called it over the radio for owner confirmation.

Ely was listening to Fox through the earphones. His shoulders began to shake.

'Watch this,' he mouthed, waving us to the window.

We looked out. The passenger door flew open and Fox was tossed from the car. He tumbled on to the pavement, all sprawled legs and spangled stockings. One of the slut heels tumbled into the gutter. Poor Cinders. Prince Charming had bombed out. The Rover shot off and Fox cussed into his D-cups while scrabbling about on all fours, retrieving his dinky sequinned handbag and spike shoe.

'Bloody bloke thought I was a tranny!' he gibbered.

'No, really?' I said. 'I wonder where he got that idea?'

'This is not working, boss. I feel too vulnerable like this.'

'Now you know how half the population feels, Fox.'

You could feel the simmering heat melting the radio contact as Fox fought to control his annoyance.

'Point taken,' he said finally.

'You can take five and change your stockings. We've a spare pair of fishnets up here.'

'I can't wait.'

'Nor me.' I couldn't resist a chuckle.

My mobile phone rang just as the show was getting interesting. I would have carried on perving as Fox peeled off his laddered spangles if the caller hadn't been my daughter Chastity on the line. Muscular male thighs and sweet sixteen daughters do not mix. Believe it or not, I do have some integrity.

'Hi, Mum,' she chirruped. 'Thought I'd better remind you about parents' night.'

Parents' night! Grief. I hated parents' nights. Half the teachers made me feel I was ten again and a complete moron, while the others tried to avoid eye contact because they'd been nicked for something.

'As if I'd forget,' I lied.

Since my latest promotion, Chastity had attended boarding school, the theory being I wouldn't have to worry about getting home every night, keeping up with the laundry and putting hot dinners on the table. It also meant I didn't have anyone updating the calendar.

'It's tonight.'

It was? Damn.

'I'm in the middle of an operation.' It was a valid excuse. I didn't have to go. I had an abductor to catch. Infinitely preferable to sitting opposite a bunch of arrogant, smart aleck teachers discussing my shortcomings as a parent.

'You had forgotten! You weren't going to come and this is my first parents' night at Saint Immaculata's.' Sixteen years of emotional blackmail punched down the line.

My heart sank. I was a sucker where my daughter was concerned. She knew which buttons to press, and how.

'You want me there, I'll be there.'

'I want you there.'

'So I'll organise something.'

Look, I'd named my daughter Chastity in the vain hope she'd be smarter than me. And actually she was. Hey, a win!

And my mother had named me Eve. Why? Because of the original sin. But that ploy hadn't been quite so successful. Like my mother, I'd fallen pregnant after a one-night stand. Though in my case it had been a torrid weekend, but same difference. It goes without saying I hadn't seen the worthless Romeo again. My luck with men was abysmal, unless they were crooks and I was banging them to rights. This adds up to a social life as barren as the Simpson Desert. But that didn't mean I'd rather attend a painful parents' night than stay at home twiddling my thumbs, so I said goodbye to Chastity, then cursed as I stashed away my phone.

'Problems, chief?' said Burton.

'Nah.' Rule number one in the professional battle of the sexes: Never admit weakness. Never tell them when the Achilles heel of family life is pierced. 'Did you get a fix on the bloke with the Rover?'

'Yeah, he's a divorce lawyer. Leo Stark. Clean as far as a criminal record goes.'

'I doubt if he's the one we're looking for,' said Fox.

I turned to the young officer. He was taller than I'd calculated when seeing him on the street. Probably six foot without the red heels. He was rail thin, blond and cherubic and he easily cast Brad Pitt into the shade. Dreamy blue eyes were skilfully made-up with black eyeliner and mascara. Cherry lipstick emphasised his curved, full lips and made them look extremely kissable. I involuntarily licked my own. As Burton had said, Fox made one tasty chick.

I reached out and ran my fingertips over Fox's chin. It was firm, smooth and sleek. Not a hint of stubble, but I felt like teasing.

'Better shave,' I murmured. 'Don't want you giving the punters bristle rash.'

His blue eyes, no longer dreamy but deliciously steamy, held mine for a spine-tingling second. A pulse jack-hammered at the base of his exposed throat. I resisted, just, the temptation to place a finger there too, because, hey, it wouldn't have been professional.

'Yes, boss,' he said and spun away to rummage in a black sports bag for his razor.

'Why don't you think the Rover bloke is our suspect?' I said, admiring the view of his scarlet, Lurex-clad back.

'Didn't have the right smell.' He drew out the razor and clicked it on, running it over that dimpled jaw while he twisted back to face me.

I raised my brows and flicked a glance at the other two officers. Ely was eyeballing the street, but Burton had been watching our exchange. He shrugged and didn't offer an opinion. I turned back to Fox.

'Can you expand on that?'

'Not really. Just my gut instinct says he's clean.' He kept on shaving.

'And this instinct has been honed how, exactly?'

Fox snapped off the razor and gave me a bland stare.

'From my years on the street,' he said.

'Spare me. You haven't been a cop that long. You still reek of baby powder and teething rusks.'

He offered a tight, humourless smile, as if I'd hit a nerve.

'For your information, DI Rock, I did have a life before I joined the police force.'

'And it's this previous life that honed your sense of er… smell?'

'Yes.'

'I see.' My curiosity was piqued but now wasn't the time to pursue the subject. 'So we go with the smell?'

I wasn't convinced.

'Don't forget my gut instinct.'

My eyes automatically dropped to his flat belly, shown to beauteous advantage in the scarlet stretch top. It was perfect, but did it mean it was a foolproof crime-o-metre? Hmm. But I decided to give him the benefit of the doubt. At least for now.

'Okay. You're entitled to your opinion. But we'll do a follow up on him anyway.'

'Yes, boss.'

'Get back to your beat as soon as you're done.'

'Yes, boss.'

My eyes narrowed and I stared at his mild, angelic countenance. I wasn't sure if there was a lot going on behind that sweet face. Perhaps I'd been landed with a dud.

Or perhaps not.

It struck me that I could have a lot of fun finding out, now that Chastity wasn't home to cramp my style. I might miss having her around since she moved to St Immaculata's, but there was an upside to the arrangement. It meant I could indulge my addiction for red wine, Indian takeaways and cigars without Chastity – my very own Jiminy Cricket – ticking me off for my bad habits. Now there was a little ray of sunshine on an otherwise bleak home front.

The school hall was already packed. I was late by a good thirty minutes. Not bad considering my usual track record.

Chastity was nowhere in sight. I scanned the crowd. It teemed with Stepford Wives and my heart sank. I'd come straight from the stakeout in my bomber jacket, jeans and sneakers, still reeking from the chicken tikka and chapatis I'd shared with the boys. But perhaps I should have made the effort because the other mums were wearing classy clothes, high heels and expensive jewellery. Hair was coiffed, nails buffed and teeth were dazzling in their perfection. I ran my tongue over mine and hoped there were no lurking tikka spices lodged between the pearlies.

I then wondered about the state of my hair. When had I last brushed it? Not since this morning's shampoo and shower? Maybe. And that was hours ago. Best not think about it. Anyway, no one would notice in the scheme of things.

'Mum! Oh no, what have you done to your hair?'

Then again, there's always Chastity to keep one grounded.

'I haven't done anything to it.' I went to give Chastity a hug but she held me at arm's length.

'That's obvious.'

'Don't be rude. It's clean. What more do you want?'

'For you to be properly dressed for once. You look like that seventies cop.'

'Starsky? Great. I'll take that as a compliment. So what's the problem?'

Chastity did an exasperated eye roll.

'And you reek of garlic and something else…?'

Her nose twitched.

'You've had a curry. And a smoke! You said you were going to stop. Honestly, Mum.'

'Hey, can it! Are you glad to see me or not? I had to move mountains to get here tonight. I came straight from work.'

'Sorry, Mum. Of course I'm pleased to see you. Look, I've booked which teachers we have to see so we won't waste time.' My super-organised daughter handed me a printed list.

'So we do this thing together?'

'New policy.'

'Excellent.' At least I could hide my inferiority behind her straight-A brilliance.

First cab off the rank was Chastity's chemistry teacher. She was an attractive woman and would have been stunning if ever Sister Immaculata relaxed her stance on habit wearing. But she wouldn't. That wasn't the Iron Nun's style. Other church schools had slung out the habits and put a more hip spin on proceedings, but Sister Immaculata ran this joint with ramrod efficiency and discipline hailing from the dark ages. Which was one of the reasons why her school was so popular.

In her serene, low voice, Sister Mercy praised Chastity for her diligence and flair and mentioned all the extra time my daughter spent in the laboratory.

'Since when did you develop a love of science?' I whispered to Chastity as we moved on to the mathematics teacher. She just grinned, her eyes gleaming. Was I missing something here? A schoolgirl crush maybe? It could be worse, I suppose. Drugs, rock and roll, disastrous boyfriends. But no, she wasn't me. Chastity was far too smart for that.

We were about half way through a particularly bad grilling by Sister Immaculata, the Iron Nun herself, about my lack of moral example when there was a stir at the entrance.

A tall willowy blond stood in backlit splendour. His jeans were scruffier than mine and he was shrugged into a battered American Air Force jacket I coveted instantly. I'd swear there was a collective sigh from all the women in the hall, including my prudish daughter.

Good, there was hope for her yet.

A cloud of schoolgirls hovered in muted hysteria around the golden Raphael angel. He ignored them and silently, methodically scanned the hall until his gaze fixed on me. Heat suffused me in all the interesting places as I suffered a jolt of recognition: Fox.

Grief, what was he doing here?

He began to walk towards me, using the same slow, measured stride Clint Eastwood had used in the Spaghetti Westerns. Very macho. Very effective. I went from feeling like the mother from

Planet Disaster to the high school belle in a nanosecond. My kudos rose with every deliberate step trod by Fox.

His face remained beautifully bland as he apologised to Sister Immaculata for the unavoidable interruption. She actually simpered and blushed. Yuk. It wasn't pretty. Fox then smiled sweetly at Chastity before turning his attention to me.

'Can I have a word, DI Rock?' he said.

I vowed there and then he could have whatever he wanted. He'd made my night by establishing my street-cred and shutting-up the steely-spined nun who'd been reading me my rights as a parent.

Let me explain about Sister Immaculata. She'd founded the all-girls school after having a vision to educate girls in an environment of high moral calibre. And she didn't let you forget it, not for one single, sinful second.

How do I know this?

Because she's also my mother.

She'd had me before the call to sainthood, while she was still working the streets.

Falling pregnant with me put a stop to her nocturnal career and made her do some serious reality checking. It was so serious she turned her back on the dozen-men-a-night habit to embrace celibacy and a totally different sort of habit. I should be grateful.

I think.

Anyway, Sister Immaculata now reluctantly agreed we could use her office. Fox and I followed her stumpy, penguin-like figure. I was conscious of a hundred envious eyes as Fox and I walked side by side, both in our tight jeans and creaking leather. Eat your hearts out, Stepford Wives.

'Well, Fox, this better be good.' I said, acting tough as the disapproving nun closed the door on us.

A slight smile hovered around his lips, lips that were now free of lipstick and still extremely kissable. His eyes held traces of mascara, which I confess I found deliciously attractive, especially when they crinkled at the corners.

'You've had a long day, guv. I thought you could do with an early night,' said Fox. He didn't bat one angelic eyelid. He was acting cool to freezing. And I was goose-bumping everywhere to prove it.

But his baby blues were hot.

The smell of tikka, cigar smoke and leather clung about us. I decided on a rapid assessment.

'What sort of car do you drive, Fox?'

'Spitfire.'

That swung it. I love fast cars.

And leather.

And hot, hot, HOT baby blues.

'Give me half an hour,' I said. 'And we'll shoot through.'

'But you can't go yet,' wailed Chastity. 'You've only just got here. It's because of that cute guy, isn't it?'

'He's a police officer and I have work to do.' I tried not to focus on the statue of Our Lady just behind Chastity's head. I was already feeling guilty as hell. I didn't need anything else to prick my shaky conscience.

'I don't believe you.'

'Chastity!'

'And you haven't even seen my room.'

'Let's do it now, but make it quick.'

We jogged down the corridors, my sneakers squeaking on the highly polished tiles while her neat, low heels clickety-clacked.

Her room was tidy. No surprise there. Chastity was always tidy. I sometimes wondered if I'd picked up the wrong baby at the hospital. If it weren't for our replica mops of red hair, I'd go for a DNA match.

Chastity tries to tame hers into a civilised style. I let mine corkscrew to kingdom come. We also have similar wide, brown eyes. Not a lot you can do with those, except mine are sometimes a little bloodshot after a bender and hers sparkle all the time. She puts it down to the huge quantities of water she drinks. That wouldn't suit my system in a fit. I need the roughage of red wine and tobacco to bolster me for the job.

Chastity's walls were a jarring note in the clutter-less room. They were covered in a multitude of slogans. Some were about healthy living, such as giving up smoking and drinking and saying no to drugs. Others stated the body was a temple of Christ and to treat it accordingly. There was a lot about celibacy and the like.

Okay, I was proud of my little girl and wished I could be as morally highbrow. But not yet. Not with a leather-clad Fox in a Spitfire. Some things were just too, too tempting.

'Are the other girls into all this,' I said, waving a hand at the notices. Some had a red and gold double 'V' emblem stamped on them.

'Pretty much. We thought we would launch a crusade to encourage other girls to think twice before using drink and drugs,' said Chastity, her eyes glazing with fanatical fervour as she beheld a vision of her own making. I recognised that look. I got it too, but for other, more earthy reasons.

'What do the two V's stand for?'

'You don't want to know.' She giggled, blushed and then hustled me out. 'You'd better go before that yummy young cop comes searching.'

'Hey, not so fast. When did you go in for black sequins?' I held up a little black, sparkly dress that'd been hanging on the back of the door next to Chastity's chaste pink fluffy dressing gown.

'It belongs to my room-mate.' She held my eyes, daring me to call her bluff. As if I would. I trusted my daughter. Most of the time.

'I'm surprised Sister Immaculata allows outfits like these. She didn't in my day.'

'It's just for dressing up,' said Chastity. 'No big deal.'

I should've known better. My daughter doesn't deign to undertake anything that's not important. But my sensors didn't pick up the discordant note. Blame the hormones. They were focusing on something completely different.

And that something was waiting outside…

2

'ANOTHER WOMAN WAS TAKEN LAST NIGHT,' SAID SODBURY AT THE next day's morning briefing. His small, close-set eyes were doing their agitated flicking routine.

'How come we've a missing person report after only a few hours?' I asked. 'She might just have gone off with someone for the night.'

Sodbury shuffled the papers on the desk and zeroed in on the relevant page.

'She was with another girl. They'd been having a drink at the bar and then she went to the toilet. When she didn't return, her friend went to look for her. She couldn't find her, so raised the alarm.'

'You were watching the club the whole time?'

'Yeah, Rock, all the damn time.' He sounded belligerent, as if I was accusing him of incompetence. I wasn't. I just wanted facts.

'And you didn't see anyone being forced into a car or looking drugged?'

'No. Nothing suspicious happened at all. Just a usual night out on the town.' Sodbury frowned savagely, as if the world was ganging up against him. 'I can't understand why we didn't see anything. We had both exits covered.'

I ignored his burst of anger.

'What do we know about this girl?'

'Roberta Fellows, known as Bobbie. She's eighteen and apparently very attractive. She's studying at uni to be a teacher, lives in student digs and her parents are well off.'

'Like the others,' murmured Fox.

'What?' said Sodbury.

'Just thinking aloud,' said Fox.

'Who was her friend?' I asked Sodbury. 'I'll go and see her. You never know, I might turn up something.'

Sodbury furnished me with details. I glanced at the name: Maria Dellaporte. I'd seen that name somewhere recently but couldn't for the minute recall.

Burton and Ely went back on surveillance duty while Fox and I drove out to see Maria at her family's home in one of the upwardly mobile western suburbs. We talked for a while, but Maria gave us little to go on. But as we were leaving I suddenly remembered where I'd seen the Dellaporte name before.

It had been on the door of my daughter's room at Saint Immaculata's. Angelina Dellaporte was Chastity's roommate, and the owner of the snazzy dress.

'Hey, Maria,' I said. 'Do you have a sister at Saint Immaculata's by any chance?'

'Yes, Angie,' she said. 'Bobbie and I went there too.'

I showed her the list of names of the other missing women and we finally hit jackpot.

'Hallelujah!' I said to Fox as we drove back to the station.

'So they went to the same school but not at the same time,' he said. 'And some left ages ago. So where does that get us?'

'Further ahead than we were.' But I could tell he was sceptical. I ignored it. 'Let's go and rattle Sister Immaculata's cage, you never know what we might turn up.'

A few minutes later we were in the Iron Nun's office. She was sitting behind her desk and we were standing. I was going for the psychological advantage. Every little bit helped in dealings with my mother.

'Sasha Lucas, Monique Dewson, Ashleigh Johnson and now Roberta Fellows. Do these names ring a bell?' I asked.

'They are former students,' said Sister Immaculata with calm deliberation.

'And?'

'What else do you want me to say?'

'Anything that might help my investigation.'

'Investigation?' She looked at me blankly.

'Hello! You do know these women are missing?'

'Are they?'

'It's been plastered over the media.'

'You know I don't read the newspapers, Eve.' Her voice held gentle reproach and made me want to gnash my teeth.

Instead, I sighed and plonked myself down on one of the hard-backed chairs next to the desk. To hell with psychological advantages. They rarely worked with the Iron Nun anyway.

'Okay,' I said. 'These women have gone missing over the past couple of weeks. They were last seen at the Paradise Nightclub. There's been no trace of them since. Is there anything these girls had in common? Anything that links them together?'

Sister Immaculata's glasses glinted so that it was impossible to read any expression in her eyes. I was never sure if this was a deliberate ploy or not but it was effective all the same.

'They were all high achieving students.' She folded her lips and her hands and gazed at me, serenely.

'That's it?'

She smiled and remained silent so I carried on fishing.

'Were they friends? In the same class?'

'No.'

I huffed. Angels had more luck turning stones into bread than me getting information out of my nun mum. Everything with her was on a need to know basis. I'd always had to pump hard to get any pertinent facts and even then the information wasn't always forthcoming. Like, who was my father? And did he know I existed? You know, fundamental stuff.

I stood up and made to leave.

'If you think of anything, let me know,' I tossed over my shoulder as we made for the door.

'You didn't give her one of your business cards,' said Fox as we strode down one of the lengthy, polished wood corridors.

'No need. She knows my number.'

'I forgot. Your kid goes to the school.'

That was one reason. I wasn't ready to share that the Sister Theresa look-alike was my mum. The knowledge might put him off his stride, and we didn't want that, now, did we?

Our next stop was the Paradise Nightclub. It was just before their noon opening time and the previous night's debris were being cleared up, bars restocked and floors mopped and polished. Where the outside was hideous purple, the inside wasn't much better, just darker and seedier. It wasn't my idea of paradise at all.

We interviewed the club owner, Stan Zefferelli, over a cheap instant coffee served in a polystyrene cup. Classy.

Zefferelli was barrel-chested, beer-bellied and wore his dirty blond hair long with Elvis Presley-style sideburns. He walked like a duck on heat and had the nasty habit of scratching his crotch and juggling with the family jewels. He wore saggy black trackie pants with holes in the rear and a floppy T-shirt that once upon a time must have been white. It sported the faded legend that Paradise Sucked. I presumed he was referring to the club and I heartily agreed with him.

He seemed unconcerned about the missing girls but stroppy his club was the focus of a police op.

'It's bad for business,' he said and gave us a circus-standard juggling performance before taking a slurp of coffee. 'You guys will give the place the kiss of death if you hang around for too long.'

'Aren't you worried women seem to be disappearing from your club?' I said.

'People disappear all the time. It's no big deal. It hasn't put off the punters. But you will.'

'Forget it. We're not leaving until we discover what's going on. These girls weren't the type to simply go walkabout.'

Zefferelli's lip curled. He gave me a suggestive up and down.

'Never been tempted to go off with a bloke for some hot sex?' he said. 'Or are you a dyke?'

I ground my teeth and resisted the urge to dismantle his juggling act. One swift kick would have done it. Or point blank range with my .38 Smith and Wesson. But I resisted. I'm a professional.

And, anyway, he did have a point about the slinking off for some hot sex. Wasn't that how I ended up with Chastity? Four days on a boat with a blond hunk I'd picked up at a party.

In my defence, it was before I understood about safe sex, stranger danger or slip, slop, slap. So hey, I was a late developer. Who wouldn't have been with a harlot-turned-zealot nun as a mum? I met the skipper of *Wild Thing* and the rest was history. Your protected, naive convent girl went overboard. Literally.

Could the same sort of thing have happened here with these convent-raised girls? But three of them had been missing for a while so it didn't seem likely.

Apart from that, Fox and I learned absolutely zilch from Zefferelli. I decided we'd revisit the club that night and be part of the action. Perhaps we'd missed something vital.

I took Fox, as he'd got to know the layout pretty well. And with him looking so good in his spangles, there was the chance we might strike lucky and get a pick up by the perp.

We got there late and struggled through the Thursday night crowd. You'd think there was no place else to go in Perth on a steamy Thursday night. Heck, these people needed to get a life. I did a double take when I thought I saw Sister Mercy, sans habit. But I must have been hallucinating. No way would a nun trip the Light Fantastic in a sleazy joint like the Paradise. I resolved once I'd cracked the case, I would take a long holiday. And perhaps ease up on the caffeine.

Fox and I sat at the bar and tried to look as though we were having a good time. It wasn't hard. Fox was an easy companion. Hey, isn't my job a bitch?

'Tell me about your days on the street, before you joined the force,' I said to him.

Fox shrugged.

'There's nothing to tell.'

'Don't give me that.'

'I was like a lot of kids. Hung around the streets. Slept rough. Occasionally went home for a meal.'

'You have a family, then.'

'Mum and Dad split up before I was born. Mum married some corporate climber on the second time round. I was always the step-kid with the attitude. His kids could do no wrong. Then Mum and this bloke had a couple of their own.'

'A big blended family. Nice.'

Fox gave me one of his bland, dreamy blue looks.

'You could say that. It had its moments.'

I empathised. I might not have had stepsiblings but I'd had an entire school full of companions. The fact I hadn't kept in touch with any of them showed what a loner I was. Maybe Fox was a loner too.

'So what about your dad?'

'When he was in town we would get together.'

'Nice.'

'He wasn't in town much.'

'Oh.'

'But it was good when he was.' A glimmer of a smile played around his painted lips. His luscious painted lips. I resisted the urge to fan myself. Surely I was too young to have hot flashes so it must be something else.

Not wanting to go down that road, I changed the subject: 'So how come you joined the police?'

'Well-defined sense of right and wrong. I was witness to it all the time growing up. I thought I could make a difference.'

'Noble.'

'Stupid. I don't feel as though I've achieved much.'

'But you've done a heap of undercover stuff. You must be good.'

'A few lucky breaks. Good contacts. I don't feel quite so confident running around in this gear.'

'You look gorgeous.' I chuckled and he grimaced.

It's an unwritten rule of mine never to sleep with anyone on my team. This rule has been easy to abide by over the years because, when surrounded with men like Sodbury, Burton and Ely, one can resist without trouble.

But now here was Fox. In a league of his own, he was totally another matter. It was going to be hard resisting such a ripe peach.

And I hadn't been joking. He was gorgeous, either dressed in jeans and leathers or in slinks and sequins. It was enough to send my taste buds roaring. There was a definite zing in the air when he was around, and it wasn't just due to the apple-scented shampoo he favoured. But I didn't think I'd be wise to react to it. Best wait until we were both off the case and I could relax my self-imposed rule. I had standards...

We sat there for an hour or so, downing orange juices and tonic waters until our bellies were squealing in protest at the acid overload.

'I'm off to the john,' said Fox, sashaying off in his hot pink number. He was one mean sister. And I must say, I didn't think I scrubbed up half bad in my little black shift. If we didn't get a nibble tonight I'd have to do a serious rethink of our wardrobes. Maybe our cup sizes were too small to make much impact.

Actually, no. Mine was insignificant, but Foxy's D-cups were priceless.

I fiddled with the purple and white Paradise beer mat, flicking it over and over and catching it mid-air as I watched Fox wiggle away. I'd have to tell him his trip to the bathroom was causing all the men to drool. I admit I was doing a little drooling myself which caused me to bungle a catch.

As I retrieved the fallen beer mat from the floor, I glanced at its Paradise logo. It had been defaced. What a surprise. But then I looked harder. On the flipside was drawn a double 'V' in biro. It was an imitation of the design I'd seen in Chastity's room. Hmm. So some of the Immaculata girls hung out here. I should have a word with the Iron Nun. It wasn't a place I wanted my Chastity frequenting.

I nursed my drink and scanned the heaving mob of hyped-up young things gyrating on the dance floor. And then I saw it. A sparkly black sequinned frock. Now, there were probably hundreds of these dresses sold around the city, but I'd seen this one hanging on the back of my daughter's bedroom door.

The woman wearing it was young and slim with gelled hair a mass of ringlets. Red ringlets. Red ringlets like my daughter's red ringlets.

Chastity!

Maternal ire raised its ugly head, swift and sharp. What the heck was Chastity doing in a dump like this? I jumped off the bar stool and elbowed my way through the throng of sweaty bodies to find out. Progress was slow, mainly because I'm better off wearing sneakers than stilettos, but also because the dancers were too engrossed to notice me and get out my way. By the time I'd shoved into the middle of the dancers, there was no sign of her.

I spent the next few minutes circling the floor but my daughter, if indeed it was she, had disappeared. But I wasn't giving up. I'd head for the school, go up to her room and find out if Chastity was there or not. I didn't want my baby hanging out in nightclub dives and I certainly didn't want her at the Paradise where women were being abducted on a regular basis.

But where was Fox when you needed him? Probably still negotiating his stockings in the ladies.

I headed back to my seat at the bar to wait. I was angsty, tapping my fingers impatiently on the counter when someone nudged me in the ribs and began burbling on about somebody's drink. She then slapped her hand over her mouth.

'Sorry,' she squeaked. 'I thought you were a friend of mine. You look similar.'

'Do I?' I couldn't help but wonder who she'd mistaken me for, what with a Chastity clone pirouetting about on the dance floor. But before I could ask, the girl slipped off the bar stool and merged with the crowd.

Fox appeared at my shoulder at last.

'Sorry, Eve, there was a queue.'

'Always is, for the ladies,' I said. 'Come on, we're leaving.'

'But why? The night's young.'

'I have parental responsibilities. But if you want to stay, feel free.'

'I'm disappointed.' Those blue eyes shimmered. 'I thought we could chat some more, then dance.'

'I presume you meant us, to dance together?'

Those eyes shimmered some more and that enigmatic Madonna smile played around those kissy, kissy lips.

'Sorry, Foxy,' I said. 'But I'm no dyke, regardless of what Zefferelli insinuated. See ya later.'

'What?' He frowned, confused.

'Just look at you, kid!'

He glanced down at his dress.

'Damn,' he said. 'I'd forgotten I was wearing this stuff. I'll come with you.'

'I'm seriously worried about you,' I murmured as we negotiated our way through the crowd to the exit. 'If wearing a dress is beginning to feel normal.'

We briefly called into the surveillance room to let the others know what was happening and for Fox to change. I told him not to bother on my account, but he did anyway.

'You splitting already?' said Ely around a mouthful of half-chewed pepperoni pizza.

'Have to,' I said. 'I've got to track down my daughter. I think she was at the nightclub.'

Burton whistled.

'Doesn't she know about the abductions? Doesn't she read the papers?'

'I don't know what she knows, but I'm going to warn her off. I don't want Chastity becoming a victim.'

'Chastity. Great name. Will you tell her about the surveillance?' asked Ely.

'No. I don't believing in sharing my work with her.'

'We'll take my car if you like,' said Fox once we were back on the street.

'Twist my arm, why don't you,' I said and made a beeline for the Spitfire. If ever I had spare dosh, I'd be tempted to buy myself a cute little number like that.

Tucked cosily in the low-slung sports-car, we roared over to Saint Immaculata's, beating red lights all the way.

'Stay here,' I ordered Fox once we had pulled into the deserted parking lot and he'd killed the engine. 'This is personal. I'll deal with it on my own.'

I let myself in through the kitchen and used the staff stairs at the rear of the school building. Saint Immaculata's was built as a private mansion by one of the Kalgoorlie gold barons back in the 1890s. It had survived the 1980s purge on old buildings and was a grandiose white elephant, impractical but stately and perfectly suited as an old-fashioned style school.

It had been the only home I'd known until I'd spread my Dodo wings and hit the ground running to escape the cloistered strictness my mother demanded. I liked the old place, sort of. Few fond memories but it had still been home.

Once inside, I took off my stilettos. I didn't want to announce my unauthorised entry by staccato-ing over the miles of polished floorboards.

When I reached Chastity's room, I hesitated. Should I knock? It had gone midnight and I didn't want to wake her if she'd been tucked up in bed all night. But there again, it had looked awfully like Chastity out there on the nightclub dance floor. I decided not to take any chances.

I stealthily began to turn the doorknob. There was a slight scuffled noise from behind me. I turned to see what it was when something arced down and cracked me on the head.

There was a violent starburst and everything went black.

3

Consciousness returned and I realised I was flat on my back on the floor.

'It's your mum,' said a young girl's voice. It was hushed, with a hard edge of panic, and came from somewhere to the right of my shoulder. As lightning strobes decorated the inside of my eyelids, I reckoned someone had a torch trained on me and was checking me over for vital signs.

'Have you killed her?' asked another girl, this time to my left.

'No.' I recognised that voice. Chastity. She sounded confident and assured. 'I didn't hit her hard enough to kill.'

She'd been the one who'd decked me? Where had she learned a self-defence tactic like that? Heavens, I should have paid more attention to her new curriculum. I wasn't ready to confess my conscious state. I stayed still, eyes closed, letting the throb of pain buy me time.

'Shall we get Sister Immaculata?' said the first girl. I thought it could have been Angie Dellaporte, Chastity's roommate.

'Not yet. Let's see if we can bring her round,' said Chastity. 'Mum? Mum? Can you hear me?'

She shook my shoulder, hard.

'What's going on here?' This new voice was all authoritative male. I could feel my insides tingle just at the sound of him. Fox had joined the proceedings. Excellent.

Someone clicked on the corridor light and Fox must have seen me in all my glory. Legs askew, rucked hem, possibly a pool of blood under my head and dribble of saliva on my chin.

'DI Rock! Eve! What have you done to her?' His roar of outrage was nice. I can't remember the last time someone on the force actually cared if I got hurt or not. He must have crouched down next to me because I was suddenly breathing in the scent of his apple shampoo. The next moment his hands were on my head, gently searching for wounds.

'I hit her. I thought she was an intruder,' said my daughter with self-righteousness indignation. I'd swear she could make murder sound justified. It's a skill she's honed over her sixteen short years.

'Ouch!' I said as Fox found a bump the size of a walnut at the back of my skull.

'Sorry, Eve.' His hands dropped. One landed on my bare leg where my little black number had ridden up even further with the action. He rhythmically rubbed his palm backwards and forwards.

Ooo, ooo. Now it wasn't just my insides tingling.

'You're awake!' said Chastity, cutting through my sudden fog of lust. 'Thank goodness.'

'No thanks to you. What in heavens name did you hit me with?'

'My hockey stick. Sorry Mum.'

'Do you hit everyone who happens to pass by?' I was still prone, preferring the steady hardness of the floor to the erratic spinning of my head.

'Only when I think they're up to no good,' she declared. 'What were you doing skulking around the dormitories in the middle of the night?'

'I was coming to check on you.'

'I'm not a baby anymore.' There was that indignant tone again.

'I never said you were. But I wanted to make sure you got home safely.'

'What do you mean?' She sounded suspicious.

'I saw you at the Paradise Nightclub.'

'Oh pur-leese!' she laughed. It was too high pitched to be reassuring. 'As if I would break curfew and go out on the razz.'

Hell, she was my daughter. It was more than possible. And not only could I smell apples, but I could detect hair gel and the flowery perfume Chastity uses on special occasions.

'You were there,' I said flatly, broking no argument.

'Mum!' she protested.

'I don't want you setting foot in that hell-hole again.'

'I wasn't there.'

'Chastity, don't lie to me. I know it was you. Don't you realise women are being abducted from that club? Do not go there again. I forbid it.'

The girls were all wide-eyed, silent. You could've heard a flea sneeze.

'I didn't want to scare you,' I said. 'But I do want you to be safe. I'll talk to Sister Immaculata in the morning.'

Again, static silence. I had the feeling secret messages were being conveyed but I wasn't in a fit state to intercept and interpret them. I just wanted to go home, put an ice pack on my bump and sleep. I tried to sit up which caused everything to whiz around faster than the final spin cycle of my washing machine. Fox and Chastity both shot forward and tried to support me with their arms around my shoulders. Chastity knocked his hand away and gave him a ferocious glare. Fox backed off all of six inches, glaring back. There was a certain similarity about their bulldog expressions and intensity that would have been funny in other circumstances.

Foxy helped me to my feet. I swayed and he put his arm around my waist. I swayed a little more, just to indulge myself, and he tightened his arm in a very satisfactory manner.

Chastity was staring at us, still resembling an outraged baby owl.

'Go to bed,' I said to her. 'We'll discuss this in the morning.'

'Are you going to be okay with him?' she said disparagingly. 'Or shall I come home in case there are… complications?'

'I'm a big girl. I can handle myself,' I said, stung.

'I meant concussion.'

Oh.

'I knew that.'

This won a reluctant smile from her.

'Mum, you're terrible.'

'Don't worry, I'll take care of her,' said Fox. 'She'll come to no harm with me.'

Shame.

Then I encountered his bland stare and glimmer of a grin. More shameful than shame. And I grinned back.

'Make sure she doesn't,' said Chastity, intercepting his look. 'Or I'll be hitting you with my hockey stick next time!'

It was time to go before the two babes got into fisticuffs over me. I kissed Chastity goodnight and allowed Fox to lead me back to the car. In a few minutes we were parked outside my place.

'Do you want me to come in?' asked Fox. He stared straight out in front. There was no real telling if he wanted to come in or not. I fought down a silent sigh.

'No.' I said it with reluctance. I was feeling sooky and my resistance to a foxy Fox would be too low. I didn't want to take the risk that lust would impair my judgement. 'I'll be fine.'

He then swivelled in his seat and faced me.

'I don't mind,' he said. 'I'll gladly… tuck you in bed.'

Which made me feel much happier. But I declined all the same.

The next morning I slept through my alarm. It didn't matter. I was on late shift as it was my turn to watch the Paradise Nightclub. Apart from that, the day stretched out before me. The only date I had was with Sister Immaculata and, as she didn't know I was coming, I could see her whenever I wanted.

My head was tender, but I could live with it. So what to do first? I could wash the clothes, do some housework or, if really keen, tackle the garden. And of course, there was always the renovating.

I lived in the leafy suburb of Subiaco. My house was an old weatherboard with pressed tin ceilings, fancy mouldings and a pitted history of white ants. The stumps were sinking, causing the house to slump in a similar manner to my backside and boobs. Both the house and myself could do with a complete overhaul. The house was probably easier to fix; at least that didn't require bucket-loads of self-discipline, and you could employ others to do the dirty work.

It was the first home I'd ever bought and I was still trying to get a hang of actually owning a place. There were responsibilities, right? Can't just blast the landlord and complain of dripping taps, blocked drains and rusting gutters and get them fixed for you. Oh no. It's down to moi and I didn't have the foggiest.

I'd bought the house privately a couple of months ago. A work colleague's elderly mum had died and the family wanted a quick sale. The old girl had lived in the house since the war and it had the relics to prove it. The toilet was at the far end of a spartan garden. There was a separate laundry with a concrete trough. And the kitchen was an enclosed back veranda without insulation or hot running water. The shower was the only exception. There was an electric unit for instant hot water. But the water pressure was lousy and I'd promised myself a new system as soon as I had some spare cash. Unfortunately, that didn't look like any time soon.

Okay, so the house was basic, but so were my needs. Most times, I only needed a place to sleep. Food was often eaten on the run and my work took up the majority of my waking moments.

Chastity was itching to decorate her room. She had the colours already picked out. They were all shades of pink with metallic silver for a bit of relief. I was hoping she'd change her mind before the summer holidays when she intended to attack it with a paintbrush. But I might have been wishing on a star. There were only a couple of weeks until holiday crunch time.

But today I didn't fancy doing anything too domestic – did I ever? I took a trip down to the bottom of the garden for a pee and then went back to bed and slept until lunchtime. By then it was too hot to remain in bed. The sheets were no longer inviting but sticky winding cloths that stifled.

I put on a load of washing, fixed myself a piece of toast and read the paper. When the washing was done, I slung it on the old Hills hoist. I winced as clothes caught on the rusty line. Not for the first time I vowed that the ancient contraption had to go. It left horrible orange marks on all my clothes and looked hideous. It went on the ever-increasing to-do list. I then got dressed in my usual jeans, t-shirt and jacket, and headed off for Saint Immaculata's.

Oh joy. The Iron Nun was waiting for me.

'I've been expecting you all morning,' she said.

'Really?'

I was impressed. Chastity must have come clean about the previous night's escapade.

'I don't want my daughter frequenting nightclubs,' I said, going straight into attack mode. 'She's too young and too vulnerable.'

Except when armed with a hockey stick.

'It's all under control,' said Sister Immaculata. 'Don't worry yourself. Concentrate on real crime and leave Chastity's discipline to me.'

Sounded good in theory but I had the feeling I was being conned.

'You do understand why I'm so anxious? Those young women I told you about, the former Immaculata girls who've been abducted, they were taken from the Paradise Nightclub. I don't want Chastity or her friends going there in case they get hurt.'

'Don't fret so much, Eve.'

'You're being totally irresponsible allowing them to go out to nightclubs!' My voice rose in frustration. 'I don't want Chastity becoming a victim.'

'I think you're the victim here. You worry too much. Your view of society is so hopeless.'

'Oh really! I'm the one out of touch with no street sense? I don't think so.'

'You lack faith,' she said gently.

'This isn't about religion.'

'Those young women will turn up.'

I gritted my teeth and counted to ten, but too fast to defuse the surge of anger.

'Yes, they'll probably turn up, but in what state? Alive or dead? I admire your laissez-faire attitude, Mum. Unfortunately I don't have the luxury of a cloistered, sheltered life. I know what scum are out there and what they can do to their victims.'

'Have faith, my child.'

At that moment, I envied her. It was a thin, pure shaft that penetrated to the very core of my soul.

She had faith. Simple. Effective. Empowering.

I'd battled it, and for it, all my life. Faith to me was always just out of reach, a will-o-wisp defying capture but it tempted me all the same. But I couldn't embrace it. I had to have hard facts and proof. I needed evidence.

Sister Immaculata sat there, a fine example of a Chaucerian nun with her sinful, colourful background, and announced once again, with concrete authority, that those girls would reappear.

'I know they will, Eve,' she said. 'Trust me.'

Hah! I'd be crazy to trust anything she said. And our discussion was getting nowhere. I sighed deeply, feeling depressed and defeated as well as frustrated.

'I've got to go, Mum. I've got a job to do. Look after Chastity. Keep her safe.'

My next stop was the bottle shop. I bought a few essentials, like red wine to unwind and brandy for pre-menstrual days. I should also have gone to the supermarket for food staples, but I decided to leave that treat for another day. I returned home and packed the bottles away in my sparse pantry. I then headed off to the surveillance pit to watch the Paradise Nightclub.

It was one doozy way to spend a Friday night, but at least there might be some arrest-able action, which was more than I would get at home sitting in front of the television, draining a bottle of red and smoking too many cigars.

The stakeout hole was festering nicely. There were a few more empty pizza boxes, chicken takeaway containers and scrunched up milkshake cartons. Carbs and cholesterol were well catered for in this dump.

Burton and Ely were already there. Burton was watching the street through the binoculars.

'Are you going in there tonight, boss?' asked Ely.

'No. I'll watch from here. I sunk enough orange juice last night to OD on vitamin C,' I said. 'I don't think my digestive system can take too much of that junk.'

'I'll deal you in, then,' said Ely shuffling a pack of playing cards.

We did a few hands, gambling for matches, before Burton motioned me over. I squinted through the lens and spotted Anne and Ken Fellows, Bobbie's parents, outside the club. They were walking up and down the pavement, handing out sheets of paper. I guessed those sheets were posters sporting Bobbie's photograph and appealing for witnesses of Bobbie's abduction to come forward.

Even from this distance, their anguish was palpable. The droop of their shoulders and desperate appeals to passers-by gave them away. I wished I could go down there and say something that would ease their grief, but I would be grappling to find the right words.

The other three families had also placed posters and adverts around the western suburbs. They'd made public appeals on television and been interview by the media circus. Mind you, they had fallen silent on the whole deal. There hadn't been a peep out of them for a good two weeks.

I had interviewed Anne and Ken Fellows but I hadn't talked to the other three sets of parents. Sodbury had done that before I'd joined the investigative team. I wondered if I should go and see them. We weren't getting very far anyway, so it'd be worth a shot.

The Fellows couple remained outside the club until midnight before the bouncers and then Zefferelli himself asked them to move on. They gave him a poster. He appeared to thank them and then scrunched it into a ball and dropped it on the pavement as he returned inside to his Paradise pit. That man was all heart.

My shift was over by three a.m. The club cleared out and the pavements were free of punters. I was on again at eight. I went home for some brief shuteye but was too wired from gallons of caffeine and double-cheese burgers. I hooked out a bottle of wine from the fridge and turned on the television. It was a big mistake. I finished the wine and ended up sleeping on the couch, unwashed, fully clothed and totally unfit to start the new day.

4

'YOO-HOO! ANYONE HOME?' MARGOT, MY NEXT-DOOR NEIGHBOUR, tripped into the kitchen without so much as a by your leave.

It was seven-thirty the next morning and she was wearing her trademark stiletto sandals, a white denim mini skirt and a plunging fringed silver top more suited for nightclubbing than early visits to your neighbour. You'd be forgiven for thinking she was on the game or some wannabe country and western singer. In fact, she was a model who'd fallen on hard times due to her age and society's obsession with pubescent stick insects. But hey, she was usually upbeat about it.

Ten years older than me, but a lot less ragged about the edges, Margot sported long jet-black hair piled up in a high topknot, long fingernails to rival Fu Manchu and long Tina Turner legs to die for. She could happily pass as Ab-Fab Patsy's dark-haired twin sister. Not only that, she shared the same appetite for pretty younger men.

Margot had the biggest heart in the Southern Hemisphere. She was the best neighbour a girl could have, except early on a Saturday morning when my head was pounding from an overindulgence of the rough red and it was already hot enough to fry an egg on the footpath. I was out of painkillers, food and ironed clothes. I was not a happy bunny and it was made worse because it was all self-inflicted. I should have forfeited last night's wine.

Make that the week's wine.

And I should have shopped and ironed when I'd had the opportunity instead of slothfully snuggling in bed.

'You look jaded,' said Margot and laughed. I winced because her laugh resembled that of a hysterical hyena.

'Don't mince your words. Tell me how you really see it.' I slammed shut the fridge door after a futile search for anything without extra culture, and I don't mean of the Beethoven variety. I filled the kettle. At least I had an on-going supply of water and didn't have to shop for it.

'Hard night?' She clicked her tongue sympathetically and leaned a narrow hip against my kitchen counter.

'Self imposed,' I admitted.

'Another night solo?'

'Not completely. I was working for most of it.'

'Poor substitute. We'll have to do something about your social life, honey.' She snapped her fingers decisively which made her lashings of bracelets jingle and jangle. Margot dripped enough gold jewellery to re-finance South America and still have change for the poker machines.

'I've got a brilliant idea,' she said.

It was too early in the day for brilliance.

'Tell me later,' I pleaded. 'I need painkillers and coffee and then I have to go to work. You want a coffee?'

She waved her hand dismissively, causing another bout of clashing metal, and carried on with her spiel. 'But this will suit you down to the ground, Evie. Swift, sure and satisfying. No messing around. No wasted time. Just straight in there and down to brass tacks.'

'Go on then,' I said, spooning instant coffee into a mug and impatiently waiting for the kettle to boil. I was already running late and Margot's ill-timed visit would delay me a heap more.

'I'll take you speed dating,' she said.

'Huh?'

'It cuts out the wasted flab of chatting someone up. You have five minutes to work out if the bloke is worth dating or not and if he isn't you haven't wasted a lifetime's investment on him. It's like an accelerated version of a lonely hearts' club.'

'Sounds like a sop for a bunch of losers.'

'Yeah, and you're not one when it comes to dating?' she said, her eyes narrowing dangerously.

I took a sip of scalding coffee and burnt my tongue while trying to ignore her true but cruel shaft. She had a point. I sometimes felt I had Loser Lover tattooed on my forehead.

'There's a new place in town called Hit and Miss in Hay Street. We'll go together, tonight,' she said, which sounded great in theory but I was sure would be absolutely disastrous in practice.

Margot, you see, had always beaten me in any encounter with the opposite sex simply by slinging a hip in a provocative pose and batting one artful, artificial eyelash at them. Hey, when I slung a hip, it was to get a better aim with my gun. Ditto when lowering an eyelid. Maybe I should try Cupid's bow rather than a gun. And aim for the heart rather than the leg.

'Better if I meet you there,' I said. 'Then if I get caught up on a case, you can speed date for the two of us.'

'You're not going to stand me up?'

'As if.'

'Remember to dress to knock 'em dead. See you at eight.'

'I'll do my best.'

My best, as it turned out, wasn't very good. For starters, I was late. As usual. Everyone was already milling around with clipboards of pink paper and red pens. They were dressed to kill and I was still clad in my hard-day-at-the-office jeans and t-shirt. Even though the night was muggy, I had on my leather jacket. Call it a security blanket if you like. It made me feel in control.

It also hid my gun.

Hit and Miss: the place lived up to its name. It was neither a bar nor a hall, but simply a room with a scratchy, carpet-tiled floor in deadbeat brown, and neutral, corpse-beige walls. I should think it had once been an office and those running the speed dating had got it cheap. I hesitated at the door, trying to spot Margot and hoping I'd got the wrong place.

I hadn't.

She yoo-hooed me from the other side of the room and pointed to a small card table where the organiser was seated. The lady in charge was called Josie. She was a bottle blonde with fake tan and, judging by her protruding cheek bones and taut skin, she'd been stretched and nipped a few too many times for comfort. She dressed like a teenager and affected a Shirley Temple cuteness. She must have been all of sixty-five, though it was hard to tell without cutting her in half and counting the rings.

'Yes?' she said when I hovered by the table. Her voice was sugary and girly and would appeal to the older male punters, I reckoned, as would the little pink bow in her hair.

'I… er…' What the hell was I doing here? I should make a dash for freedom before it was too late.

'At last, Eve!'

Damn, too late. She who hesitates…

'Josie, meet my friend Eve. She wants to sign up,' said Margot over my shoulder. 'You're late.'

She waggled her finger and jingled her bracelets. 'You've wasted valuable talent spotting time.'

What talent? I couldn't see any from where I was standing.

'It couldn't be helped. I was busy,' I told her. 'So what do we do now?'

'Pay up front, put your name down, grab a clipboard and get your backside on a chair in front of a man.'

'Sounds…'

'Simple? It is.'

'Actually, I was going to say clinical.' Though cynical was also appropriate. And awful and horrendous and a complete waste of valuable curry-eating, wine-drinking, cigar-smoking time.

Josie handed me a form.

'You have five minutes with each person. You fill in the scorecards provided and anyone with a score of ten-plus should be a good match. Five and over aren't bad either. You might just need more time to find common ground. We take no responsibility for what goes on between consenting adults. Good luck.'

Good luck? After that spiel, I reckoned I needed it. I looked at the registration form the Barbie doll grandma had given me and tried to spend an inordinate amount of time filling it in. If I spun it out long enough, the clock would strike midnight and I could return to the ashes and pumpkins and miss the ball altogether.

'Oh for goodness sake, do it later. You'll miss out otherwise,' said Margot returning from the back-blocks of the room to hassle me.

By now I'd got an eyeful of her get-up. She'd stinted at nothing in the fashion stakes. She had on a leopard-skin boob tube that revealed a great deal of her womanly charms, and a red leather mini skirt. Her red snakeskin heels I'd swear were circus stilts and made her at least seven foot tall. She was all woman. I wondered which men here would be game to take her on. Even a milkshake with Margot on the other end of the straw would be more than a lot of these mousy types could handle.

Margot grabbed me by the arm and sat me down in the nearest vacant chair.

'Go for it, kid,' she said and skittered away back to her dark corner, where she obviously had someone tasty baled up. It took me a split second to realise there was a man sitting on the other side of the small, round, café-style table.

Feeling acutely embarrassed and avoiding all eye contact, I said, 'Evening.'

I purposely left out the 'good' bit, because, as far as I could see, there was nothing remotely good about the night. I'd be more gainfully employed watching the Paradise for perps. Or feeding my face with takeaway chilli chicken masala.

My taste buds tingled instantly at the thought. Finding love and companionship in a nanosecond sucked. But you knew where you stood with an Indian.

'Do you believe in miracles?' the man said. His voice was creepily quiet, like crumpled tissue paper in an airtight room. I gave him a swift once over. He was no miracle, I could tell him that for nothing.

'Actually, no. Especially not tonight,' I said instead.

He had an uncanny resemblance to Elton John. Or was that Elton's mum? That was scary enough on its own. But his smile owed everything to Alfred Hitchcock. Bring on the psycho. Eek! Eek! Eek!

I wasn't totally surprised when he said, 'I do. I believe in miracles.'

I shut my eyes in disbelief. He wasn't going to start singing that old Hot Chocolate number, was he? Hell, I hoped not. His nasty smile widened so I could easily count the fillings in his molars.

'There's a French proverb that says miracles only happen to those who believe in them. I think tonight is my lucky night,' he said.

I shuddered and I didn't care if he noticed. 'Not with me, mate. I think our five minutes is up.'

I abruptly pushed back my chair. The legs caught on the cheap carpet mats and the chair went tumbling. Everybody's head turned to stare. I'm not sure, but I think I was making an impression and not necessarily a good one. I picked up the fallen chair and tucked it back under the table. I straightened my jacket, subtly readjusted my gun holster and then cast my eye about for another vacant lot.

There was only one. The man was a bear. He was big and brown and hairy. And he looked sort of familiar. I purposefully sauntered over.

'Evening,' I said again. 'May I sit down?'

'That's the idea.' He looked me up and down. 'Nice to see you've made an effort.'

He waved a paw at my jeans and leather.

'You have a problem with the way I dress?' Was this part of the five minute get-to-know-you stuff? He wouldn't win any best-dressed awards either. His charcoal grey jacket was rumpled as if he'd slept in it for a week and there were dangerous stains on his maroon tie. I should think he hadn't bothered to change his shirt for several days. His tie for several decades. He was a businessman's disaster. He smiled without warmth.

'Most the women here are dressed to kill. Either you wanted to make a statement by being different or…'

'How do you work that one out?'

'By dressing so contrarily to the other ladies, you instantly attract every man's attention.'

'And my other reason?' I might as well hear it, even though I knew I probably wouldn't like it.

'You're butch.'

'Oh. I see. Well, we've only got five minutes. Do you want to spend it trading insults?' I asked sweetly, trying not to grind my teeth. Surely I didn't look butch? I was a mother for goodness sake. The bear should get together with Zefferelli so they could swap bad impressions.

'Yeah, why not? It'll make a change from sugar-coated innuendos.'

I'd recognised him by this stage. He was the bloke in the gorgeous silver Rover who'd tried picking up Fox.

'Okay,' I said. 'It's my turn. You're the type of man who picks up prostitutes for lunch, male and female.'

His eyes narrowed.

'You're a hooker,' he said flatly.

'Worse. I'm a cop. But even that's not as bad as being a divorce lawyer.'

The bear leaned back in his chair. If he leaned back any further, I was sure the chair legs would snap. I was tempted, in a juvenile sort of way, to stick out my foot and push the chair the last centimetre or so, just to make certain.

'So you know who I am,' he said. It was a statement, not a question.

'Leo Stark. Married and divorced three times – I hope you give yourself cheap rates. You own a small practice in Subiaco, have a very nice Rover on lease and you need to attend Weight Watchers before heart disease and diabetes overtake you. At a guess, I would say you're moderately successful as a lawyer, hit the booze too hard and are a pussycat where unsuitable women are concerned. How do I score?'

He was silent. His eyes were still narrowed so I couldn't read any expression in them. I should think it was a learned lawyer tactic. He stroked his beard with one large paw. There was a signet ring on his pinky but from this distance I couldn't make out what was engraved on it.

'You don't score. Our five minutes have expired.' He rollicked the chair back on all fours and then left without a backward glance.

I watched him go all the way. He negotiated the tables like a huge sea-faring galleon avoiding treacherous rocks. For a big man he moved with surprising grace. He waved to Josie and then left the Hit and Miss. Why was he in such a hurry to leave? I wasn't *that* ugly or that butch. Maybe he didn't like police officers. It was common enough but it still bothered me. Did Leo Stark have something to hide? Or was he fed up with the whole speed dating game? I know I was, and I'd only been there ten minutes.

In fact, I was very tempted to follow him out. But before I could put the thought into action, Josie rushed over to my singleton table.

'What did you say to Leo?' she demanded with a squeak. 'He never leaves early. Were you rude?'

'She was rude to me,' Mr Psycho piped up.

'And she hasn't even bothered to speak to me,' said another of the losers.

'I'm learning how this whole thing works, okay? Back off, the lot of you.' I felt like drawing my gun to underscore my frustration.

'No need to get snitchy,' said the Barbie grandma. 'There's still time for you all to mingle and get to know each other.'

She then eyeballed me with one of her china-blue eyes. The other was pointing to the ceiling. I guess the plastic surgeon hadn't had the expertise to fix her squint.

'We don't want trouble, Eve,' she admonished. 'Play by the rules or you'll be expelled.'

Grief, this sounded much too much like Saint Immaculata's. Get me out of here!

'Now here comes one of our new clients. Do try and be nice.' She took hold of my arm in a surprisingly strong grip and led me to yet another small, round table where a salesman type in a blue suit sat with a smug, self-satisfied gleam in his too-familiar eyes. I swung a panicked glance around the room for Margot. She must have picked up my vibes because she was standing up and staring in our direction.

'Help!' I mouthed.

She smiled and did a little finger wave back and then returned her attention to whoever she was speed dating. No escape there, then. She obviously didn't want to squander her precious five minutes of chat-up time. I would have to bear it then. But not without a reward, that was for sure. I promised myself a treat if I got through the next five minutes without gagging.

I squared my shoulders and met my opponent.

'Hello, I'm Eve,' I said with as much warmth as a chilled watermelon.

'I wish I could say I was Adam,' he smirked back. 'But my name's Den. You can call me Tiger.'

I failed the treat challenge and gagged.

5

THE BLOWFLIES AND SPRINKLERS HAD BEATEN US TO THE BODY. THE flies were fatly swarming over the sharp blue suit and not doing much for the image. And the bore water sprinklers had soaked the lot, further diminishing the fashion statement.

It was Sunday morning and already it was too hot and glary for someone who preferred vampire hours. Especially when last night's red wine and Indian curry were curdling my insides. I should have been at home languishing in the Land of Nod, but murder didn't accommodate shift work timetables and Sodbury had booked the day off for a family party.

It was down to my team and me.

The body was face down in a sorry strip of scrub on the perimeters of a small park. The park itself overlooked the Swan River and was a haunt of mothers and toddlers during the day, and wackos at night. This morning, it was the sole domain of police officers.

'Want me to turn him over?' said Ely who'd beaten me to the crime scene by several minutes and was antsy to get on with the job.

'Yep, if all the crime scene pics have been taken.' I chewed on an antacid tablet while Ely rolled over the body.

I stopped chomping when I spied the dead man's face. He looked marginally better dead. Not much, but better. Alive he'd sported a supercilious, self-satisfied sneer that I'd learned to detest in a flat second. What was his name? Len? Ken? Den? Though he'd said to call him Tiger...

I hadn't.

'Know him, boss?' said Ely watching my reaction with interest.

If I'd possessed a weak stomach, coupled with my bender last night, I'd probably be throwing up half-digested masala over the bottlebrush bushes by now. But I'm not the sensitive type, which is probably one of the reasons why I didn't score terribly highly the night before. Actually, I don't think I got one tick. Can you believe that?

'Define know,' I said to Ely.

'What's his name?'

'Not sure. Something boring.' Except for the tiger bit, but I wasn't going to share that little gem with Ely.

'So how come you recognise him?'

'I've seen him around.'

'Recently?'

'Last night.'

'This is getting better. Where?'

'On the razz.'

I was being pathetic. I couldn't come clean. Inwardly I squirmed while outwardly I affected a nonchalant stance. The jeans and leather bomber jacket helped but with the temperature rising, the leather would soon have to go. It's one reason I hate summer. It's hard to maintain attitude.

Ely was shaking his head at me.

'You can't be more specific?' he said with a slight smile.

I was positive Ely was trying for a rise. I'd discovered in the short time I'd worked with him, that he loved pushing people's buttons. And especially mine. I ought to get him transferred before he ended up the main character in a homicide investigation, with me as chief suspect.

'Is there any ID on him?' I abruptly changed the subject.

'Nope. Wallet's been taken. No car keys. Nothing.'

'Unhelpful.'

'And with all due respect, chief, so are you.'

I scowled at him but before I could think of a suitable retort, one of the young officers handed me a nametag. It had been bagged in plastic to preserve any evidence.

'We found it in the car park,' said the officer.

'Looks like a conference tag,' said Ely squinting at it through the clear plastic.

'Dennis Phipps. What's with the hearts?'

I grabbed the bag and stared. Yep, there were sickly pink hearts bordering the rectangular plastic badge. I'd worn a similar one last night. Mine had ended up in someone's wheelie bin. I'd wanted no mementoes of such an abysmal night.

Burton and Fox sauntered over the wet grass towards us.

'Glad you could join us,' I said.

Burton was looking like I felt, but Fox was a blinding ray of sunshine. He shone sunny side up and was good enough to eat, with or without seasoning and side of fries.

My nerve endings began to fizz. I wanted Fox so bad I could taste it. But it was a no-go. I had my career to think of, which meant no dating the rank and file under my command.

But Fox had set up this itch. To scratch it, I needed a man who wasn't a police officer. But they were the only breed of male I seemed to come across, except, of course, for the crooks. Or my car mechanic. Come to think of it, he was in the crook category. Yesterday, Margot's suggestion had sounded sort of promising, in a loser kind of way, but it was turning out to be a bad move. I might have to confess to my colleagues that I had to pay to get a date. How humiliating.

'Any ideas yet on how he died?' I said.

'No, boss. We'll have to wait for the post mortem. From here it looks like drowning by sprinkler,' said Ely.

'I'll arrest the council gardeners now,' offered Burton, laughing.

'That's what I like, a bunch of jolly jokers early on a Sunday morning,' I said.

'Beats going to church,' said Burton.

'I beg to differ. I could do with some uplifting worship.'

'Bad night, chief?' Burton tried to look concerned but failed.

'She was out on the juice with this geezer,' chipped in Ely helpfully.

All eyes were suddenly on me. I could feel the sweat begin to trickle from under my boobs and creep towards my waistband. Damn, the jacket would have to go. I made a big play taking it off so I could avoid all eye contact for a good long minute. But it wasn't enough. The boys were still regarding me as Exhibit Number One as I hooked my finger under the collar and tossed my jacket over one shoulder.

'Is that true, DI Rock?' asked Fox. His blue eyes were intense but otherwise unfathomable.

I couldn't deny it, so I shrugged a yes.

'He was a friend?'

'Grief, no!'

'An acquaintance?'

'Barely that.'

'Come on, Detective Inspector,' said Ely giving my rank full credit. 'Lighten up. Give us something to go on.'

He was right. It didn't make it any easier though.

'Okay. I met him at the Hit and Miss in Hay Street.'

Blank faces.

'It's a… speed dating joint. I went there last night around eight thirty and left an hour later. This bloke was there.'

'He was one of your dates?' said Ely. 'Phew, you must have given him a hard time.'

'Thank you, DS Ely.' I hoped the sarcasm was loud and clear.

'A pleasure, DI Rock.'

'I was with him for only five minutes.' I'd moved on to an IT nerd after that. The brief meeting hadn't fared much better. Ditto the telecommunications engineer, a waste disposal expert – which translated to garbo – an accountant and a financial planner who was really there touting for business.

'At what time?' asked Fox, sticking to gleaning the facts, bless him.

'About nine, I suppose. Maybe earlier.'

'What did you talk about?'

That was classified stuff. But in a nutshell, Tiger had boasted about his sexual prowess and asked me what my preferences were in kinky sex. I'd told him I was a police officer and sex offenders were my specialty, which brought about an abrupt end to conversation. At least he hadn't knocked over his chair in his haste to get away from me.

'This and that,' I said evasively. 'We didn't hit it off so we didn't actually manage to talk for our allotted five minutes.'

'So it was classed as a miss,' said Ely and grinned.

I rolled my eyes to show him how much I appreciated his humour and then looked down at Dennis Phipps' waxy face. He was being zipped into a body bag and taken off to the morgue, away from our curious eyes. And the flies.

'I suppose we better see who he speed dated after me. Maybe that will shed some light on his last moments. Ely, you get an address for him. Burton, go with the body. Fox, you can come with me.'

'Where are we going?' he asked as we drove away from the park.

'To my place.'

'I see.' He sounded surprised. Even a touch pleased. He shifted a little in his seat so I was aware he was looking at me as I drove. It was rather disconcerting. I didn't dare to peek and see what sort of expression he had on his face. As it was, the air was crackling nicely, like a well-done piece of roast pork.

'That's made my day,' he said.

I quickly squashed any anticipation he might be feeling.

'Relax, Fox. We're going to call on my neighbour. It was her suggestion that we went to the Hit and Miss last night. She'll probably have a number for the organiser.'

'My mistake. Sorry.'

'There's nothing to apologise for.'

Yet.

I parked the car in my driveway and we walked across Margot's lawn and down the side of the house to the backdoor. As I expected, she was in the kitchen. And she looked as though she'd had a good, long, h-a-r-d night.

She was still in her leopard skin top and leather skirt, but minus the high-rise sandals. Her hair was a mess. Some of it hung down to her bare shoulders, the rest was anchored to her head with grips and bobby pins. Mascara underscored her eyes. There were no traces of scarlet lipstick. She had a coffee in one hand and a cigarette in the other and looked delighted to see me.

'Ms Saviour of the Universe! What a nice surprise.'

'Morning, Margot. Can I have a quick word?' I said through the fly-wire of her backdoor screen.

'Hell, honey. 'Course you can. Wanna coffee?'

Then she spotted Fox.

'Well....' she said. 'Who do we have here?'

'DS Fox. He's working with me on a case.'

'Hi, sweet thing. I'm Margot and I'd work on a case with you any day of the week,' she said, giving him a suggestive wink.

She seemed totally unfazed by her unkempt appearance. If it had been me, I would have slammed the door and bolted for the bathroom to try and perform a dramatic change. But then I'm not an Amazonian former model with cheekbones to die for, and legs and cleavage that would distract the most critical of male eyes. I needed all the advantages that a hairbrush and mascara could give.

'Come in the both of you and sit yourselves down while I fix a fresh brew,' she said, opening the door wide.

I didn't say no. When the call had come through about the dead body in the park, I'd scuttled out of bed, thrown on some clothes and left the house without breakfast. My body was yelling out for caffeine.

Bless Margot.

'You're up bright and early,' she said conversationally as the perk machine popped and purred and did its aromatic magic stuff. She sat down and leaned her forearms on the table, giving Foxy a good eyeful of that distracting cleavage.

Fox cleared his throat and shuffled his feet and gave a good impression of trying not to look.

'I thought it was your day off, darl,' said Margot.

'Rearranged shifts. Story of my life.'

I was itching to find out how Margot's evening had panned out but I didn't want to probe on the succulent details with Fox listening. Some things you just couldn't share with a man present.

I knew she'd been out late because I hadn't seen her come home. I'd sat on my veranda until midnight or so, pungent mosquito coils burning a charmed circle around me while I ate my chilli chicken masala and sunk my wine.

It had been too hot and humid to stay inside the house. The place had absorbed the summer heat while closed up all day and once again the sea breeze had failed to materialise. There'd not even been a brief puff and the place had been a sweltering furnace. Once upon a time, when people had lived in smaller houses on bigger blocks and street trees were large and leafy, the sea breeze could ruffle through the western suburbs and refresh the wilted streets. Now, people demanded two-storey homes right up to their boundary line and trees and gardens were out of vogue. The sea breeze couldn't penetrate the concrete jungle. So it just went around or over and left the suburbs to slow cook the summer away. Because of this, I had added the acquisition of an air conditioning unit to my list of necessities for the house. I couldn't afford it, but I didn't think I could live without it.

Anyway, Margot had been a dirty stop-out and I wanted the nitty-gritty, low-down details. But for the time being I had to be content with drinking a wicked cup of strong coffee and getting the number of Josie Lambert, the Barbie gran of Hit and Miss fame.

'Why do you want her number?' asked Margot as she wrote it down on the back of an old envelope and handed it to me. I noticed she had lost a couple of her scarlet Fu Manchu nails. Probably embedded in some bloke's back. It must have been a good night.

'I need to ask her some questions about her clients.'

'You're not going to bust her? I wouldn't have invited you along if I thought you'd make trouble.'

'As far as I could tell there's nothing I could bust her for. Do you know something I don't?'

She didn't answer directly, but obliquely said, 'She doesn't mean any harm. She's offering a service.'

Eek. I didn't want to go there. Was there more to the Hit and Miss than speed dating? Was Josie a pink, fluffy Madame? Had I been at a call girls' convention?

'I just need to chat with her about someone. It's not about her organisation or activities,' I said hastily.

We finished our coffee and left Margot lighting up another cigarette. We drove to the station to find out if any details had been found on Tiger Den and to ring Madame Josie for a chat.

Ely and Burton were working the phones. Fox got us a couple of drinks from the water dispenser while I rang the number Margot had given me.

Josie must have been sitting on the phone. She answered on the first ring.

'Josie Lambert?' I asked, though I recognised her saccharine sweet voice from the night before.

'Yes, speaking.'

'Hi, you might remember me. We met last night. Eve Rock.'

The sweetness turned sour. 'Yes, I remember you. What do you want? To apologise?'

'Apologise for what?' My hackles rose immediately.

'For disrupting the evening.'

'I did not!'

'I don't want you coming back. Ever.'

'I don't intend to.'

'Good.' She put the phone down on me and I stared at it in surprise.

I hit redial and got her again on the first ring. Again the sweetness instantly turned sour when she realised it was me.

'Don't hang up!' I said and quickly introduced my police credentials.

'I've done nothing wrong!' she hissed.

'I didn't say you had. I just want some details about one of your clients.'

'Who?' Suspicion rippled down the line.

'Dennis Phipps.'

'Why?'

'He turned up dead this morning,' I said brutally. 'I need to contact his next of kin. I want all the details he put on his enrolment form.'

I waited while she booted up her computer and then she rattled them off.

'Thank you, Ms Lambert. I'll send someone around within the hour to get a copy. Can you remember what time Dennis left your establishment last night and who with?'

'Why?'

Grief! It was like getting information out of Sister Immaculata. Same tight-lipped drill.

'Because I need to piece together his last movements.'

'He left with a group. I think they went to the Paradise Nightclub.'

That cesspit again.

I must check if the boys on duty last night were taking pics of the place. It would aid the investigation somewhat if we could pinpoint who had been with Phipps.

'Will that be all?' said Josie.

'For the moment. Thank you.'

I dropped the receiver in its cradle and massaged my temples. What a great way to start the day.

Ely was waving a piece of paper at me across the office.

'Dennis Phipps. Forty-eight. A greeting card salesman. Lives in Scarborough. Wife and two kids,' he said.

I looked down at my pad where I'd just written Josie Lambert's information. I read it aloud.

'Dennis Phipps. Forty-eight. Greeting card salesman. Lives in Midland. Wife, no kids.'

'Different Dennis Phipps,' said Ely with a shrug.

Burton then came off the phone.

'Dennis Phipps. He was a greeting card salesman for one of the big companies and lived in Fremantle.'

'Do you have an age?' I asked.

'Forty-eight.'

'Any kids?'

'One.'

'So,' I said. 'Do we have three different Dennis Phippses or do we have one very naughty, but dead, polygamist salesman?'

6

WE VISITED EACH WIFE IN TURN, STARTING WITH THE ONE LIVING AT
the Fremantle address.

The red brick home was in a state housing street. A broken bike
lay on a coarse grass lawn. Judging by the rust, the bike had lain
there for some time, indiscriminately watered by the rain, sprinklers
and stray dogs. There was no vehicle in the carport and it didn't
look as though one had been there for a very long time. Dead
leaves gathered in dusty corners together with cardboard boxes.
The whole place wore a tired and neglected air.

Fox rang the bell. We didn't hear a chime, so he knocked as
well. While we waited I took a quick squizz out the back. Mrs
Phipps' Hills hoist was in the same league as my relic, except that
hers listed slightly to one side and had limp grey boxer shorts
hanging on it. The hoist added as much class to her garden as it
did to mine.

Finally the door opened. A woman of around fifty stood there
in a black polyester tracksuit that fitted her corpulent figure much
too snugly. She had pink rubber thongs on her feet and her long
greying hair hung down in uninspiring hanks either side of her
faded face. It needed a good wash, cut and blow dry as well as a
whole bottle of double strength colour. Any colour. But then she'd
still have the same face. It was a face that catalogued her defeat by
life. She didn't strike me as the other half of Tiger Den. I thought
we'd made a mistake.

'Yes?' she said.

'Are you Audrey Phipps?' I asked as I flashed my police badge.

'What's he done now?' she said tiredly. 'I'll give him a big clip round the ear, see if I don't.'

'Who?' I said.

'My son. Derek. Isn't that why you're here?'

'No, actually I'm more interested in your husband Dennis.'

'You're wasting your time, then. He shot through years ago, when Derek was little. The sod.' She had a low, defeated voice, matching her surroundings.

'Do you have a picture of him?'

'I might have. Why do you want it? Is he in some sort of trouble?'

'I'm just trying to establish if we have the right Dennis Phipps.'

'I see.' Though she didn't look as if she did. 'Wait here a minute.'

She returned with a faded snapshot taken at the beach. Dennis grinned at the camera, bared-chested for all to see. It wasn't a good look. There was more hair on his head and he had a thinner face, but you couldn't mistake that cocky self-confident smile. It was our dead salesman all right.

'So you haven't seen him recently?' I said.

'No, luv. As I told you. He buggered off years ago.'

'Were you divorced?'

'No. Never saw the point. I didn't want to get married again, and I doubt if Dennis did.'

You'd be surprised, Aud, I thought.

'I'm sorry to have to inform you that your husband is dead.'

She stared at me blankly.

'Dead? Heart attack or something?'

'We're not sure at this stage. We're investigating.'

'So it was suspicious, then?'

'We always investigate sudden deaths. It's procedure. We'll be in touch again shortly.'

'What about the funeral and stuff?'

'I'll let you know when the body can be released. I'm so sorry Mrs Phipps.'

'Don't be. And what will happen to his things?'

'Nothing at this stage.'

She was still asking questions about Tiger's last will and testament as we backed out the driveway. It was the most animated we'd seen her. She jauntily waved us off as if we were old friends. Perhaps we were. She didn't strike me as a woman who had a wide circle of intimates.

I couldn't help wondering what the other wives were like, and it didn't take long to find out.

Scarborough Sue was a bottle blonde of indeterminate age. She had on a tight white t-shirt, white tennis skirt, bobby socks and sneakers. Her skin glowed bronze. She jogged to her small white Nissan car as we pulled in behind her.

'If you're Jehovah's Witnesses, I'm not interested,' she announced. 'Please remove your car. I have an appointment.'

I ignored her and got out the car.

'Mrs Susan Phipps?'

Her eyes narrowed.

'I might be.'

I flashed my badge and introduced myself.

'Are you married to a Mr Dennis Phipps?'

'Yes.'

'Is he here?'

'No.'

'Do you have a recent picture of him?'

'Of course.'

'May I see it?'

She sighed.

'I do have tennis to go to.'

'I need to confirm an identity,' I said.

'Come this way.' She slammed the car door and pinged the locks with her remote control. She jogged with compact, tight movements to the front door and unlocked it.

The house couldn't have been more different to Audrey Phipps' place. Aud's was all grey defeat and neglect. Here was white and clean and uncluttered perfection.

We followed Sue Phipps into the family room where two blonde children sat in front of the television watching cartoons. The boy was about ten, the girl maybe eight. They paid us no attention.

Sue marched over to a white shelf filled with tastefully framed photographs. She picked up one in a plain silver frame. It was a studio shot, sponged-suede background in blue, with Tiger Den looking like the toothpaste salesman of the year.

'This is your husband?' I confirmed.

'Yes, that's Den.'

'I'm afraid I've got some bad news.'

Her nostrils flared slightly and she held on to the white counter that divided the family room from the kitchen.

'He's been hurt?'

'Would you like to sit down?'

'No. I'm fine where I am. Just tell me what's wrong.'

'He was found dead early this morning.'

Her eyes flicked from me to Fox and then back again.

'Where?'

'In a park. In Nedlands.'

'How?' Her knuckles whitened to the same shade as the counter as she held on grimly.

'We don't know yet. Would you be up to identifying the body?'

'Of course. I suppose I'd better cancel my tennis match.'

Fox and I shared a swift glance. She was taking this remarkably well. Unless what we'd actually said hadn't sunk in.

'Is there someone who could be with the children?'

Sue made a couple of cryptic phone calls and then went and changed her sports skirt for a pair of white jeans. Obviously white was her thing.

'When did you last see your husband?' asked Fox while we waited for the neighbour to appear to baby-sit the children.

'Saturday afternoon. He had to go out for a business dinner and said he'd stay over because it was a regular boozy event.' She sounded rigidly controlled and I wondered how close she had been with her husband.

'You didn't think that strange?'

'My husband was away a lot on business. He travelled throughout the week and usually spent the weekends at home. Sometimes, like last night, he had a function to attend. It was just how things were.'

'So you only saw him regularly at weekends?'

'Yes.'

'How long were you married?' I said.

'Ten years. Ah, here's Sylvia now. Thanks for coming round at such short notice, Syl.'

'No sweat. There's nothing wrong is there?' said Sylvia who was a bouncy brunette with braided, beaded hair. She was wearing a yellow sundress and had bare feet with ringed toes. 'I came as quickly as I could.'

'I'll tell you later. It's about Dennis…' Her voice suddenly cracked. She rammed her knuckles against her mouth to stop the rush of emotion. 'He's dead! Don't tell the children…'

'Omigod! Sue!' Sylvia rushed to put her arms around Sue. 'You poor thing. Of course I won't tell them. Take as long as you need. I'll hold the fort. The kiddies will be fine. Don't worry about them. Just get through this, girl.'

Every woman needs a great neighbour, I decided, and gave thanks for my own next-door angel.

Sue Phipps declined having a friend or relative to accompany her to the morgue. She said she was quite capable of identifying her husband and anyway, who else could be expected to do it? She was his wife.

We could have given her an alternative comprehensive list, but decided to leave that until a later date, once the shock of his death was over. A woman could only cope with a certain number of nasty surprises at any one time.

We drove to the morgue. Sue positively ID'd the corpse and then we took her into an interview room.

'Do you feel up to answering a few questions?' I said.

'I suppose.' She shredded a tissue between her fingers, the control not quite so visible.

'Can you think of anyone who might want to hurt Dennis?'

'No. Why would they? He is – was – a nice bloke. He never harmed anybody.'

'How were things between you?'

'Fine. You're not suggesting that I killed him?' Her voice rose accusingly.

'I'm not suggesting anything. Just trying to get a picture of the man, his family life, work, recreation. That sort of thing.'

'There's not a great deal to tell. He was a good dad. A good provider. Loved the beach. Worked hard. Travelled a lot in his job. He was a card salesman and went around all newsagents and gift shops in the state.'

'I'm sorry to have to ask this, but did he have affairs?'

'You're kidding, right? He wouldn't have had time.'

'Did you know he'd been married before?'

'Den? Come off it.'

'Did you know he frequented the Hit and Miss speed dating agency?'

'You're lying.'

'That's where he'd been the night he died.'

'But he was at a conference.'

'Witnesses saw him at the Hit and Miss.'

'They lied.'

'They didn't.'

'Well then maybe he was forced by politeness to attend with a crowd of delegates. That happened sometimes. He'd have to go to clubs and bars. It was all to do with networking.'

'He was on his own.'

'I've had enough of this. I'm not going to listen to anymore of your lies. I'm leaving.'

'I'll have someone take you home. We will need to talk to you again.'

After she'd gone, Fox and I joined the others.

'Any news on how Phipps died?' I asked.

'Broken neck,' said Burton. 'Quiet, clean and effective. No weapon necessary and no fingerprints.'

'Any signs of a struggle?'

'Nope.'

'So he possibly knew his killer.'

'Maybe.'

I briefed Burton and Ely on our conversations with Audrey and Sue Phipps while I ate a sausage roll from the vending machine. It was breakfast and lunch rolled into one, and not very appetising. The machine coffee wasn't much better but at least it washed down the flakes of papery pastry and cardboard sausage.

'Do you want us to do the death knock of the third Mrs Phipps?' said Ely. He was itching to get out of the office. So was I, but sometimes you have to sacrifice yourself for the troops.

'You guys do that. Fox and I will look through the Saturday night surveillance pics.'

'We've already been through them,' said Burton. 'And got copies of everyone who went in and out of the club from nine-thirty onwards.'

'Bless you, my children.'

'I hate it when you go all religious on us,' said Ely. 'Reminds me of Sunday school. Save it for those who need it.'

'If anyone was in need of salvation, Ely, it would be you.' I gave him an evil grin.

I skimmed through the pics. It didn't take me long to find the relevant frames. There was Tiger Den himself, his arm around one of the painted ladies from the Hit and Miss. I planned on taking the photos to Josie Lambert later, to put names to faces.

I flicked on through the pack and stifled a yawn. I rolled back my shoulders to try and inject a bit of life into my body. Suddenly a pair of hands landed either side of my neck. I jumped.

'Be still,' said Fox and he began massaging my tired muscles while he peered over my shoulders. 'Are these last night's Paradise shots?'

'Sure are.' I bit back a deeply appreciative moan as his long, strong fingers worked their magic. It was totally unprofessional, but it felt soooo good.

Too good.

My insides started turning to mush while my thighs began to

quiver and my breasts tingle. The photographs slipped through my fingers as I gave myself up to the pleasure of Fox's hands. I absently watched the pictures spill. They slithered over the desk. I sighed. I wanted to do the same.

And then I saw a familiar spotty top. Fighting the desire to just let it be, so I could keep indulging my erotic fantasies under Fox's fingers, I reached out and studied the slightly blurred photo more closely. Fox stopped massaging to look too. He leaned further over my shoulder so our cheeks were almost touching and his breath caressed my skin.

'Isn't that your neighbour?' he said.

'Sure looks like it.'

So Margot had been at the Paradise too. I transferred my attention to her companion. I stared at him disbelievingly and, I admit, with a bit of annoyance. It was the mammoth, Stark. So when did they link up? He'd been long gone by the time I'd left the Hit and Miss. Unless, of course, he'd been hiding around the corner, waiting for my departure so he could return to the speed dating fast track without my caustic tongue to slow things down.

Hmm. He went on my list of people to hassle. It would be a pleasure.

I then realised that Fox was staring at Stark too.

'She's with that loser who tried picking me up at the Paradise!' he said, his voice rising in outrage at the remembered humiliation.

'Want to come and interview him with me?' I said.

'You bet. I wouldn't miss it for the world.'

'That'll be our treat for tomorrow, then. Lucky us. And lucky Mr Stark.'

'I hope he's guilty,' said Fox and tossed the photo on to the desk.

'He's innocent until proven. Remember that.'

'Yes, boss. But I bet we can pin something on him.'

'That's not the attitude, Fox.'

'Sorry. I got carried away.'

As I had just about, with his massage. Phew. I really should be more careful.

Sitting side-by-side, shoulders occasionally brushing, we sifted through the other photographs. We didn't make any more positive identifications, so I shoved the lot in a large buff envelope to show to Josie later.

Next I read the medical report. It said that Dennis had had a Chinese meal an hour before his demise. A lemon chicken with crispy noodles and spring rolls. Foolish man. He should have had a king prawn jalferezi for his last supper, with onion bahjis and garlic nan. Yum. My taste buds burst into life just thinking about it and then my stomach gurgled to reinforce my love affair with Indian food. I dragged my senses back into line and continued to read.

Phipps had suffered from fallen arches and enlarged adenoids. He was asthmatic, was without his appendix and he'd had sex that night. Euewk! It was a shame I had to know that. I wondered who the unlucky tigress was, and eternally thankful it hadn't been me.

The reports read and digested, it was time to talk to Josie again. I needed to find out who Dennis had partied with. I also wanted to pump Margot for more information. She'd been in the loop that night. Maybe she could shed some light.

But Josie first.

'Come on, Fox. Let's go interview the Hit and Miss Madame.'

It was too hot now to wear the jacket and so the shoulder holster had to go. Luckily I always kept a spare shoulder bag in the bottom drawer of my desk for such emergencies. I grabbed it and shoved in my gun.

'Time to rock and roll, Foxy. Let's go.'

7

Sunlight wasn't flattering for Josie Lambert. It revealed too many flaws in the nip and tuck landscape of her face. She was wearing a kimono the colour of cheap cab sav, with a writhing golden Chinese dragon emblazoned across the shiny material. There was a gold bow in her hair and slippers on her feet to match the dressing gown nightmare.

She seemed resigned to see us and silently stood by to let us walk into her small, neat unit where the predominant décor was sugar-mouse pink. It didn't go well with her get-up. Or mine.

'I have the print-out of Dennis Phipps details,' she said in her saccharine soft voice. 'There's not much on it. I don't ask for a great deal of private information from my clients. I think it's up to the individuals to learn the pertinent details from each other.'

'Five minutes isn't long to learn someone's history,' I said. And all I'd done in the allotted time was trade insults.

'The five minutes is a taster. If there's enough interest to pursue the relationship, then that's the time to find out more.' Her tone implied that I'd failed to water anybody's taste buds.

Then I had an unexpected flash of a bearded bear. Leo Stark. Why the sudden newsflash? He hadn't appealed to me in the slightest. Or had he? Damn. I must be getting desperate if I was fantasising about alcoholic, overweight lawyers with a penchant for Paradise prostitutes. I blamed Fox. If he hadn't kick-started my sex hormones I wouldn't be slathering over anything remotely male.

I glared at him and he raised his eyebrows inquiringly.

'Yes, boss?'

'Nothing. Just thinking.'

'Keep me posted,' he said with a wary smile.

I returned my attention to the Barbie doll grandma.

'So Josie, Saturday night was Dennis Phipps first time at the Hit and Miss?'

'Second. He'd been the Saturday before.'

'Had he been successful? You know, as in getting dates?'

'Yes. Of course.' She scowled at me for doubting that he wouldn't.

'So who did he link up with?'

She gave me an impressive list. I whistled.

'Just about a full house.'

'You were the only one who got below five points with him.'

'What did I score?' I asked out of morbid curiosity.

'None.'

I heard a muffled snort behind me. Fox obviously found the whole thing very funny. I didn't.

'My loss,' I said. Josie didn't respond. I don't think she liked me very much either. Another nil score. I was doing well.

'Can you name any of the people in these photographs?' I asked Josie, emptying the big envelope on her breakfast bar.

She put names to faces of all the Hit and Miss clients, and a few extras for good measure. She certainly knew a lot of patrons of the Paradise. Maybe we should have her on the payroll for Operation Paradise. It would save us a lot of legwork.

While we were there, we also took the names and addresses of those who were at the Hit and Miss on the two Saturday nights Phipps had attended. We then left Josie filing her nails or doing whatever a Madame did in the middle of the afternoon.

I was beginning to run out of steam after my early morning start. And the heat was really getting to me. All I wanted to do was strip off and stand under a cool shower.

I gave Fox a sly glance. I didn't mind sharing the shower… And then I remembered. Sharing showers with police officers under your command was not a brilliant career move. Life's tough at the top. But at least I had some control over working hours.

'Let's call it a day,' I said to him. 'We'll go through this list tomorrow.'

'Suits me.'

'You got plans?' I asked as we pulled into the station forecourt and I parked by his spunky Spitfire.

'Yeah. My dad's in town. I'll go catch up with him. Maybe ride a wave or two, share a beer.'

'Sounds cosily macho. Enjoy.'

He hesitated.

'Do you want to join us?' He said it rather doubtfully, probably wondering how his dad and new boss would mix.

But it was too early to begin meeting the folks. That smacked of commitment and we hadn't even kissed.

Yet.

I grinned at him and waved my hand.

'Oh no! I don't want to encroach on some male bonding. I have better things to do, but thanks all the same.'

When I reached my hotbox of a house I flung open all the windows to let out the stifling, stale air. Instantly more hot, stale air flooded in. It was one of those horrible, muggy late afternoons that just keep getting hotter and hotter, when everything feels warm to touch – the glasses in the cabinet, the water from the tap, the kitchen towel, the chair. Roll on the day when I could afford air-conditioning.

I peeled off my sweaty, sticky clothes and stepped into the shower. I turned on the cold tap. A lukewarm trickle came out. I kept turning until it was supposedly on full blast. Still only a trickle. I hit it. The pipe clanked but the idle tinkle of water remained the same sorry dribble.

There was only one thing for it. I shut off the water, pulled on a black singlet and pair of red bikini underpants and padded out to the backyard. I pulled the hose and sprinkler into the middle of the so-called lawn and then turned on the hose. I waited for the hose water, hot from the day's sun, to run out before lying flat out on the parched grass, eyes closed, arms and legs akimbo, and letting the cool fake rain splatter over my overheated body.

I hadn't done this since a child. I don't know why, because it was heavenly bliss. Everyone should do it once in a while.

When my body had sufficiently chilled so I felt slightly more human and less like a combusting amoeba, I finally opened my eyes. The ground around me was a sodden swamp. I reluctantly stood. The party for one was over. I wiggled my toes in the wet sand and allowed the sprinkler to wash off the small sticks, dried grass and dirt that stuck to my body.

A slight movement on the edge of my peripheral vision snagged my attention. I swung around and caught sight of a face peering over my fence. It was hard to see clearly through the streaming water but I was pretty damn sure I didn't know the person.

Immediately my cool good mood evaporated and I went rigid.

The man disappeared as I marched over to tell him exactly what I thought of him spying on me. I grabbed an old flowerpot, a relic from the previous owners when the garden had been cared for, and up-ended it so I could elevate myself over the fence and holler abuse at the Peeping Tom, yelling that he'd be locked up and dealt with if he continued his nasty, grubby little games.

He high-tailed it down the rough back lane. The lane used to serve the old homes when earth closets were the go but now was a glorified car park, rubbish tip and playground for the local kids.

Ace detective that I am, I couldn't help but notice that the man was no ordinary Peeping Tom. He had on red trousers and a red jacket trimmed in white. His boots were black but he was missing the red hat and white beard.

Great, I was being perved by one of Santa's jolly helpers.

And then the bottom of my flowerpot gave way and my foot went through the fatigued black plastic, scratching me from ankle to knee. I extricated my foot with difficulty. Blood tricked down my shin as I limped over to the tap, shut off the sprinkler and disconnected the hose so I could wash the wound.

The sun still had a bite, but I reckoned it had gone down somewhere around the world so it was time for a reviving red wine to blot out the day's sordid events. As I stripped off and climbed into a pair of brief shorts and another black singlet, there was a yahoo! at the back door.

'Come in, Margot,' I called out from the bedroom. 'I'll be with you in a sec.'

'I'll open the wine,' she called back.

I towel-dried my hair until it frizzed in all directions. I tried snagging a comb through it but gave up and left it to do its own thing, as per normal.

Margot had the glasses out and wine poured by the time I padded barefoot into the kitchen. On the table was a plate of crackers with olives, sun-dried tomatoes, and slivers of cheese.

She'd fixed herself up from the morning's catastrophe. Her hair was brushed and swept neatly into its fifties beehive. The faux leopard-skin boob tube had been replaced by a tiger-striped version and the mini skirt was a brown leather one as minuscule as the one she'd worn the previous night. Her broken nails were fixed and re-painted fuchsia pink.

'Josie called me,' she said as with clinked glasses and I took the first delicious sip. 'She said Dennis Phipps was dead. Is that why you wanted her number?'

'Yes. Did you know him?'

'Is this official questioning or what?' she asked, her eyes narrowing suspiciously.

I was surprised she asked. What was the big deal?

'If you have any information that might help the investigation, then you should give it to me,' I said in what I hoped was a reasonable tone. 'There's a murderer on the loose.'

'He was murdered?'

'Yes. Of course.'

'How do you know?'

'It was pretty obvious. His neck was broken.'

Margot shuddered and slugged back half of her wine in one hit.

'I didn't have my five minutes with him,' she said. She sounded defensive, almost sulky. 'The session broke up before I'd got the chance.'

'But you all went partying together after the Hit and Miss.' I said it as a statement. I knew that's what had happened. I had the pictures to prove it.

'You know about that?' Her eyes flickered and I experienced a corresponding niggle in my belly which I hadn't expected. Hey, what was I missing here?

'What's your problem, Margot?' I said easily, sipping the plonk, keeping my eyes steadily on her, trying to sound nonchalant. She was my neighbour and friend, after all.

'There's no problem! I just hate talking to the police. I always feel as guilty as hell.'

I laughed, my sudden pang of professional tension easing.

'That's just your misspent past catching up with you.'

'What do you know of my past?' There was that bristling suspicion again.

I flapped my hand.

'Only what you've told me. Relax. I'm not here to arrest you.'

She drained her glass and swiftly filled it again. She crunched on a cracker and then grinned.

'Sorry. I'm being stupid.'

'Don't worry about it. I have that effect on a lot of people. It's an occupational hazard.' I took another sip and then said, 'Did you see who Dennis hooked up with during the evening?'

'No, Eve, I was too busy hooking up with someone myself to notice.' She smacked her lips together. 'Boy, was he worth it!'

'You mean Leo Stark?'

Her brows rose almost to her hairline.

'How did you know that?'

'I was just presuming.'

'Yeah. Leo is a nice man. A very nice man.'

Perhaps. I'd reserve judgement.

I demolished a cracker and said, 'Is it usual for everyone to go off together after the dating session?'

'On a good night.'

After my speed dating experience, I'd hate to think what a bad night was.

'And Saturday rated well?'

'Very.'

Grief, I wasn't convinced, but I let it go out of kind neighbourly feelings.

'On a completely different matter,' I said. 'Have you ever had trouble with Peeping Toms?'

'Around here?'

I nodded.

'No, darl. This is a decent neighbourhood.'

Except for perving santas.

We drained the bottle. Margot was all for sinking another but I was bushed. I kicked her out and went to bed.

8

I CRASHED AND SLEPT LIKE THE DEAD UNTIL MY PHONE WOKE ME. IT was still dark. The magpies were carolling in the moonlight and my tongue was stuck to the roof of my mouth. As for my hair, it was sticking up so much it was brushing the cobwebs from the ceiling.

I grabbed the phone and barked a sharp yes.

'Sorry to wake you, boss.' It was Ely. 'They've fished a body out of the Swan River. A young woman. Dark hair. Maybe in her early twenties. No older. Perhaps younger. Hard to tell.'

'Is it one of our missing girls?'

'Possibly.'

'I'll come right on over. Where are you?' He gave me directions. I terminated the call and scrambled together the first clothes that came to hand: jeans, t-shirt, sneakers. And leather jacket, just in case there was a chill in the air.

There wasn't, but what the hell.

Fifteen minutes later I was on the foreshore close to the university looking down at the sad, bloated face of a dead girl. Shoulder length hair streaked across her puffy skin like black seaweed, her eyes stared, and her mouth was opened on a silent scream. At a guess, I'd say she'd once been pretty.

Anger rose within me. It didn't seem right she was lying here at my feet. But then sudden death never felt right. The sun would soon be rising on a new day that this young woman would never see. What a tragic waste of a life. Why had she done it? And would my Chastity ever think to end her own life? It was a constant, niggling fear that occasionally gave me the sweats at night, what with all the media attention on teenage suicide and Chastity's strive and passion for perfection.

She was destined to fail and I didn't want that for my baby. I'd tried to instil in her a sense of detachment from life's miseries so she wouldn't be continually disappointed, but she had a Pollyanna view that was hard to shake.

'Any ID?' I asked Ely, controlling my voice, playing down the concoction of fermenting fear and wrath boiling in my stomach.

'Not on her. The divers are dragging the river.'

I studied the girl again.

'It's hard to tell,' I said. 'But I doubt if she is one of ours.'

I squinted out over the Swan. Lights twinkled back. There was the soft lap of the water and occasional splash caused by the police divers. It should have been a nice balmy end of night. But as often happened, the darkness hid terrible sins.

'You know,' I said to Ely. 'We must be roughly opposite where Phipps was found.'

Ely followed my gaze.

'I suppose,' he said. 'Yeah, not far off.'

'I wonder if the deaths are connected.'

'That would be stretching coincidences.' He shrugged. 'I reckon she's a suicide case. She's about student age, getting close to exams. Probably couldn't take the strain.'

'The uni exams were over weeks ago.'

Ely didn't miss a beat.

'Wasn't looking forward to the results, then. Or was depressed about Christmas. Lots of people get depressed about Christmas. I know I do as my wife goes into spending overdrive.'

'She hasn't got a wife,' I said dryly.

'But she might've hated Christmas anyhow. You know, with all the rellies coming out the woodwork and the tensions on who is going to spend Christmas with whom.'

'That's your nightmare, not hers.'

'I was just tossing ideas around.'

'How about we suspend all theories until the pathologist tells us how she died, hmm?'

'You were the one who started it,' he said, nettled.

'And I'm ending it.' I grinned. Sometimes I liked being the boss. I looked at the girl a third time. She was wearing black and blue lycra crop top and shorts with florescent lime green strips to warn motorists of her presence. I frowned. She didn't strike me as being dressed for a suicide drowning. Not that there's a dress code for suicide, but she just didn't look right for it.

'I bet the divers find a bike,' I murmured.

Ely bit back a laugh.

'There you go again. Theorising. You can't help yourself.'

'And I bet you she was murdered. This was no suicide.'

'What do you want to bet?'

'A bottle of red.'

'Done. Easy as taking candy.'

I rolled my eyes at him.

'Says you. Makes sure it's a good red. I don't want any rubbish.'

'Who says I'm buying?'

'Me.' I waggled my eyebrows. 'It's in the bag.'

'Hah!'

I smiled sweetly. 'Let's go over to the park.'

'Now?' He looked aghast.

'It's beginning to get light.'

'What about breakfast?'

'Is that a whine I detect, DS Ely?'

'No!'

'Good. We can eat later.'

Ely followed me in his car around to the other side of the Swan. We parked where we'd found Dennis Phipps' vehicle.

'Okay,' I said, standing on the shore and squinting at the scene. 'What do you reckon that the girl saw whoever killed Phipps so the murderer decided to take her out, too?'

'Farfetched.'

'Why?'

'It was past midnight when Phipps was murdered. The girl wouldn't have been out cycling then.'

'She might have been coming back from somewhere. A job or a party.'

'Dressed in cycling gear?'

'She'd changed her clothes or something. I don't know, Ely. Stop making it difficult. But it doesn't alter the fact that the gear she was wearing was designed for night time cycling with all the reflectors across the clothes and shoes. We need to find out who she was and where she was going.'

'But tell me, boss, how did the murderer disentangle themselves from Phipps, get out the car and catch a speedy cyclist? The girl would have been long gone.'

I stared at the parking lot and back over to where the body had been discovered.

'Perhaps Phipps wasn't killed in the car? Maybe they were sitting on the grass looking out across the river? Maybe Phipps was already dead and the murderer was laying him out on the grass and the cyclist, misinterpreting the scene, stopped to see if help was needed?'

'And then got done too,' supplied Ely. 'I suppose it's possible.'

But he didn't sound convinced and I wasn't sure I was, either.

We walked it through a couple of times and then we looked around for bike wheel marks, not that we expected to see any after all the police activity yesterday. We wandered back down to the shoreline. The sand was all poached and messy. No telling if a body or bike had been thrown in.

'Time to eat,' I said to Ely.

'No argument with that, boss.'

We filled our bellies with a double fry-up at a breakfast bar close to the station and then fronted up for work. It was still only early and the day stretched ahead like a highway on constant rush hour. It was a chance to catch up with paperwork before the real work began.

But before I got immersed in the boring pen-pushing routine, I flicked through the yellow pages. Building contractors came a little after bridal wear. Maybe it was just listed alphabetically, but I realised later it was sorted by mental and physical suffering.

Hiring a builder was very like getting married. You had to bite your tongue and learn to live intimately with another person's crazy, irritating and irrational foibles or the whole relationship would fall in a heap. I ran my finger down the copious columns of contractors and randomly selected a handful of those located in my suburb. Only one answered my call and I agreed to meet him at my house late that afternoon.

Fox and Burton came in at eight. We briefed them on the early morning find. By that stage we had a name and a bike.

She was Thelma Freeman, a twenty-year-old student, and she'd been coming back from working a late night dishwashing shift at one of the big city hotels. Her bike was fished out close to the park. My theory that she'd witnessed the murder was looking good, though I didn't completely rule out the possibility she'd been killed for other reasons.

'We'll need to interview her work colleagues and friends and establish some background,' I said. 'You can do that, Burton. In the meantime, we'll concentrate on Phipps. Anyone got any ideas on why he was murdered?'

I wrote MOTIVES on the big whiteboard that took up most of one wall in the office. On the other wall was a similar board that had on it the abduction details. The face of Bobbie and the other three girls stared back at me reproachfully. At least Thelma hadn't been one of them. I didn't want the ex-Immaculata girls turning up dead. Though what they must be going through…. I shut my mind on that. Until something surfaced, the abductions were a cold trail. There was no point stressing.

'Come on, fellas. Use those brain cells. Think up some good solid motives.'

'The usual,' said Fox. 'Greed, jealousy, money, justice, revenge.'

'Good start,' I said, writing them all down.

'My money's on jealousy, what with all those women in the equation,' said Burton.

'That's too logical,' said Ely. 'Not every murder is a stereotype.'

'True,' I said. 'But most motives boil down to the basics. They don't have to be that clever. I'm with Burton. I reckon one of his women got wind of his polygamy and didn't like it. How did you go with the third wife yesterday?'

Ely flipped open his notebook.

'Lina Phipps. Thirty. Blonde, tall with legs to die for.' He clutched his heart and shuddered in mock ecstasy. 'She's a dancer at an inner city strip joint and believes she's his first wife.'

'How long had they been married?' I asked as Fox answered a ringing telephone.

'A year.'

'One busy boy,' said Burton. 'How did he do it?'

We were all considering this with too much unprofessional hilarity when Fox got off the line.

'That was Tara Oakes,' he said and looked at us expectantly.

I shrugged.

'Do we know her?'

'She read about Phipps' murder in the newspaper this morning. She claims she's his mistress.'

With that the phone rang again. In fact, it rang a lot. By the end of the day we had five other women from around the state claiming Dennis Phipps was their man. Every name went on the whiteboard. We had our work cut out interviewing the far-flung callers and establishing whether or not they were crank. But I left that for the boys. Fox and I had a pre-engagement to see Leo Stark. Not that he knew it.

We rocked up to his Subiaco office. It was in one of the small, tree-lined sun-dappled streets off the main drag where old workers' weatherboard cottages had been converted into tasty, expensive businesses harbouring medical specialists, financial consultants and lawyers. It was just before lunch but Stark had beaten us to it. The remains of a pie were adhered to his red stripy tie and beard.

'Mr Stark,' I said brightly as his receptionist showed us through. 'We meet again.'

I held out my hand but he didn't take it.

'I must admit, this meeting doesn't fill me with joy,' he said not even bothering to stand.

'You're all warmth, Leo.'

He looked me up and down and then his lip curled sarcastically.

'Good to see you make an effort to dress nicely for work.'

I hadn't been home to shower and change since the early morning wake up call. It was one of my failings. Once I was on the road, I didn't give my appearance much thought. Actually, no thought. This always bugged Chastity. It obviously bugged Stark too. It was the second time we'd met and the second time he'd had a dig at my clothes.

I don't know why it irked him so much. What was a little river mud on creased, unwashed jeans? And face it, he was no Giorgio Armani clotheshorse.

'Leave my attire out of the equation, Stark, and just answer the questions.'

He smiled. There was still no warmth. I bet I hadn't scored a point on his Hit and Miss dating card either.

'Which are?' he said. He picked up a pen and began to doodle on a yellow legal pad.

'You know Dennis Phipps was found murdered on Sunday morning?'

'I read it in the papers this morning.'

'Did you know him?'

'No.' His eyelids did that hooded thing, hiding any expression that might flitter across the supposed mirrors of his soul and give him away.

'But he was at the Hit and Miss.'

'Not when I was there, Rock. You know that. You were there. Did you know him?'

I ignored his question and carried on with my own.

'You didn't return later?'

'No. I went to a bar to get the bad taste of my final date out of my mouth.'

Thanks a bunch.

'But you joined some of the Hit and Miss clients later?'

'Yes. Why ask? You obviously know the answer.'

'How did you link up?'

'A friend came and got me.'

'Who?'

'Margot Jolley.'

At least that tallied.

'How did she know where to find you?' This was asked more to satisfy my own curiosity rather than for professional need-to-know reasons.

'She rang me on my mobile.'

'Can you tell me what happened?'

'All the deliciously sordid details?'

'Just the relevant ones, Stark.'

He sighed with forced, long-suffering patience and tossed down his pen.

'We got to the Paradise a little after eleven. Had some drinks, did a little dancing and then decided to call it a night.'

'Who was Phipps with?'

'No one in particular.'

'Who did he leave with?'

'I don't know. I left before him.'

'With Margot?' Again it was me who wanted to know. It wasn't essential to the investigation.

'On my own. Pleased about that, Rock?'

Actually, I was. Horrors. I schooled my face into a cool, bland mask. I didn't want him thinking I was interested. Show no weakness to the enemy…

'If you think of anything else, call us.' I gave him my card and walked towards the door, Fox close on my heels. As I reached it, I halted Fox with my hand.

'By the way, Stark,' I said. 'Meet DS Adam Fox. I believe you fancied giving him one last week.'

'Fox?'

Fox delivered one of his sweet angelic smiles.

Stark frowned a wide crease between his thick bear eyebrows, and then recognition dawned and he said a very rude word. Fox and I ducked out the door with huge cheesy grins on our faces. Sometimes I got a real kick out of my job.

'I think that went well,' I said to Fox once we were back out on the street and heading for the Spitfire.

'He likes you,' said Fox.

'Who? Stark? Do me a favour.' But I felt a secret thrill. There was something about Stark.

Mind you, there was something about Fox, too.

'He was drawing hearts all over the paper.'

'Really?' I'd been too busy eyeballing him to notice that.

'He doesn't want to, though,' carried on Fox. 'Those hearts all had swords sticking out of them. I think he's scared of you.'

The feeling was mutual.

'You talk a lot of rubbish.'

'I can feel it in my belly.' He slanted me one of his devastatingly attractive looks and I felt that thrill again. Maybe I was simply sex starved and any and every man was beginning to look good. Though I had to admit, Fox did look exceptionally scrumptious.

'You talking about that street-wise instinct again?' I said, patting Fox on his flat stomach, enjoying myself. 'I don't know, Foxy, but I reckon you're just hungry.'

He smiled enigmatically.

'Could be,' he said.

While we ordered a couple of Lebanese rolls, my mobile rang. It was Chastity. I left Fox to collect the food while I went outside to talk to her.

'Mum,' she said. 'You didn't come and see me yesterday.'

'Was I meant to?' I mentally started going through my calendar. Which concert or sports day had I forgotten?

'It was Sunday.'

Sunday. Student free day. Oh bother. It hadn't registered. The days often blurred.

'Sorry, kiddo, but I was working.'

'Again?'

'Since my promotion I've been dealing with more of the gritty stuff. I'm on call if something big happens.'

'So what happened yesterday that was so big?' I could hear the emotional thumbscrews being put into place.

'A body turned up in one of the local parks.'

'Anyone I know?'

'I'm not discussing it with you.'

'I'm not a baby anymore.' Her voice rose in a plaintive wail.

'Chastity, I can't talk now. I'll pop round to see you tonight.'

Her voice suddenly dropped.

'Have you got that tasty cop with you?'

Fox was now standing in front of me with two dripping rolls. The aroma of chicken and garlic wafted around me along with a hint of Foxy's apple shampoo.

'Yes and he's got our lunch.'

'I won't hold you up, then. Bye Mum. Love you.'

'Love you too.'

We sat down on the wooden bench outside the Lebanese restaurant.

'Organising a date?' said Fox with a wry smile.

'Yes, with my daughter.'

'She's cute,' he said, his smile widening appreciatively.

'Yes, she is and if you go anywhere near her I'll break your knee caps.'

He chuckled.

'Relax, Eve. She's too young for me. I prefer older women.'

Goosebumps racketed over my entire body. And if you go near me, I felt like saying, I swear I'll self-combust. Instead, I just grinned back and took a big bite of my roll and chewed with a nonchalance I was far from feeling.

There was a slight movement just on the edge of my vision. I turned my head in time to see Father Christmas ducking behind a parked car. I abruptly stood up and stared, shielding my eyes against the sun with my free hand. The man slowly lifted his head.

This time he had on a full white beard and red pom-pom hat, but I would have sworn it was the same man who'd been eyeballing me over my garden fence. When he saw me staring, he took off at a fast trot, scaring a couple of kids who were walking a dog. One of them began to cry while the other watched open-mouthed as the big fat man disappeared down a side alley.

'What's up?' said Fox around a mouthful.

'I'm not sure.' I sat back down. 'But I think I'm being stalked by Santa Claus.'

Fox laughed and then choked over his roll.

'Serves you right,' I said. 'Didn't your mother ever tell you it was fatal to laugh at someone when your mouth was stuffed full of food?'

'Sorry. Do you want me to go and bust him?'

I shuddered. I could well imagine the flak back at the station if we did that.

'No. I can handle it. But not a word to the others or I'll have you demoted.'

'Scout's honour. But if he turns dangerous, let me know and I'll come galloping to your rescue on Rudolf.'

'You sleigh me, Fox.'

'Ouch. That was a bad one.'

'They get worse.'

9

WE SPENT THE AFTERNOON SIFTING THROUGH PAPERWORK, TRYING TO work out who had the motive and opportunity to kill Phipps, and not getting very far. I decided to interview Lina Phipps and personally find out what she had to say about Tiger Den. Ely came with me, as he'd interviewed her before and reckoned he'd built up a rapport with her. I think he just wanted to have another squizz at her legs.

It was four o'clock but Lina was still in her jammies. The fact they were yellow silk and moulded around a voluptuous figure made Ely's day.

'Lina,' he said with a smile. 'We need to ask you a few more questions.'

'I gotta get ready for work,' she said, slouching onto the doorjamb as though it was a big effort to stand up.

'This won't take long,' said Ely who then introduced me and confidently walked past the yellow-haired woman in her yellow pyjamas and into a cluttered lounge.

Lina padded barefoot after us. She half-heartedly picked up an emerald green satin cushion from the couch and tossed it to one side.

'Find a seat, why don't you?' She draped herself along the whole length of the couch and stared at Ely with bold blue eyes. There was nothing of the grieving widow about Lina. She was definitely more of the merry variety. And I could understand why Ely thought they had a rapport. I should think every man who met Lina thought he had a rapport with her. She oozed sex.

'Can you tell me when you last saw your husband?' I asked.

Lina didn't bother to address me. She spoke directly to Ely.

'Friday morning. He woke me up, had his wicked way and then left for work.' She winked suggestively at Ely.

'Didn't you make him breakfast?' I inquired sweetly.

For the first time she flashed a look at me.

'That was breakfast, darling,' she said.

'You don't appear too upset by his death,' I ventured.

'Of course I'm upset. I just don't wear my heart on my sleeve.' She returned her attention to Ely where her sultry gaze was rendering him useless.

'Did you know Dennis was already married?' She cast me another irritated glance.

'Don't be daft. He was married to me.'

'So you don't know about his wife and son in Fremantle?'

She sat up, her feet landing on the floor in a rustle of silk.

'He was divorced? He never said.'

'So he never mentioned any other women?'

'Dennis was faithful. His needs were simple and I gave him everything he wanted. He didn't need to have another woman. I was more than enough for him.'

'Actually, he was still married to his first wife. He never bothered divorcing her.' I watched her reaction. Disbelief followed closely by anger.

'Is this true?' she demanded of Ely.

He nodded.

'The bastard. So he was a bigamist?'

She shrugged, grappling again for her sangfroid. 'He must have had a good reason. He wouldn't want to hurt me.'

She got up and began pacing the room, kicking away magazines and cushions that were scattered on the floor.

'Would he have gone to work on Friday?' I asked.

'Of course. He had to go to Kalgoorlie or somewhere. I don't – didn't – keep a tally of his movements. He travelled extensively, though he only got paid peanuts. I used to ask him why he did it, but he loved being on the road, loved his job, loved the people he met. He was one happy and contented man.'

He was a sleaze, but I kept my opinion to myself.

'So you didn't see him at weekends?'

'Sometimes, but not often. I work weekends and sleep most of the day. That's why Den organised his trips then. He'd leave early Friday and come home Monday night. It suited us.'

Ely and I exchanged knowing glances. It had certainly suited Tiger Den.

Lina couldn't tell us anymore and so we left. I had my appointment with the builder and got back to my place as a smelly, noisy, battered red van, with the legend 'Ferrari Builders – We Tackle Anything' painted on the side panels, pulled up.

A small, rotund Italian bounced out of the van and then bounced his way over to me. He had greying dark hair sprouting from ears, nose and neck but little on his nut-brown scalp. His grubby t-shirt strained to cover his watermelon shaped torso and he wore shorts that clung to his body I don't know how. He had the shortest, hairiest and stumpiest legs I'd seen on a grown man and disreputable plimsolls on his feet. But his smile was wide and friendly.

'Meeses Rocks?' he said offering a hairy hand the size of a pizza plate. 'I Dom Ferrari. I coma to look at your place.'

We spent an exhausting couple of hours cataloguing the disasters of my house and Mr Ferrari scribbling furiously in a small yellow pocket notebook with a stubby red pencil.

'So you'll give me an itemised quote?' I asked.

'No problemo. I do thata now.' He ripped a miniscule page from his soiled notebook and showed me his calculations.

I was pleasantly surprised. It didn't look that much, considering.

'And if I agree to this, you can get the work done before Christmas?'

He'd been assuring me throughout the two hours that it would be a piece of cake. That nothing was too difficult, however awful it appeared to be. He had lots of family who could pitch in to help.

They were a team. An efficient team. They were Ferraris, were they not, and all that sort of jazz.

Now he said, 'Lady, you betcha. No problemo.'

He gave a friendly wide grin that showed big yellow teeth in his sun-bronzed face. He was like a cuddly benign troll and I was charmed by his bonhomie. To cap it all, he said the work was manageable, affordable and could be done by Christmas. What a bargain package. How could I resist? So I didn't.

Mr Ferrari left in a cloud of black smoke, his broken exhaust shattering the relative quiet of the street, while I belted inside and raced for the shower.

It had been a long, hot day and I needed to wash the day's grime from my body before going to see Chastity. The shower lived up to expectations and squirted some lukewarm spit over me. I fantasised about the new shower system Mr Ferrari had assured me would be top priority. What a great Christmas present to myself. In spite of the pathetic dribble, I persevered and washed my hair. I then donned clean jeans and t-shirt, fast, as I was already late.

As I went to leave, I remembered my washing was still hanging on the line from Friday. It would be sun-baked to a crisp. Best get it in before it disintegrated completely. I headed for the backdoor and stopped. No washing. The horrible, lurching Hills hoist was empty. Someone had stolen my laundry!

Grief, they must be sick. My knickers were well beyond their use-by date and my t-shirts needed an overhaul. Only my favourite jeans had been worth the effort. I kicked the veranda post and then swung around to go back inside.

And there, by the door, was my washing, neatly folded and stacked in my bleached cane laundry basket. Margot must have got sick of seeing the colours fading away to grey before her eyes and brought it in for me. What a star. I must remember to thank her.

I got to Saint Immaculata's by eight. Chastity was sitting on the grass near the car park with a bunch of friends. When she saw my car, she bounded over to me like an overgrown red setter puppy, all bouncy curls and gangly legs.

'Mum! I've been waiting ages.' She launched herself at me and hugged and kissed me as if we hadn't seen each other for years.

'How's the head?' she asked, a slight crease furrowing her otherwise perfect brow.

'I presume you're talking about the hockey stick attack?'

'I'm so sorry, Mum. Did it hurt much?'

'Yes. But I forgive you. It's good to know you can handle yourself in a crisis. Did you get a pass from the Iron Nun so we can go out for a coffee?'

Chastity giggled.

'You shouldn't call her that. It's disrespectful. But yes, she said we could go out.'

We had coffee at a restaurant overlooking the Swan River. The cups were large, the coffee creamy and the pecan pie was to die for.

'You'll get fat,' said Chastity who'd declined dessert.

'I've hardly eaten all day, so give me a break.'

'You know school ends on Friday,' said Chastity after we'd chitchatted for a while.

'Already!'

'Duh. It's almost Christmas.'

'There are weeks and weeks to go.'

'Three.'

'Yikes.' I suffered an immediate cold sweat, which wasn't a mean feat considering the temperature was still in the top thirties. I hadn't bought a single present or card and the way bodies kept disappearing or dying in my patch, there wouldn't be any time to rectify the problem.

'What have you got me for Christmas?'

'Do you want the truth or an excuse?'

'So you haven't got me anything? No big deal. Can I choose my own present this year?'

I regarded her suspiciously.

'What did you have in mind?'

'Driving lessons.'

'You're too young.'

'I'm old enough to get my learner's permit.'

'You're still too young.'

'Aw, Mum. There's a driving instructor coming to the school next term and I'd really like to enrol.'

I looked at my baby. She was a fledgling young woman, almost ready to fly into the world. My heart contracted in love and awe and fear.

'Please Mum?'

'I'll speak to your grandmother.'

As we drove back to Saint Immaculata's, I said casually to Chastity, 'Does Sister Mercy ever hit the hot night spots?'

I sensed rather than saw Chastity tense.

'Why do you ask?'

'I thought I saw her the other night.' And I had a surveillance photo on my desk which looked awfully like her too, but I wasn't going to tell Chastity that.

'She'd be easy to recognise because she always wears a habit. You know that.'

'She wasn't in a habit this time.'

'Couldn't have been Sister Mercy, then.'

I don't know why, but I knew Chastity was lying.

'Are you covering up for her? I wouldn't blame her for wanting to wear something nice. I know Gran is a stickler for old traditions. I'd be the first to admit that can be hard on a young woman. But I'm curious.'

'We don't mind Granny's strict ways,' said Chastity calmly. 'And Sister Mercy is a great supporter of fundamentalism.'

'I see.'

'Do you, Mum?'

'Actually, no. I tried to distance myself from all that years ago.'

'But you sent me to Saint Immaculata's anyway.'

'Yes.' Go figure. Perhaps I was more like my mother than I

cared to admit. I wanted the old-fashioned morals and integrity drummed into my only child, even if I was a little hazy over them myself.

'How's your secret society going? You know, the one with the double Vees?'

'It's going well.' She gave me a pixie grin. 'In fact we're going great guns.'

'Want to tell me about it?'

'No. It's secret.' She wrinkled up her nose. 'Though I might one day.'

I decided not to push and changed the subject.

'I've got the builders moving in to do some renovations on the house. You might want to stay on with Gran for a couple of weeks. The water and electricity will be turned off at odd times and there will be a lot of dust and mess and noise.'

'Will the work be done by Christmas?'

'That's what was promised me.'

'Christmas in our own home. I can't wait.'

Blow Christmas. A decent shower in my own home – I couldn't wait!

I dropped Chastity back at school and headed home, only stopping to buy a chicken korma with pilaw rice and keema nan for my dinner. I ate it sitting out on my front veranda. The orange glow of streetlights dampened the lustre of the starlit night. Crickets and frogs serenaded me along with the muted roar of the traffic. All was right with the world at that precise moment. I took a large bite of nan, savoured the flavour and then almost choked.

Because I saw him.

Santa Claus sans red suit. I'd swear it was him.

He was in the shadows across the road and he was watching me as intently as I was him. I forced the food down my clogged throat as I grabbed for my gun. Damn, but it wasn't in my shoulder holster. I'd forgotten I'd taken it off and put the gun in my bag after forsaking my leather jacket for the inevitability of summer. I wasted valuable time rummaging for the bag under the empty takeaway paper-sacks. Then I leapt off the veranda, taking half the cartons with me, and scurried across the grass.

'Hold it,' I yelled. 'Police!'

But Santa had already sunk into the shadows and disappeared at a dogtrot. I ran up and down the street for a while but the scent was cold.

I got back to my dinner and that was cold too. It had also been found by Margot's ginger tomcat Horace who was daintily picking the chicken out of the korma.

Excellent.

I huffed and muttered and cursed as I tidied up the debris, shoving everything into my wheelie bin. Then to cap it all, Margot yoo-hooed me. I wasn't in the mood for company but it didn't look as if I had a choice. She was primed for action.

'Was that you making all that racket?' she said, flopping down in one of the two chairs I kept on the veranda and setting down a bottle of red and two Woollies' wineglasses. She was dressed in a low cut top with diagonal zebra stripes, her black miniskirt and four-inch stilettos. She looked as though she was expecting a client any minute now.

'Yeah, that was me,' I said, shoving the gun back in my bag. 'Just overreacting to the shadows.'

I didn't want to alarm her by airing my fears I was being stalked.

'Was that a gun you were waving or a plastic toy?'

'A gun.' I really didn't want to talk about it.

'Are you a good cop?' she asked after we clinked glasses and had our first mouthful of cheap wine.

I winced at the red's roughness hit the back of the throat and said with a wine-rasped hoarseness: 'Well, I didn't make it to DI without showing some grit and flair. I also have boundless enthusiasm and determination to do a good job.'

And a cast iron stomach so I could drink whatever came my way with the good, the bad and the ugly.

'You dig righting the wrongs of society.'

'Something like that.'

'Though it's not always black and white.'

Well, not like her top that was making my eyes going all waggily. It was a good job I wasn't epileptic.

'No,' I said. 'But the law is a good benchmark.'

'I'm glad you're a good cop and that you're my next-door neighbour. It's comforting to know you're on the case to find Den's murderer. I don't mind telling you, I'm scared. It's rather close to home having one of our own murdered.'

'Try not to worry, Margot. We're doing our best. I have every confidence we'll nail the person who did it.'

'So you reckon you'll find him?'

'Or her.' I shrugged, slopping some of the wine, which was no big loss. 'The murderer is not necessarily a man.'

'Why do you say that?'

'I've a hunch it's a woman, that's all.'

'No! Get away! Surely a woman wouldn't be strong enough? The news report said his neck was broken.' She sounded amazed.

'A fit woman, using the right technique, could do so easily. And if he knew her and was lulled into a false sense of security...' I realised I was thinking aloud and stopped abruptly. I didn't like discussing my cases outside work. It wasn't professional. Margot was regarding me intently.

'Go on,' she said. 'It's fascinating stuff.'

I waved a hand in the air.

'No way. No talking shop. I've had my fill for the day. But I do want to say thank you to you for bringing in my washing.'

Margot laughed and slugged back some more wine.

'Don't thank me, darl, thank the hunk who was floating about in your garden this afternoon.'

'I beg your pardon?'

'Burly and beefy with untidy reddish-blond hair. Dangerously sexy in my opinion.'

'Did you recognise him?'

'Nope. But I sure would like to have my laundry folded by him, anytime.' She gave a throaty chuckle.

Dangerously sexy? I had no idea who it could have been.

Fox? Nah, he was not a burly beefcake but sleek angel. Then who? I wasn't as excited as Margot to find out. I already had one nutter stalking me. I didn't relish the idea of two, even if he was domesticated.

10

Bang, bang, bang.

I was woken by an army of Italian midgets who raided my house at seven o'clock with a total disregard for my very necessary beauty sleep. I staggered out of bed. A squizz in the hall mirror confirmed my hair was a red, curly mess. My eyes matched the same description. Thanks, Margot. Last night's wine had been rougher than rough. Not that I'd cared much after the third glass.

'You're keen,' I said to Ferrari when I opened the door and squinted at him and his motley troll family.

'Meeses Rocks, if yous wanna us to get it all a finished by Christmas then a we gotta get started.'

'Fine. I'll just make myself decent and then I'll be with you.'

I snagged up the laundry basket containing the neatly folded clothes and headed for the bathroom. The shower dribbled over me and I fervently rejoiced that soon – very soon – I'd have steaming jets of pure hot water.

Dressed in my favourite jeans and a lime green t-shirt that did nothing to detract the redness from my eyes, I met the building crew. I couldn't remember all their names but then I presumed they wouldn't be around long enough to get closely acquainted. They'd be gone before Christmas.

Hah! I should've known better!

I skipped breakfast because the kitchen was suddenly too crowded. It appeared the Ferrari family needed freshly brewed tea and a discussion on tactics before any hammers or screwdrivers were wielded.

I went straight to work. Today I was going to visit the parents of the original three missing girls. No deviating. The case was lying heavy on my conscience. I know I had a double murder to investigate, but there was a chance these girls were still alive. Hadn't Sister Immaculata told me to have faith?

I caught up on my outstanding paperwork and then studied all the surveillance photographs. I hoiked out the one of Sister Mercy. I'd bet my police pension that the slinkily dressed babe was her. There was also a back shot of a blonde in a familiar black sequinned dress. Angelina Dellaporte, Chastity's roommate? Maybe.

Have faith, my mother had said. Well, I was trying.

I also had a niggling little feeling I couldn't quite put my finger on. But give me time. I was trying to have faith on that too.

Later in the morning, Fox and I visited all three sets of parents. They were the fastest interviews on record and we didn't get much out of them. I turned to Fox once we were back in the squad car and said, 'Okay, what do you reckon?'

'Boss?'

'Something's not right.'

'Can you clarify?'

'Well, they're too serene, too unruffled. If I'd had Chastity abducted, possibly murdered, I'd be a gibbering wreck and turning the city upside down. But they're all acting as if their daughters have gone away on school camp.'

'Maybe they're on drugs from the doctor to stop them from worrying.'

'All six parents? I think not. I think they're stonewalling us. Something's not right.'

Have faith, she'd said. Hmm. I wondered if the Iron Nun was involved…

'Let's go and see Bobbie Fellows family too. I'd be interested to see how they are faring.'

On Friday night, when I'd seen them outside the Paradise Nightclub, Anne and Ken Fellows had appeared stricken with grief. Today, the contrast was astounding. Anne had been to the hairdressers and looked almost perky and Ken was back at work.

'What's going on, Mrs Fellows?' I said as she set down a tray of freshly brewed coffee and fragrant, homemade shortbread. I mean, who makes shortbread when their daughter has gone missing? In fact, who makes shortbread, period, in this day and age?

We were sitting at a wrought iron and mosaic tiled table under a flowering jacaranda tree. A lone purple petal floated down and landed in the sugar bowl. Cicadas sawed around us. It was hot and perspiration prickled my skin.

Anne Fellows fumbled a cup and shot me a nervous glance.

'What do you mean?'

'You don't seem that upset about Bobbie.'

'Oh? But I am...'

'And definitely less upset than you were a few days ago. Do you, perhaps, know something we don't?'

'What do you mean?'

I sighed and tried not to growl my frustration.

'Have you had news from her?'

She fidgeted with the cream jug and poured a huge dollop of double thick into my cup. I wasn't complaining. I love cream, but I felt she was trying to avoid the question.

'Mrs Fellows?'

'We want you to drop the investigation,' she said with a sudden spurt.

My mouth dropped open and then snapped into action.

'Four girls have gone missing, abducted by heaven knows who, and being subjected to goodness knows what, and you want us to stop investigating?' My voice rose in disbelief.

'Roberta and the others have probably taken themselves off. Having a bit of a rest or a holiday or something.'

'Without telling you?'

'Girls have their little secrets you know,' she said defensively.

Didn't I know it. Chastity was a case in point. But that didn't change the fact Bobbie had disappeared during a trip to the Paradise toilets and had left her friend kicking her heels at the bar. Strange time to go walkabout, and so I told Anne Fellows in a few clipped words.

'Have you heard from the kidnappers? Had a ransom note?' I pushed.

'No!' Her emphatic denial convinced me.

'But you have heard from Bobbie?'

'No.' Less convincing. She wasn't a natural liar. But I let it pass.

'It's an offence to withhold information, Mrs Fellows. We'll be in touch.'

'What is going on?' I demanded of Fox when we were cruising back to the station.

'Search me, Eve.'

I contemplated that statement, from the purely personal aspect. Fox's jeans were so tight you wouldn't need to search them. Then again, a strip-search would be ever so enjoyable…

'I might just do that, Foxy,' I said and I think my voice might have purred like that of a fat, contented cat. Blame it on the cream.

Fox briefly swung his eyes from the road and snagged mine. His smile was sultry sweet as he said, 'I'll look forward to it.'

Purrrrr.

'The chief wants to see you,' said Burton when we blew into the office a few minutes later.

'What for?'

'No idea.'

It didn't take me long to find out. Operation Paradise was being trashed. Just like that. No discussion. No reason. Just the parents wanted us to butt out and the chief had agreed to it.

My good mood pinged.

I saw red.

'Why? Are you all Masons or something and done funny handshakes to stymie the Op?' I stormed at him, heedless of whether or not I offended the hierarchy.

'You forget yourself, DI Rock.'

'Young women have disappeared! They might be suffering torture and abuse or are already dead. Don't you care?'

'Their parents are no longer worried about their whereabouts.'

'Why?'

He gave me a steely look that could have shattered an iceberg at a hundred paces, but I was reared on those sorts of glances and so it bounced off me as I raged around the room. He let me rant on for all of thirty seconds before I was summarily dismissed from his presence.

'You have a murder investigation to run. I suggest you get on with it,' he said as I wrenched the door almost off its hinges and stomped back to the operations room to let rip among the boys.

Sodbury was already packing away reports and statements into filing boxes and stripping the photographs of the girls off the information board. I roared up to him, impotency fuelling my wrath.

'Did you fight to keep the operation going?' I demanded of him.

Sodbury shrugged. 'I don't have the time or energy to argue the toss, Rock. It's not the first operation ever to be suspended and it won't be the last.'

'Don't you feel any responsibility to find these girls?'

'Nope. I'm not paid to. I've got my work cut out.'

'But these girls might still be alive and praying for the cavalry to save them!'

'Not this officer, honey. I've got a drug bust coming up.'

I ignored the patronising 'honey' tag and stared at him suspiciously. I felt I was being fobbed off. 'I haven't heard of any drug bust. When and where is it happening?'

'It's very hush-hush. Need to know basis only.' He gave me a supercilious glimmer of a smile and I felt like punching out his lights. 'You don't need to know.'

'We are on the same side, Sodbury,' I said through gritted teeth. 'And I want a very, very sound reason why you're letting Operation Paradise die without even a squeak.'

He sighed.

'Okay. You win. I'm not crazy about the operation being canned either. But all I can tell you about the drugs raid is that it's happening any day now and involves some undercover cop whose been working on the investigation for months and reckons now's the time to pull it off.'

'I'm not letting Operation Paradise go,' I vowed as Fox and I headed off to interview Sue Phipps for the second time. 'I care about those girls, even if their parents and the powers-that-be don't.'

'You live up to your name,' chuckled Fox. 'Solid and immovable.'

'I think I'll accept that as a compliment.'

'Do. It was meant as one. But what about your Christian name: Eve? The perpetrator of the original sin? The first to succumb to temptation? Do you live up to that part of your name too?'

'You're a detective. You find out.'

'I shall,' he said as he drove up the driveway of Scarborough Sue's house and stopped the car. He swivelled in his seat to face me, his baby blues burning with an intense inner heat, and I almost shivered and gave the game away.

Almost.

I wanted him to work harder to find out just how much temptation I could withstand.

'Eve,' he said softly and my insides liquefied. He reached over and lightly tugged one of my red curls that was spinning crazily out of control along with all the others. 'You're very beautiful.'

'This is very unprofessional behaviour, Fox,' I said and hoped he didn't detect the hint of sudden huskiness edging my words.

'True. We'll have to wait until knock off time.' He made it sound dirty and sinful and delicious.

'Shame,' I said on a regretful sigh. 'But them's the breaks.'

I legged it from the car before I succumbed to Eve's temptation curse and grabbed him by the shirt, hauled him into my lap and ruined all my professional decorum. I think he realised because I could hear him chuckling behind me as I knocked on the door.

But I ignored him.

Cool Sue wasn't at home so we went next-door to see if her neighbour knew where she was.

Sylvia answered our first knock. She was in a turquoise sundress today with plenty of rings on her fingers and toes and chains around her neck, wrists and ankles.

'Hi, guys,' she said breezily. 'You after Sue? She's staying at her mother's for a bit of support. I'll give you the address. Come in while I find it.'

Her beaded, braided hair clacked noisily as she walked into the airy family room.

'Grab a seat. Want a drink?'

We declined. I wandered over to the large glass doors that opened up to a large sunken swimming pool the colour of Sylvia's dress.

'Nice,' I said.

'Yes, isn't it. Mind you, I worked hard to afford it.'

'What do you do?' I inquired as she scribbled the number down on a pink post-it pad.

'I'm a sex therapist.'

'Goodness. What a job.' I waggled my eyebrows and grinned.

'That's hard work?' said Fox with an answering smile.

She fluttered her lashes at him.

'You'd be surprised, DS Fox.'

She'd remembered his name. I was impressed. Then on second thoughts, I wasn't. Any red-blooded woman would remember all Fox's vital statistics.

'Actually, Den was one of my clients,' she chirruped.

'You didn't mention this the other day,' I said, only marginally surprised that Tiger Den needed sex counselling considering the number of women in his life. I wouldn't have been surprised if he was having time management counselling, too, to work out how to keep them all satisfied.

'Well, I forgot. I had been giving him counselling for a while but we'd stopped.'

'Why?'

She gave a self-conscious giggle and a slight red tinged her cheeks.

'It's a bit embarrassing.'

'Try us. We're very broadminded, aren't we DS Fox?'

'Very.' He winked at me and I felt my own temperature rise. I shoved back down the mercury so I could concentrate on Sylvia.

'We became lovers,' she said. 'I know that was unprofessional but it just happened. Please don't tell Sue. It's so awkward and silly and she'd be devastated.'

'I see,' I managed to say, though Fox appeared struck dumb. What did that bring the count to? Nine, ten, eleven women? What was Dennis Phipps? The font of all sperm?

'I was trying to help him,' Sylvia gushed on. 'Sue didn't understand his needs. Actually he didn't really need a therapist. He just needed love.'

I was amazed and didn't bother to hide it.

'You bought that corny old line?' I said.

'What do you mean?' She pouted and I was reminded of Lina. Perhaps Den had preferred his women dumb.

'He had at least three wives and six girlfriends and now you tell us you were his lover too. I reckon once we're finished, we're looking around a dozen women in Dennis' hectic love life.'

'A dozen? Ridiculous. You must be exaggerating.'

'Give or take one or two, but no.' I began ticking them off. There was a girl for every port of his life. Dennis Phipps had been like a landlocked sailor riding the waves of lust through Western Australia. No wonder the state used to sport the legend The State of Excitement. Dennis must have personally coined the phrase.

'When did you last see him?' I asked.

'Saturday morning.' A single tear slipped down her cheek and she sniffed. 'He slipped around while Sue was playing tennis and the kids were watching cartoons.'

'To have sex?' asked Fox bluntly.

'No, DS Fox, to make love. We loved each other. He talked about leaving Sue and marrying me, but decided he couldn't do that to Sue and the kids. He was very thoughtful like that.'

'Sylvia,' I said shaking my head in disgust. 'He had a wife and son he'd deserted in Fremantle, another current wife in Midland and all these other women in between. He was using you, Sue and all the other women.'

'I knew about the other women, but they were all in his past. He'd moved on,' she said, her chin in the air. 'Sue didn't know about the others though. Unless you've told her?'

'Not yet, but we'll be telling her today. Tomorrow it'll be in all the newspapers and I don't want her finding out like that.'

Sylvia blew her nose hard and wiped her brimming eyes.

'I'm going to miss him,' she said.

'I'm curious. Please tell me,' I ventured. 'What was so special about him?'

'Of course, you never met him. It's like that old song, "To know him was to love him".'

Was she serious? I tried not to gag.

'Really?' was all I could manage.

Fox came to my rescue.

'So any ideas why someone wanted to kill him?' he said.

She shook her head and blew her nose again.

'It must have been an opportunistic killing. No way did anyone hate him. He was totally loveable.'

'You can still say that after hearing about all those other wives and women?' I said.

'He was confused which was why he came to me in the first instance. He was a lonely, lovely man.'

Again, I tried not to gag.

'You okay, boss?' asked Fox as we drove away. 'You had a funny look on your face back at Sylvia's.'

'I was trying not to throw up. I only met the bloke once, but I felt like killing him immediately. He didn't inspire one jot of love in me. He was a sleaze.'

'So really we should be checking out your alibi.'

I grinned.

'Looks like it. I must be the only woman in the Southern Hemisphere who didn't fall for his charm. Mind you, Sexy Sylvia could be a suspect.'

'Why?'

'Angry he wouldn't leave his wife for her. It might have especially griped if she'd heard about all his other women during sex therapy sessions and knew he was capable of shedding the old to put on the new. We've only got her word for it she didn't care about his past. I think we should do some digging.'

Next, we had the unpleasant job of informing the wives about each other. Ely and Burton told Lina, Fox and I told Audrey and Sue. It took some convincing but eventually Lina accepted it, Sue was shattered and Audrey couldn't have cared less. The lovers knew that wives were in the equation, so we didn't bother telling them. They would read all about it in Wednesday's newspapers.

The day ground to an unsatisfactory end. My team had annoyed half the women on the planet and we were no closer to finding the murderer. And we didn't have one solid suspect.

The only bright ray of sunshine was perched on the edge of my desk, in tight jeans and a black t-shirt, with a gun holster strapped to one superb, muscular shoulder. I don't think it was my imagination, but I could feel sex vibes vibrating through the air like jackhammers.

And it would soon be knock off time. Mmm, mmm.

And then Foxy's phone rang.

'Dad! Hi! Yeah, almost done here,' he said his eyes seeking mine in hot blue promise of after-hours delight. 'Ah, you want to meet up.'

Fox mouthed to me 'do you want to come?' and I mouthed back a definite 'no'. It was still too soon to meet the folks. And we still hadn't damn well kissed.

'Where?' he was saying to his dad and putting a heartfelt appeal in his eyes for me to join them. It was a good job Burton and Ely had left for the day or tongues would be wagging faster than a dog with a hambone. As it was, if this continued, we'd have to up the air-con as there was so much heat radiating between us.

'The yacht club bar? Sounds great.' He grabbed my sex-sweaty hand in his warm dry one and mouthed a please. How could I resist with megawatts of sexual sizzle coursing through my veins?

I gave him the thumbs up. Fox lit up like one of the Christmas trees adorning Hay Street Mall.

'Dad, do you mind if I bring someone?' He sounded like a kid with a fancy treat. And then his face fell to his leather tooled boots.

Obviously Big Daddy did mind. Darn it.

'Yes, it's a woman,' he said and added furtively, as if it explained everything. 'It's okay. She's a cop.'

His dad was less furtive. I could hear his response to that little gem loud and clear.

'They're the worst kind,' said Father Fox and he was laughing, hard.

'Gee, thanks,' I said as Fox abruptly terminated the call.

'It's not like it sounds.' His eyes flickered. He was lying.

It was just like it sounded.

'Don't worry about it, Foxy,' I said brightly. 'I've things to do anyway. We'll get together some other time.'

'Like tomorrow night?'

'You betcha.'

Fox left soon after with another apology on his lips and a promise of nights to come. With that I had to be content. His relationship with his old man was touching. I envied him. I didn't even know who my old man was.

I was now alone in the office, and I was hot and cranky. Things were not going my way on any front. I hated that Operation Paradise had shut down. I hated we had no concrete leads for Dennis Phipps' murder. I hated my house was invaded by Italian trolls. And I hated I'd been cheated out of a sizzling hot date. At least the trolls would be moving out by Christmas and I'd eventually get a date with Fox. But there were no guarantees we'd find the missing girls or Phipps' killer.

I took yet another look at the surveillance pictures. Something was bugging me. I laid them out on the table. There were the Hit and Miss clients going in. And here they were coming out. So what?

Then it struck me. Not everyone was accounted for. Too many had gone in, but not enough exited. There was Phipps, arms around a couple of women that Josie Lambert had named, and there were those same women coming out a couple of hours later but without Tiger Den. There was Leo Stark going in with Margot but coming out alone. But who did Margot come out with? Like Den, she wasn't among the pics either.

I systematically went through all the photographs and found six people unaccounted for, and one of those was dead. But we'd had both exits covered. How had we not seen them leave the club? What was it about the Paradise, I wondered, that people went missing so often and so easily? It was time to have another word with Stan Zefferelli.

But not tonight. I was bushed.

By the time I finally made it home I was looking forward to a cool shower, sinking some wine and having a calm, quiet smoke of one of my cigars before hitting the sack.

But, as usual, I shouldn't have projected and tempted fate. I'd already been disappointed once tonight. And yes, the sanctuary of home wasn't to be.

For starters there was a large skip parked outside my house and there was enough rubbish on the lawn to start my own salvage yard. What had the Ferrari boys been doing? It didn't take me long to find out.

They'd been causing chaos and mayhem, Italian style.

Dom Ferrari was still in residence.

'Ciao, Meeses Rocks, yous have good day?'

'Busy, thank you Mr Ferrari. You obviously have too.' I stared in dismay at the huge cracks in the walls that hadn't been there when I'd left this morning. They were wide enough to drive a double-decker bus through them. Actually, I exaggerate. They weren't quite that big. More community bus size.

'Don't yous worry about thems cracks,' he assured me. 'Thems will be fixed after we finish re-stumping the house. After that, the house no longer sag. Good, eh?'

'Good,' I said faintly. 'But I had no idea there would be so much mess.'

'Hey, lady. Yous have to break eggs to make omelette. Didn't your mama never tells yous that?'

'Of course. I understand.' Just. But I felt like blubbing anyway. My darling house. My garden. My tranquillity. All trashed by trolls.

'I see yous tomorrow, lady. Have a good night.'

I stood on my scrap-heap lawn and watched him drive off in a bilious cloud of exhaust fumes. I was just about to turn around to go indoors when another car drove past. The driver slowed down and gave me a good long look. It took me a moment to realise he was Santa, but only because he wasn't wearing a pointy red hat or I would have been quicker.

'Oi!' I yelled grappling to get my car keys out of my back pocket so I could jump into my car and follow him. But the exercise took too long. The jeans were too snug. The yellow-haired Santa accelerated away before I could get his registration number. Rats.

Feeling rattled, I locked the front door behind me. I took a couple of steadying breaths and then decided to inspect the bathroom. I needed a good lathering to get rid of the day's trouble and grime.

I stopped on the threshold and my heart sank. There was a large cavity where the ceiling used to be and lots and lots of plaster chunks and ancient dirt over the shower, basin and floor. Once again the sprinkler alternative was looking good.

I stripped down to basics and showered under the hosepipe. At least the builders' junk hadn't permeated into the backyard. Yet. And for the first time since I'd bought the house, I was glad I had an outside toilet. At least I could contemplate without builders' dust up my nostrils and their mess assaulting my eyes.

11

I SPENT A RESTLESS NIGHT. THE SEA BREEZE HAD AGAIN FAILED TO deliver its cool promise. The bedroom was hot and airless. On top of that, I had too many things on my mind: men, murder and missing girls. I tossed and turned so often I felt like one of those barbequed chickens impaled on a spit.

In the end I gave up trying to sleep. I glanced at my clock. Five o'clock. A good time to hit the streets and give my running shoes a pounding and my brain a rest. I slung on a black sports crop top and pair of matching shorts, dragged my hair back in a multi-coloured scrunchy that didn't go with my red hair and then limbered up on the back veranda with some stretching exercises.

I unlocked the gate at the bottom of my garden and did a gentle jog along the back lane. Staffies and kelpies barked through the fences at me, some baring teeth, others presenting waggly backsides desperate to be loved. They were like the men in my life.

Wattle birds were busy in the gums beating up the smaller birds. And I was gasping before I'd run one kilometre. Too many curries and cigars, and not enough exercise.

I got back forty minutes later and sluiced myself in cold water from the hosepipe. The earlier enthusiasm of sprinkler showers, of recapturing childish pleasures, was fast losing its appeal. In fact, it sucked. I wanted a decent shower.

I dressed in my usual gear and slung a couple of pieces of stale raisin bread into the toaster. I desperately needed to do some food shopping. My cupboards were as bare as Ma Hubbard's. Good job I didn't have a dog to feed.

As I was up so early, I did some washing and got it on the line as the Ferrari boys turned up. They were my cue to leave and I was back at the station by seven. I might as well have lived at the joint. At least the showering facilities were better.

The boys and I spent the morning checking and cross-checking statements. Nothing new turned up. I told them about the nightclub patrons supposedly failing to reappear and Fox volunteered to accompany me to see Zefferelli.

'How was your evening with your dad?' I asked Fox as we sped towards the seediest nightclub on the block.

'Good.'

'So what does your dad do?'

'Not a lot.'

'He must do something.'

'Messes about on his boat. Sails where he wants to.'

'A free spirit, then.'

'Something like that.' He laughed but I didn't get the joke.

We parked right outside the ugly purple-painted nightclub. Zefferelli was not thrilled to see us.

'What do you want?' he said ungraciously.

'Not going to offer us a drink, mate?' goaded Fox.

'No time. I'm busy. Unlike you civil servants, I have to earn every cent. No cushy number for me.'

'Just a couple of quick questions about Saturday night,' I said.

'I've already told your lot I didn't know the murdered geezer.'

'So you say.'

'It's the truth.'

'Well, I've got a problem with your place, Zefferelli.'

He looked ready to throw up. Maybe he thought I was going to slap a condemned sticker on the club and close it down. Now there was a happy thought.

'Relax,' I said. 'It's nothing too hard. But I know a certain number of people came into your club that night but the same number didn't leave by conventional means. Do you have any other exits to this joint that we don't know about?'

Zefferelli licked his lips and ran a pudgy hand over his slicked back hair. Not that it needed rearranging. The grease was doing a great job keeping the Elvis hairstyle in place.

'Zefferelli?'

'No,' he said and began frantically wiping the bar top with a dubious coloured cloth.

'And yet we have six people unaccounted for and one of those was Phipps.'

'Phipps?'

'The dead man.'

If he rubbed the bar any harder, the Laminex was going to need replacing.

'How did Phipps and the other five get out of the club, Zefferelli?'

He didn't answer.

'If you don't cooperate, we'll have to haul your sorry carcass down to the station.'

He shot me a glance of pure loathing.

'There're only the two entrances. Those people left after the club was closed.'

'You had a private, unlicensed party?'

'No. The bar was shut down. I've got some rooms that I let out to… valued customers.'

There was an expectant silence.

'Go on,' I prompted, wanting him to spell it out.

He sighed.

'You know, to use if the mood takes them… Sometimes people don't want the hassle of going back to someone's place. Especially if there are complications.'

'Such as?'

'A wife or partner.'

'I see.' Finally a breakthrough. Whoever Phipps had been with was probably the last person to see him alive. And as for Margot,

I wondered who she'd scored with. I'd have to ask during one of our boozy evenings.

'Do you know who Phipps shared a room with?' I asked Zefferelli.

'No. He just ordered the room. I was surprised he knew about it, because it's not general knowledge.'

'So he was with a regular then?'

'I didn't see who he was with. I told you.'

I guessed he was lying but there was little more we could get out of him at this stage.

'Would you like to come out to dinner tonight?' Fox asked as we drove through the glary afternoon streets back to the station. The city was groaning under the weight of Christmas streamers and bunting. Shops were decorated with flashing fairy lights and mock snow. The temperature was thirty-eight degrees in the shade. Roll on a white Christmas.

'Eve?'

'Possibly,' I said, to buy myself a little more conscience-searching time. Adam Fox was special, but could I cope with the complication of an in-house affair? Yes, no, maybe.

'Hey, that sounds keen.' His voice was deceptively neutral. I'd like to think he was as interested in me as I was in him.

'No hot date with your dad tonight?'

'He's busy.'

'Where did you have in mind for dinner?'

'My place…'

My blood began thrumming a merry tune. A lust haze descended. It was a good job Fox was driving. I might have hit a candy cane decorated lamppost and that wouldn't have looked good on my report card.

'Sounds… interesting. Where is your place?'

'I live on a boat.'

Like his dad. Hopefully it wasn't the same boat…

'Oh.' I said and pondered the irony of that little gem. I'd had some of my best sex on a boat, and then ended up pregnant with Chastity. Let me say this now, if things did progress with us, I would be much more careful this time round.

'It's moored at the yacht club.'

'Okay. Sounds good. I'll bring the wine.'

I tackled the afternoon's work with a buoyancy that was brutally punctured and deflated a couple of hours later when Fox apologised, once again, because he had to cancel.

'Don't tell me, your dad wants a drinking partner.'

'My mum this time. She called to say she's got plumbing problems she needs me to sort out. I'm sorry, Eve. How about tomorrow night?'

'Fine,' I said, but it wasn't. I felt miffed and cheated. Because I had plumbing problems too, on top of a cancelled date. So I went to the firing range and let off a few practice rounds with my gun to vent my frustration and then knocked off early to buy food staples and check on the progress of my house.

I was out of my car and halfway up the garden path when I spotted Santa peering at me over the top of the skip. I yelled and took off after him, but was so intent on trying to catch him, I tripped over some piping left by Dom Ferrari or one of his crew, and fell flat on my face.

Oof! The air whooshed from my lungs and my shin screamed pain. I rolled about in agony, clutching my leg and attempting to breathe through gritted teeth.

'Are you alright, darl?' Margot came tottering over the grass to view the damage. She was wearing skyscraper silver stilettos that matched her boob-tube dress.

I mimicked a landed blowfish for a few seconds before finally finding my voice.

'No,' I said. 'I hurt.'

'A nice drink of wine will make you feel better,' she assured me, patting my head.

I sat up and wrenched up my grass-stained jeans to inspect the damage. Thank goodness the recycled fashion of flairs was back.

Not only did it make it easier carrying a gun on the inside leg, it also meant easy access to hurt shins.

'So that's where you keep your gun,' said Margot marvelling.

'Sometimes.'

'Where else?'

'Wherever it doesn't spoil the line of my clothes,' I said with a half laugh. Me, fashion queen cop. As if I cared about the line of my clothes. No, I was more interested in the creep who was stalking me. 'Did you see that man by my skip?'

'What, Santa?'

Was there anybody else?

'Yes,' I said as patiently as possible.

'Sure. He was in your garden earlier and brought in your washing. I reckon it's cute. Not everyone has their own special Father Christmas to do the domestic chores.'

I sat there open mouthed for a count of five slow ones.

'Have you seen him around much?' I finally managed to articulate.

'Most days. Usually morning and evening. He doesn't hang around once you've gone to work.'

Great.

'But you said this neighbourhood didn't attract Peeping Toms.'

'He's no Peeping Tom, babe. He's Santa Claus.'

I shook my head. That wine was sure looking good.

Margot said I could shower at her place. I went into my house to get some clean clothes, a towel and a bottle of wine. The bus-sized cracks were still bus sized. The mess was about the same. I couldn't see any detectable improvements. Dom Ferrari must still be breaking eggs.

But at least my laundry was neatly folded.

'Do you fancy coming to a party with me?' Margot asked as we sat on her front veranda and ate cheese on toast. 'I haven't got anyone to go with and I don't want to rock up alone. It's not good for my image.'

'Sure,' I said. It would probably be the only Christmas party I'd be invited to. I wasn't big on parties. I was too much of a loner. Or was it because I was a cop? 'Who will be there? Anyone I know?'

'Maybe,' she said with a shrug. 'It's tomorrow night. You can borrow my red dress if you don't have anything suitable. It'll go well with your colouring.'

Dress? She wanted me to wear a dress? Grief. I only had one dress and I only wore that on very special occasions. Like going undercover at the Paradise Nightclub. Why would I wear it to a party?

And Thursday night was meant to be Hot Fox Night.

I was about to tell her I already had a date, and one I didn't have to dress up for, but then I thought it would do Fox good to know I had other fish to fry. Let him sweat for a night or two, just like he'd made me sweat.

But I still wasn't sure about the dress. Margot went and got it, tossing it over the table. I caught it and held it up, squinting in shock. It didn't look big enough to be a dress. More a sock.

'Don't you have some red heels to match this scrap of nothing?' I said, knowing full well I had nothing remotely suitable in my wardrobe.

She thought for a moment and then shook her head.

'No, sorry, Eve.'

'But you were wearing a snazzy pair the other night.' I remembered her tottering about at the Hit and Miss in scarlet neck-breakers.

'Oh, those. I broke the heel.'

'Shame. They would have been ideal.'

'They don't make them so good anymore,' she said. 'The heels are always busting. It costs me a small fortune.'

'Margot,' I said, suddenly remembering something. 'Do you ever use rooms at the Paradise Nightclub?'

Margot slanted me a cautious glance over the rim of her wine glass.

'I might do.'

'No need to sound so cagey. I'm just curious.'

'There are a handful of rooms upstairs,' she reluctantly conceded, shifting uncomfortably in her wicker chair and I don't think it was her micro boob-tube dress that was causing the discomfort. There wasn't enough of it. Margot was a minimalist where clothes were concerned.

'And?' I prompted when I realised she wasn't going to elaborate.

'They're open for hire.'

'For?' This was like pulling toad teeth. Why had she gone coy on me?

She squirmed again and took a gulp of wine.

'You don't want to know, darl.'

'Actually, I do. That's why I asked.' I tried not to sound snaky but she'd try a saint in this mood.

'Favours,' she said with the greatest reluctance.

'That's one way of describing it. I presume you mean sex.'

She nodded slightly and avoided eye contact.

I swirled the wine around in my glass and watched the red whirlpool as I digested this piece of information. Perhaps I hadn't been far off in my estimation of Margot's clothes. Perhaps she was on the game. Perhaps being a masseuse didn't pay all that well in the scheme of things and she had to supplement her income. I didn't blame her. It was one of the oldest professions in the book and one that had gainfully employed my mother. Until, of course, my arrival put the kyboshes on her career and she saw the light.

'You haven't mentioned these rooms before.' I gently chided, thinking it would have been rather helpful to the investigation if she had.

'They're not general knowledge. They're meant to be secret. How did you find out?'

'I'm a detective. That's my job.'

'Well, anyway, it's no big deal.'

Says who? From where I was positioned, this was a bit of a breakthrough.

'You used one of the rooms on Saturday night.' I delivered it as a statement, not a question.

'So?'

I expelled a pseudo-patient breath between my teeth.

'You never said.'

'Because it was private business and nothing to do with your case.' Her voice rose defensively.

'So you're not going to let on who you were with?'

'Are you asking me as a friend or as a cop?'

'Does it matter?' I was surprised how suddenly belligerent she'd become.

'Yes. As a matter of fact, it does. The whole reason for those rooms is so we can be discreet. There are reputations to protect.'

'I see.' I didn't like to point out the bleeding obvious and tell her that this was a murder investigation and so people's reputations counted as zilch. 'Did you know Phipps used one that night too?'

'No,' she said. 'I didn't. The bottle's empty. I'll go get another one.'

I sat on my own in the semi-dark of the veranda and waited. The street was relatively quiet. The neighbour opposite walked by with his black Scotty dog and a boy zoomed by on his skateboard, skilfully swerving around the old guy. And then I realised I was being watched. The hairs on the back of my neck went into erectile malfunction. How long had this been going on?

The man was half in the shadows. I'd like to say it was the tip of his cigarette that alerted me to his presence, but he wasn't smoking. It was only sheer fluke I spotted him. He'd stepped back to avoid the skateboard as the kid rocketed by him, the little skateboard wheels rattling over the cracks in the paving stones like a train belting along railway tracks.

I ceased breathing. I tried to focus on the bloke while appearing to drink my wine. Not a brilliant ruse. My glass was empty. I hoped his night vision was as lousy as mine. The crucial thing to establish was whether or not this was my stalking Santa. He wasn't wearing red, so that took the main piece of evidence out of the equation.

Margot reappeared with a bottle and she began to uncork it.

'Hey, Margot,' I said evenly. 'Don't look now, but there's a guy lurking in the hedge at number eleven. Do you reckon he's my laundry-folding Santa?'

Like a pro – and of course she may have been one – she made a big production of opening the bottle and then swivelled slightly to fill our glasses, glancing in his direction as she did so.

'Could be. Same build. Same age, perhaps.'

He moved slightly. He was now on the edge of the light thrown by the streetlamp. He was bulky. I couldn't establish the colour of his hair, but I think it was light rather than dark. Margot was right. He looked about the same size of Santa. And he was definitely staring in our direction.

Right. That was all I needed. Let's haul his butt and find out what was going on.

'I'll be back,' I said and levered myself out of the wicker chair.

'How very Arnie and macho of you. Do you want me to come too?'

'No, thanks. Keep the wine cool. If I'm not back in fifteen minutes, call the cops.'

I limped my way across Margot's lawn towards him. He retreated into the shadow of a huge Plumbago hedge. I kept advancing. He must have realised my intent and began walking briskly down the path.

I began to jog. He glanced behind at me and then picked up his pace. I ran faster, trying to disregard my painful shin. He zipped around the corner and dodged the old guy with the Scotty. But I was quicker. I bounded forward, sprinted a few metres and then performed a running rugby tackle, pulling him to the ground. He hit the pavement hard and we grappled about in an undignified heap or legs and arms.

Momentum and adrenaline were on my side. I held the advantage and was spread-eagled on top of him, chest to chest, thigh to thigh. He felt taut and muscular and I hoped he wasn't going to get difficult. I wouldn't stand a chance overpowering this guy if he turned nasty. I opted for mental superiority over physical, which was a doubtful ploy but all I had at such short notice.

'Quit struggling,' I said with a breathlessness that robbed the command of authority. 'I'm a cop and you're under arrest.'

His chest was moving underneath me. It took me a moment to realise it wasn't moving due to exertion. He was laughing!

'What's so funny?' I demanded, wondering what my next move would be because things weren't panning out great so far.

'Don't you remember me, Red?' His voice was deep and rough, like raw whisky on a cold day.

'Should I?' Great, a former collar. Just what I needed. He was probably stalking me to deliver a grudge payback. I began doing a rapid inventory of wackos I'd arrested but there were too many to count.

He grinned.

'Hey, babe, am I that forgettable?'

'Obviously,' I said tartly.

'I'm cut to the quick. Surely you remember, sweetpea? We shared some very, very special time a handful of years back.'

'Nope. No bells.' I gave him a gimlet glare which was lost in the dusk.

'Let me prompt your memory. The Swan River. A boat. Moonlit nights lying on the deck. Shooting stars, splashes of jumping fish, waves slapping against the hull. It was romantic, Red.'

I arched back to get him in better focus. In the half-light, between streetlamps, I stared at his face.

And stared.

Something stirred and yawned in a deep recess of my brain. Then the locks tumbled and unleashed things I considered better left buried.

A searing memory long repressed took form and suddenly roared to vibrant life. Hell, yes! I remembered. It had been the best weekend of sex I'd ever had. Steamy and sweaty and totally inspired.

My blood started to pound in my temples. I stared, aware that my stomach's contents were in motion. They were doing a very good impersonation of a Ferris wheel, complete with flashing lights and gaudy music.

The prone man had craggy features which reflected a life well lived. His hair was long, sun-bleached and messy. He would have been about fifty, give or take. It was hard to determine the colour of his eyes. But that didn't matter. I knew what they were like. They were blue. Not just any old blue. But sun-kissed, shallow sea blue that became the colour of wild indigo deep-water ocean when aroused.

The Ferris wheel spun faster, making my blood fizz and pop like homemade ginger beer on a forty-degree day. It flushed through my veins and I felt like throwing up, which wouldn't have been a very dignified thing to do. But my system was in shock.

Because, oh my goodness…

This man was Quinn.

Chastity's father.

12

CAREFULLY I PEELED MYSELF OFF QUINN'S IRON BODY. HE STOPPED my retreat by holding both hands on my jean-clad bottom so our pelvic areas were closer than close. Some would say too close. It didn't help the Ferris wheel sensation. I was in the downward arc at the moment with my stomach dropping to the very centre of the earth.

'You remember,' he said with satisfaction.

'I do now. Yes.' I scowled down at him, cross I'd been jolted into remembering him, annoyed he'd crashed back into my life, angry he'd given me the creeps by spying on me. 'Now let go of me.'

'Why? This is how I remember you. Hot, flustered and passionate. You're still one hell of an attractive woman, Red.'

I pulled back and flipped my hand under my flairs and hoiked out my gun. I aimed it square at him.

'Let go or I'll shoot.'

Quinn immediately released me just as the old guy and his dog came snuffling up. I didn't know if it was the gun, or the appearance of the man and dog that had been successful.

'You need a hand, girlie?' said the old man. 'Want me to call the cops?'

'No, thanks. I'm a police officer. I've got him covered.' In more ways than one. Groin to groin. Heat to heat…

'Yell if you need me, girlie.'

'Thanks, I will.'

He shuffled off, yanking the dog along with him as it tried to stop and sniff Quinn's ear. Quinn grinned up at me. The grin was fleetingly familiar. But then I suppose it would be, him being Chastity's dad and all.

'It's been some time, Red. I've often wondered where you were and what you were doing.'

'I erased you from my memory,' I countered, still steadily aiming the gun at him.

Goodness, I had loved him with an intense fusion of virgin passion and romantic love.

But, boy, did he cause me to grow up fast.

We'd met at a party and instantly clicked. He'd taken me to his boat and we didn't leave it for four whole days. And nights. The only reason I went to shore was because I had an appointment with the police academy. When I returned to the jetty, the boat had sailed away and with it my hopes and dreams and first love. A little of my soul died that day, but I did a huge amount of emotional maturing and vowed never to be so stupid again.

And then, weeks later, I'd discovered I was pregnant.

I'd tried to find him, to tell him. I only had his first name and that of his boat, appropriately called *Wild Thing*. I trawled the yacht clubs and asked around, but Quinn had disappeared.

And now he was back. Why?

'Why have you been stalking me?'

'Stalking?'

'For the past week you've been spying on me. You even took in my laundry. Twice. Do you deny it?'

'Do me a favour. I've got better things to do with my time than hang around taking your smalls off the line. Tonight was the first time I've seen you in ten, fifteen years.'

Sixteen, actually. Almost seventeen. But I let it go. I didn't want to alert him I'd been counting, and why I knew precisely how long it had been.

'Pull the other one. What do you want?' I had a sudden flash of panic. He didn't know about Chastity, did he? Was that why he'd suddenly turned up out of the blue? I moved the gun closer.

He ignored it and continued staring at me with those mesmerising blue eyes.

'Tell me, Quinn. Why are you here? Why now?'

'I was curious. I heard about this spunky, flaming-haired cop with candy lips and puppy-soft eyes who had more guts than most men. You'd talked about joining the force so I wondered if it was you.'

'Who would spin you such a yarn?'

'Ah. Never reveal your sources.'

'Are you a journalist?' I asked suspiciously.

'Nope.'

He twisted his golden-maned head to one side as we heard someone click-clacking down the pavement at high speed.

'Eve, honey. Is that you? Are you okay?' Margot trip-trapped around the corner and stop dead as she saw me sitting on top of Quinn.

'Well, well,' she said, a laugh catching in her throat. 'You caught him, then.'

'I did.' I slid my gun back into its ankle holster and climbed off Quinn.

'Shame,' he said. 'I was enjoying that.'

'Get up and get out. I don't want to see you hanging around here again.'

'I swear it was my first time,' he said, slowly getting to his feet and brushing off the dirt. I don't know why he bothered. The jeans were threadbare old and should have been chucked in a charity shop ragbag years ago. His checked lumberjack shirt, which he wore loose over a dark t-shirt, was frayed and button-less, and his shoes were dirty canvas.

He was taller than I remembered, and broader and woollier. He'd been battered by life's experiences and looked all the more dangerously sexy for it, dash it.

The Ferris wheel spun into its upward arc and my stomach went into orbit. Liquid heat swept through my entire body.

Omigod, I was going to have a lust attack.

I clenched my fist and gritted my teeth and tried to dampen my bubbling libido.

This was getting serious. And ridiculous. Quinn was the third man in a week who'd fired up my sex hormones. I needed to get laid so I could begin to view men calmly once more and not try to mentally undress them and jump their bones as soon as they looked at me.

But I knew I wasn't totally lost. I took comfort from that fact. How did I know? Because I didn't fancy Dom Ferrari, that's how. Or Sodbury, Ely, Burton...

I pulled myself into gear and gave Quinn a hard stare of the Iron Nun calibre.

'You can go away, anyway,' I said. 'I don't want to see you again.'

'Don't bet on it, Red. I think you'll find destiny has other plans.' And he gave a deep-chested chuckle.

We waited until he'd driven off in a khaki jeep and then we went back to the veranda to polish off the wine, Margot rustling along in her tiny tin-foil dress, and me limping like a lame dog.

'Do you reckon he was the man you saw in my garden?' I asked her.

'Don't think so, darl. And face it, Eve. He doesn't look like the sort of guy who'd put on a Santa suit and fold the laundry for kicks.'

She had a point. Quinn was not a fancy dress sort of guy. Or domesticated.

As I stared into the bottom of my near empty glass and wondered about him, Margot asked me how Chastity was going at school.

'You are so damn lucky having that kid,' she said.

'I know it.'

'I always wanted kids,' she sighed, her mouth turning down dolefully. 'But my rat of a husband didn't want to play ball.'

'I didn't know you'd been married.'

'It was a lifetime ago.' She didn't extrapolate and I didn't push. 'You never talk about Chastity's dad.'

Had she picked up about Quinn? Well, I wasn't ready to extrapolate either.

'She was the surprise result of a brief affair.'

'That would have been hard.'

'For all the difficulties of being a single mum, I wouldn't change a thing.'

'You're a very lucky woman.'

'Yeah. Sometimes life gives us a break where we least expect it.'

As I left, Margot reminded me to take the dress. I'd shoved it down the side of the chair and hoped she'd forget it. No such luck.

'It should fit you a treat, darl,' she said. 'You'll kill 'em all wearing that.'

I eyed the red dress suspiciously and wondered just who I'd be killing if I poured myself into the scarlet scrap of shiny material and fronted up at the party.

I didn't sleep well that night. I was creeped by the two uninvited men lurking around my house. One I felt I could just about deal with – as long as he didn't get fresh. And, of course, if I could keep my hormones in check. But Santa Claus might be a nutter, which was a totally different ball game.

I tried locking all the doors and windows, but the Ferrari trolls had done a good job at rendering my doors unshuttable. It could have been something to do with the cracks throwing out the alignment, though why I thought that I couldn't imagine. *Not*. So I slept with my gun under my pillow and a pile of saucepans in the doorway as an early alert system.

I woke up in a pre-dawn cold sweat. I was positive there was an intruder in my house even though there was screaming silence. And then the saucepans spectacularly clattered to the floor. I grabbed the gun and let off a round. Seconds later, with the light on and shades of sleep shattered beyond redemption, I found I'd shot and destroyed my black pedestal fan. And Margot's cat was streaking out the door

I flopped back on to my bed to let my heart quit its adrenaline tattoo. I eyed the fan. Bang went my only sop to air-conditioning. And bang went ten years off my life.

The shooting was reported by a neighbour, probably the old guy with the dog, and resulted in the local cops turning up a few minutes later. I was dressed and ready for them. I flashed them my badge and assured them everything was okay. Sleep, though, was a thing of the past.

I dumped the broken fan in the skip and then made a cup of tea. I sat on my back step, viewing the sorry state of my garden, and wondering why Quinn had suddenly materialised. There was no avoiding it. His appearance caused my stomach to churn.

13

THE BOYS HAD HEARD ABOUT THE FAN SHOOTING BEFORE I MADE IT into the station. There was a lot of ribbing and I felt like whipping my gun out again and shooting the lot of them, just to make a point. It took a while to focus them on work rather than my early morning target practice. I had to bribe them with sticky buns from a nearby bakery but even then there was the sly dig here and there.

We spent the day going through alibis and statements of all the people we could find who knew Tiger Den. I cancelled my date with Fox and, to show there were no hard feelings, we went together to interview the women who had been at the Paradise with Phipps. By doing so we discovered the one who had actually shared the room with him.

Her name was Dusty Marlowe and she was a well-known hooker from the seedy part of town, which meant the vicinity of the Paradise.

'You can't bust me,' she complained when we found her lounging on the corner of the street leading to the Paradise Nightclub. She was in fishnets and a tight-fitting red dress that looked similar to the one Margot had lent me the night before. 'I'm doing nothing wrong.'

'Relax, Dusty,' I said. 'I just want to talk to you. Get in the car.'

'No way. You talk now and you talk fast or my man will come along and give me a hiding.'

'You and Dennis Phipps got it together on Saturday night,' I stated. 'What time did you leave the club?'

'I left – let's see – maybe at two.'

'And Phipps?'

'He was sleeping like a baby, ducky.'

'So you left him there?'

'Yeah. Honest. You can check with my girlfriends Beryl and Margot.'

'Did you take his wallet?'

She acted outraged and banged the bonnet of the car with the flat of her hand.

'What do you take me for, DI Rock? A fool? He was the sort who'd come back for more so why would I roll him? No, I just took what he owed me and left the rest.'

'Where did you put the wallet?'

'Back in his jacket. Where else?'

Fox and I cruised to a café. We ordered two cappuccinos and reviewed Dusty's statement.

'Do you think she's telling us the truth?' said Fox, taking a sip of his coffee and leaving a white moustache. I resisted wiping it off. The way my hormones were playing up, I might have him across the table and naked in two seconds flat and I didn't think the coffee-drinking public were ready for that sort of display on a hot Thursday afternoon.

'We can check her out, but her friends will probably cover for her anyway.'

'The Margot she mentioned, is that your neighbour by any chance?'

'Yes, 'fraid so. She was in one of those rooms too. I think she's on the game, but I haven't asked her outright. She's already on the defensive. I'm using the softly, softly approach.'

'Hookers! Why do they do it? Why not get a proper job.'

'Maybe they can't. Don't knock them. Sometimes it's purely a matter of survival.'

'You sound sympathetic.'

'I am. My mother was one.'

'Oh. Sorry. Me and my big size tens.'

'Don't worry about it. She's now a nun.'

Fox opened his cute mouth but not a lot of sound came out. And what did was strangled.

'Okay,' I said as Fox valiantly tried digesting my news-bite. 'The medical report put Phipps' death between two and four. Dusty left him asleep at two. Thelma Freeman, the murdered girl, left her dishwashing job a little after two. How long would it take her to cycle from the hotel strip to the park?'

Fox looked relieved he could now deal with something less dangerous than my colourful family history. He pursed his lips and calculated. I stared at his lips and lusted.

'Twenty minutes, give or take five.' He hazarded.

'So,' I said. 'That narrows it down to maybe two thirty, quarter to three. So was it someone lying in wait for him? Or one of the Paradise mob? Or was it a random, opportunistic murder?'

I sighed. 'The frustrating thing is, no one except Derek Phipps has a cast iron alibi.'

Derek, Phipps' son, had been arrested for causing a disturbance and been banged up in a cell for the tail end of Saturday night. He might not have been very happy about it at the time, but it had got him off the hook for murder.

'Sue says she was in bed asleep, as does Lina, Audrey and Sylvia and all the mistresses. They were all alone because Dennis wasn't in their bed. He was too busy being murdered.'

'One of them is lying,' said Fox draining his cup and leaning back in his chair. His jacket casually slipped open to reveal his holster. It also revealed his tightly muscled chest under a snug black t-shirt.

Yum.

'It's not necessarily one of them,' I said, clearing my throat so my voice wouldn't husk. His baby blues glinted. They reminded me of another pair I'd only just encountered. I purposely pushed away the memory. Now was not the time to think of Quinn. It was never the time.

'Shame about tonight,' Fox murmured. 'I was really looking forward to getting to know you better.'

'Save it, Foxy,' I drawled with a cool nonchalance I was far from feeling. 'There'll be plenty of other opportunities.'

But the atmosphere had changed. High voltage electricity crackled between us. I licked my suddenly dry lips and watched Fox's blue peepers zero in on the movement. I licked again and his nostrils flared.

'Do that a third time, Eve, and I'll have to take you right now, on this table.'

'Big talk,' I said, pleased he was as sexually primed as I was. 'But we've got work to do.'

I scraped back my chair and sauntered out of the café, making sure my hips swayed with a hint of suggestion. Fox sucked in a sharp breath and followed me to where his Spitfire was parked in a side street.

'You can't get out of this date tonight?' he said in a low, bedroom-come-hither voice that sent shivers to all my interesting places and beyond.

'No can do. Sorry.' I slanted him what I hoped was a smouldering, sexy, woman-of-the-world glance. 'You'll just have to keep it on ice.'

His step faltered and I shot him another saucy look. His hand snaked out and he grabbed my arm, swinging me around and pinning me against the side of the Spitfire. He moved one denim-clad, muscular thigh between my legs and leaned into me so I could feel the heated length of his body.

'You drive me wild, Eve. Have done ever since I first saw you. I've got to have you. Got to taste you...'

'Careful, Foxy,' I said. 'You'll dent the body work.'

'To hell with the car,' he muttered.

I smiled slightly.

'I meant mine.'

'Oh.' He fractionally pulled back that fantastic body of his and I pushed my advantage. I put my arms around his waist and spun him around so this time he was up against the Spitfire and it was my leg insinuating itself between his lean thighs.

'I'm not adverse to a little tasting, myself,' I said, pushing into him and watching the streak of red heat infuse his smooth, clean-shaven cheeks. Our eyes locked. The oxygen count plummeted to zilch and millimetre by millimetre our mouths got closer…

'Hey!' said a deep, gravel-pit voice behind me.

I jerked back as Fox's eyes widened in surprise.

'Hey, Red!'

Quinn? No! My worst nightmare. Except perhaps having the Iron Nun muscling in on the action.

'Get lost, Quinn. Can't you see I'm busy,' I said through gritted teeth, not bothering to turn around.

'First you unhand my son, then I'll consider it.'

Son? Son! Good grief. I turned around, unlocking my grip on Fox fast and spinning to face Quinn. I grappled with his pearl of information and did my best to discount it.

'Your son? Do me a favour. He's too old to be your son.'

'I was a sexually precocious eighteen-year-old.'

I didn't doubt the truth of that particular statement, even if I was having trouble with his first one. I'd had firsthand experience of his precocious-ness. Quinn's smile glimmered, his eyes were watchful, amused, quizzical even. And he didn't look as though he was joking about the son part.

I glanced at Fox. He wasn't falling over himself to deny Quinn's claim. He just looked shell-shocked but that could have been due to our hot-kiss-interruptus fall-out.

Was he Quinn's son?

Omigod.

I rapidly thought about it some more. The similar blond hair. The hot blue eyes. The instant chemistry.

And then it hit me.

OMIGOD!

Fox was Chastity's half brother.

I did a quantum leap. If Quinn had done the right thing and married me when I'd fallen pregnant with Chastity, then I would have been Fox's step-mum.

Goodness, too sick for words.

I sucked in a huge breath to try and clear my brain.

'I think I'm having an Oedipus moment,' I said and pushed away from Fox. His hand came up to stop me, but I sidestepped it.

'I think you've got your Greek mythology wires crossed,' said Quinn with a dry chuckle. He was as sloppily dressed as the night before and he hadn't bothered to shave. And he appeared to be enjoying my discomfiture.

'Actually, Dad, I think she means that – Ouch!' I trod on Fox's foot, just in case he was going to say something about Chastity. I didn't want Quinn to know. The fallout would be disastrous.

'What?' said Quinn.

'Nothing,' said Fox with that blandness I'd come to associate with him when he didn't want to give anything away. Quinn narrowed his eyes and stared first at Fox and then at me. He obviously knew Fox well, knew he was withholding something.

'Are you sleeping with my son, Red?' he asked quietly.

'None of your business,' I said.

'Not yet she isn't,' said Fox at the same time.

'You've good taste, Adam. Eve's hot stuff.'

'So you two know each other,' said Fox. 'No need for introductions.'

'It was a long time ago,' I said seething at Quinn for his hot stuff comment. 'But I didn't realise his close relationship to you.'

I should have though. It probably accounted for my instant attraction to Fox. He looked like Quinn had sixteen years ago, before life and experience had ravished his dreamy, golden handsomeness.

'If I had, you wouldn't have seen me for dust.'

'You two have history?' said Fox with a quirky smile. 'Tell me.'

'It's classified information. I'm not saying a thing.'

'I like a girl who doesn't kiss and tell.'

'Cut it out, Fox.' I glared at him and he delivered one of his sweet angelic smiles.

'So do I,' said Quinn and so I glared at him too.

'I think the next few days are going to be extremely interesting,' said Quinn, stroking his stubbly chin, his eyes twinkling in a too disturbing fashion.

More interesting than you can imagine, mate, I thought and wished I'd never met either of the Fox men.

'I wish you luck, son.'

'Thanks, Dad.'

'But be careful where Eve's concerned. Remember her namesake brought the downfall of Man. Eve Rock also has that lethal gift.'

'Oh please!' I said huffily. 'Get a life.'

He grinned and tugged one of my curls then cut his eyes to Fox.

'Keep a clear head tonight, Adam. I may need you.'

'You're going to launch it tonight?'

'All set to sail.'

I snorted.

'Still messing about on waterfronts, Quinn. Don't you ever grow up?'

Fox bit back a laugh and Quinn delivered a heart-stopping smile and didn't comment.

Was I missing something here?

14

I NEEDED THERAPY AFTER MY OEDIPUS DAY. I ALSO NEEDED RED shoes, for the party. The therapy would have to wait until it was a civilised time to drink wine and I didn't have to drive. The shoes were more pressing. The party was in two hours.

Thank goodness it was late night shopping and that my daughter had broken up from school and was free to act as quality control manager. I hated shopping and rarely hit the mall. Chastity loved shopping and knew all the best places. I picked her up from Saint Immaculata's as soon as I'd finished work.

'When can I move into the house?' she asked as we targeted the mall and fought with the pre-Christmas shopping frenzy. *Six White Boomers* was being played on the PA and there was enough glitz and tinsel to rival Hollywood.

I patted her shoulder.

'It'll be a while, kid. The place isn't secure at the moment. Even I'm spooked about staying there.' I didn't tell her just how spooked I was, or that'd I'd annihilated a fan and almost turned Margot's cat into a colander. I didn't want to worry her. 'In fact, I'm thinking of moving into Saint Immaculata's.'

'Not a good idea, Mum,' she said promptly.

'Why on earth not? You've got plenty of space, especially as all the other girls have gone home. And you've got hot showers. Believe me, that's a very big plus. Also, you've a kitchen that's functional, efficient air conditioning and wide screen TV in the staff room. What more can a girl ask for? I tell you, it's paradise compared to our house.'

'But staying at the school will cramp your style.'

'I have no style, baby.'

She chuckled. It was low and full of warmth. It reminded me of Quinn. And Fox.

No!

'Seriously, Mum. It wouldn't work. I'll make a deal with you. I won't whinge about coming home and you don't hang out at the school. Done?'

'I think you're up to something.'

Chastity opened her eyes so wide they were in danger of popping out. She looked like the cutest kid on the block. But I wasn't fooled. She was stone-walling, but I didn't have the time to find out why because I needed shoes and I'd already had my fill of the commercial world.

We zipped in and out of the shoe shops until we found a pair of sparkly red shoes with spike heels. They weren't as stacked as Margot's stilettos, but they weren't far off. They were hugely too expensive and I didn't want to waste hard earned dosh on shoes I'd rarely wear.

I'd rather buy a replacement fan.

'But the shoes would be a good investment,' said Chastity with teenage logic. 'We can both wear them.'

'These aren't suitable for you!' I protested.

'Why not?'

'They're too high. You'll break your ankle. Maybe your neck.'

'I've worn higher.'

I didn't ask where because I didn't want to know the answer. She might say the Paradise and then I'd have to act the concerned, hard-line, party-pooping parent, which would put a real dampener on our frivolous shopping expedition.

'And they are far too tarty.'

'But you're going to wear them,' she pointed out.

'That's different. I'm borrowing a dress from Margot and I need shoes to match it.'

'I see. Margot's lent you a dress.' She nibbled her bottom lip and then said, 'Are you trying to attract a man, Mum?'

'No.'

Definitely not. Life was already too complicated, what with the two Foxes literally breathing down my neck. Why would I want to attract another male and have a testosterone trio to contend with?

'What gave you that idea?'

'Because you're borrowing Margot's dress. That's pretty radical for you.'

'Wearing any dress is radical. Now let's get these shoes off and try on some others. I'm running out of time.'

I had one of the expensive red shoes strapped on and the other off when I saw him. Actually, I sensed him first. The hairs on the back of my neck prickled. I stopped trying to unbuckle the shoe and swiftly cased the joint.

There he was – Santa Claus in all his rosy red glory.

He was standing at the shoe shop entrance and staring at the two of us like you'd stare at a drink through glass after being in the desert for three days without water. I could handle his obsession, just, if it had been only me. But with Chastity, I felt sick to the pit of my stomach. I did not want this nutter perving at my daughter.

There was only one thing to do. I would have to arrest him and be done with it.

I jumped up and bolted towards the door with one shoe off and one shoe on and running like Quasimodo, oblivious to the shouts behind me. Shocked horror streaked across Santa's face as he saw me bearing down. He backed out of the door, bumping into a couple of shoppers before he legged it down the mall, white beard flying. I heard Chastity and the shop assistant yelling after me, but I didn't stop. I was determined to catch him.

I hobbled and hopped as fast as I could, dodging shoppers and trolleys and children and buskers and Christmas trees and carol singers and every man and his dog. But the going was rough. The single high-heeled sandal almost broke my ankle. Santa disappeared into one of the big department stores and I tumbled after him.

Now I was in strife.

There must have been a good twenty Santas milling about the

jam-packed floor handing out lollies and gifts to children. Great. How was I going to spot my stalker in the midst of this lot? I could call for a line up, but how sure could I be of his identity? All Santas looked the same to me.

One of them came up to me and offered me a candy cane. I reluctantly took it, trying to see beyond his white beard and moustache and work out if it was my stalker or not. He wished me merry Christmas. I did likewise and he moved on.

Ten candy canes later, I finally gave up and limped back to the shoe store where Chastity, very red faced and cross, was waiting for me.

'We'll have to buy those shoes now,' she declared with blunt satisfaction, as if the scene had been my fault. 'Because you soiled one of them.'

'That's one way of putting it,' I said and apologised to the shop assistant who was regarding me warily. I didn't blame her. I would regard me warily too.

'So are you dating that yummy blond cop?' Chastity asked as we stowed the shoes in a classy black and gold bag into the boot of the car. She licked her rum and chocolate ice cream we'd purchased in a fit of indulgence.

'No,' I said shortly, trying to ignore the flash of regret. How could I enjoy a steamy fling with Fox if he was Chastity's half-brother? It just wouldn't be right whichever way I looked at it. And believe me, I'd been looking at it from all angles. Fox was not a man you wanted to give up in a hurry.

'Oh, shame.'

I could feel her assessing me out of the corner of her eye and wondered what was coming next. I didn't have to wait long.

'He is rather cute. I wouldn't mind going out with him. I bet he's one hot kisser.'

'Chastity! Don't even think about it,' I said repressively.

'Aw, Mum. I'm a big girl now.'

'Not big enough. Anyway, he's much older than you.'

'Age doesn't come into it.'

'It's important.'

'He is a lot younger than you and that didn't seem to faze you a couple of days ago.'

'That's different.'

'Are you just being horrible because he hasn't asked you out?'

Stung by her condescending tone, I said, 'He has asked me out, but that's immaterial. If I want to date a bloke I don't have to wait to be asked. I'm more than capable of doing the asking.'

'"I am woman, hear me roar,"' she sung under her breath. 'Perhaps I'll take a leaf out of your book and ask him out the next time I see him.'

'Over my dead body. There's no way you're going to date Adam Fox. Dating him is not a good idea. Trust me on this.'

'At least give me a better reason than age.'

He's your brother! It'd be incest! I felt like shouting. Instead, I said, 'Why can't you just accept the answer is no?'

'Would you have at my age?'

Good point.

'Chastity,' I sighed. 'I promise I'll tell you the reason soon but not now. There's a cast iron reason but I'm having a hard enough time getting my own head around it without sharing it with you.'

'Is he gay?' she said after a pause.

'No. Let it drop.'

'Okay, but I won't forget,' she warned.

Oh goody.

I dropped her back at Saint Immaculata's and took the liberty of showering and washing my hair there. It was an orgasmic moment, standing under the hot shower with good solid water pressure rattling over me at a zillion knots. My needs were simple: lashings of hot water, lashings of hot curries and lashings of hot sex. At the moment, the curries seemed the only item I could guarantee on a regular basis.

After indulging myself for far too long in the shower, I headed for the war zone that used to be my house. The Ferraris had gutted the bathroom and kitchen. The cracks were wider, the skip fuller and the floors were covered in rubble. Great. I must invite one of the homes beautiful magazines to come and take pictures.

I studied the underside of my tin roof from the dusty aspect of the kitchen because the ceiling was now in the skip outside my front door. I sighed and hoped Dom Ferrari knew what he was doing because I hadn't asked for a new kitchen ceiling. I hadn't thought I'd needed one.

I visited my little oasis of a toilet at the bottom of the garden, enjoyed a slice of nature watching the resident black spider eat a fly, and then squared my shoulders and prepared to do the makeover of the century.

As I stomped back through the kitchen and slammed the fly-wire door, a lump of wood the size of a cricket bat fell and narrowly missed bonking me on the head. I squinted back up at the roof. Any more low flying missiles? I'd have to have a word with Ferrari about safety. I did not want to be killed in my own house, by my own house.

All too soon I was standing in front of my bedroom mirror wearing the red dress and hyperventilating. This was not me. The dress could have doubled as a milkshake straw. The spike heels looked terrific and I'd painted my finger and toe nails scarlet to colour co-ordinate. My freshly washed hair was bouncing in all directions as if I'd had my finger in a live light socket for five minutes. My face was that of a stranger. I'd put on more makeup than I usually did to bolster my flagging confidence.

If I'd been in jeans, I would have felt sensational. But in the red straw dress and war-paint, I felt underdressed and vulnerable. So I strapped my gun to my inner thigh and hoped no one noticed if I walked like a constipated duck.

Margot tripped over to my front door and knocked two minutes later.

'Yikes, what a mess,' she declared as she crunched over the builders' dirt.

I groaned.

'I know. I look dead scary.'

'Hell, not you, darl. I meant the house. No, you look stunning.'

'Oh.' I did a double take. 'Well, thanks. And you look pretty stunning yourself.'

She did. Her tiny gold dress appeared to be sprayed on. She had matching gold shoes, gold eye shadow, gold nails and gold sparkles over her bare shoulders and across the twin tops of her breasts. Her eyelashes were so thickly coated and long that I suspect she was wearing double falsies and her lips were coated in rich Picasso-red lipstick. She meant business.

I felt dowdy in contrast, but I didn't care. I'd dressed up to please Margot and not let her down in front of her friends. It wasn't as if I had tarted up to score.

We got a taxi to the party. It was at a private residence in one of the outer rural suburbs where people kept racehorses for pets instead of cats. The house was a mansion that fronted the Swan River. It was big and bold and ugly and smack in the middle of a vast acreage of lawn that could have been spray painted it was so green. No trouble with water restrictions here, then. The owners were probably buying off the water corporation or pumping water straight from the Swan. Palm trees were in abundance and there was a huge sunken swimming pool complete with fountains, waterfalls and mock boulders to give it a lagoon affect. The grounds were littered with fairy lights, decorated Christmas trees and beautiful people. The whole set-up screamed money.

So how had Margot, with her loose and lowly connections, had been invited? No doubt I'd find out later.

We were given chilled champagne and fiddly finger food that wouldn't satisfy a hamster. We wandered around the vast patio, swilling the champers and chatting to Margot's mates. I didn't know a sausage until Josie Lambert appeared.

'Oh,' she said without enthusiasm. 'You're here.'

'Hello, Josie, nice to see you too,' I said and raised my glass to her. 'Cheers.'

She was wearing a cyclamen party frock that had seen its heyday in the fifties and she had another of those ridiculous prissy bows in her hair. She gave me a cold stare and didn't return the salute.

We circulated some more and my heart beat a little faster when I saw a Santa Claus sitting in a mock grotto close to the swimming pool. Of course, there were a lot of Santas knocking around the city this time of year, but I still had a tug of apprehension it might have been my own red-suited stalker.

There weren't any children at the party but it didn't stop Santa from being busy. Women were sitting on his knee and he was giving out small colourful bags to people. The party was particularly rowdy around the grotto. Rock on, Santa.

A little later on, I spotted a couple more of the Hit and Miss clientele.

'Don't tell me this is a giant speed dating convention,' I said to Margot in sudden panic. 'If it is, I'm off.'

'Relax, Eve. This is like a corporate Christmas party. A thank you for all our hard work over the year.'

'What sort of work?'

'Massages and other hands-on services.' She winked one gold-plated eye and gave a dirty laugh.

'Goodness,' I said and didn't know if that was much better than speed dating. I wished I hadn't come. This was not my idea of fun.

'Darling Margot!' A man in his fifties, trim and impeccably dressed and with a face that was vaguely familiar, strode up to Margot and kissed her on both cheeks. 'You finally got here.'

'A girl has to take her time to dress up,' she said and batted her metre-long lashes.

'And it was worth it,' he said. 'You look sensational.'

By this time the penny had dropped. He was Hugo Maine, a big note financier who often made it on to the gossip columns as well as the business pages. I didn't know much about him professionally since I'm not an avid reader of the business section, but if the media gossip was anything to go by, he owned a lot of rich man's toys. And women.

'Hugo, meet my good friend Eve,' said Margot.

'Delighted,' he said, taking my hand in his warm damp one and holding it for much longer than was strictly necessary or polite. 'I always enjoy meeting Margot's... friends. Maybe we can get together sometime soon?'

Not in this lifetime, mate. He made my flesh crawl. I had no illusions about what he was suggesting.

'I'm very busy,' I said, not wanting to be overtly rude and spoil Margot's relationship with him, but wanting him to realise I wasn't available.

'I'm sure you are, an attractive woman like you.'

'I'm Margot's neighbour, Mr Maine, not one of the... er... girls.'

'There are advantages when you work for me,' he said matter-of-factly. I had to admire his style. Straight to the core and no flummery.

'Such as?' I was curious how far he would take this.

'I look after my own.'

'I can look after myself.'

'I pay well.'

'I have a job.'

'I pay better.'

'And it has a sound pension plan.'

'You're a professional woman?'

'Probably your definition of professional and mine are different.'

'So what do you do?'

'I'm a police officer.' That told him straight but he didn't seem fazed. Okay, so his eyes flickered ever so slightly but then a smile that was as sincere as a priest's spread across his tanned face.

'Always good to have the police on board.'

I bet it was, I thought and wondered what his next move would be.

'If you get tired of the force, or want to earn a little extra something, give me a call.' He slipped his hand into his tux and brought out a business card. I held out my hand but he tucked the card into my cleavage and then walked away.

Yuk. What a sleaze.

I hoiked out the card as if it sported the Black Spot.

Margot drained her champagne and said, 'He likes you, girl. You should take him up on his offer.'

'No, thanks.' I tore the card into tiny shreds and tipped it in an ashtray. Gut instinct told me to keep far away from the likes of Hugo Maine.

'Shouldn't have done that, Eve,' Margot said. 'He's not a man to cross.'

'I don't want another job,' I said mildly.

'A bit of extra cash could sure help you finance your renovations.'

'You have a point but I still don't think it's a good idea.'

We refilled our glasses, burnt our fingers on the latest offering of food brought around by waiters wearing chefs' hats and black and white checked trousers, and watched a few couples dancing.

'You going to introduce me to your friend, Margot?' said a voice behind us. I turned and saw the bearded, fuzzy bear hulk of Leo Stark.

I raised one brow.

'I hate to disappoint you, Stark, but you and I are already acquainted.'

His eyes widened in shocked recognition and then he gave a grim smile.

'You had me there, Rock. I thought you were a new honey.'

'Again, sorry to disappoint you.'

His eyes devoured my lack of dress and excess of flesh.

'I hate to admit it, but you look ravishing tonight,' he said. 'It's nice to see you do know how to dress up and impress a man.'

'It's not too butch for you?' I said dryly.

'Butch it is not.'

'But don't get too carried away with my change of image. I borrowed the dress from Margot.'

'You should wear her stuff more often. It suits you.'

In spite of myself, I was pleased by his compliments and blamed the champagne.

'You can be as feminine as the rest of them,' he said.

I didn't want to shatter his illusions by telling him about the gun strapped to my inner thigh.

'And it's good to see you can wear a tie without food interfering with the design,' I countered.

We grinned at each other, in one accord for a change. The hatchet buried in the ground rather than in each other's backs.

'Want to dance?' he said.

I doubted if I could with my high heels, but I accepted anyway. At least there was a lot of him to hold on to if I tripped.

'So I hear this is some kind of end of year work bash,' I said, as Chris de Burgh sang about Romeos in the rain and Stark expertly led me around the specially constructed sprung dance floor.

'Yeah. This is always a good one.'

'So what do you do for this high flyer?'

'I'm his lawyer. I've handled a couple of his divorces and pre-nups.'

It was corny, but *Lady in Red* began to play and Stark crooned away in my ear, causing goose-bumps to skitter over my bare skin.

'You really do look gorgeous tonight,' he said. He oozed sex appeal and again I blamed my response to him on the champagne. My darned attraction to the opposite sex was getting out of hand. If my hormones danced any faster I was going to be a steaming mess. I let Stark nuzzle my neck and then lifted my head and stared into the bluest of blue eyes that were regarding me over Stark's left shoulder.

Oh damn.

15

'I THINK THIS OUR DANCE,' SAID FOX, SMOOTHLY STEPPING FORWARD and taking me from Stark.

'I don't think so, pretty boy,' said Stark, tugging me back with more force than finesse.

'Hey, quit fighting,' I said. Between them they had ruined the Lady in Red song and they were going to ruin my dress if they kept manhandling me. I didn't have a lot of confidence in keeping the wretched thing in place and I had no wish to be de-frocked and left standing in only red stilettos, underpants and a gun at Hugo Maine's fancy Christmas party. I'm not that into Merry Christmas.

I pushed myself away from Stark as Margot came to the rescue and wrapped herself around him.

'Come on, baby,' she said. 'Dance with me instead. You can finish your dance with Eve later.'

He went with her but scowled at Fox. A bad bear robbed of his honey.

I was scowling at Fox too. Where had he sprung from all of a sudden? Wasn't he meant to be with his dad, playing on boats?

'You look good enough to eat,' said Fox, reaching for me and moulding me against his hardness.

And he looked highly edible too. A tuxedo suited him. Made him very dashing and debonair. He nipped my earlobe. Eek. It was time to play it cool.

I arched away from his mouth.

'Yes, well, my dress does rather resemble a hot dog.'

'I love hot dogs.'

'Hmm, okay, so we won't go there.'

'What are you doing here?' he asked, pulling me near again.

'I could ask you the same but I suppose your dad crews for Hugo Maine.'

'Dad doesn't crew for anyone. I told you before, he's a free spirit.'

I huffed and didn't respond outwardly to Fox's fingers skimming up and down my back. I kept my spine rigid and my hands impersonal. It wasn't easy. Because inside, I was mush.

'Why so uptight,' murmured Fox. 'You were steaming this afternoon.'

'That was before I knew about your family genes.'

'You go back a long way with Dad, huh?'

I remained silent.

'He did seem mighty interested when I described you to him.'

I didn't tell him that Big Daddy had made an unscheduled visit to my house to suss me out. But then I wasn't telling him a lot about Big Daddy.

'You're vulnerable here,' Fox went on.

Bleeding obvious. Being held so close by him was giving me heart failure.

'I think you should leave.'

Oh yes? Was this a come-on line?

'And you?' I said.

'I have to stay a bit longer.'

Oh. So it wasn't a come on.

'Why?'

'Can't say. But you should head home as soon as.'

'I'll think about it.' I didn't like other people making my decisions and telling me what to do. So I decided I'd stay until the bitter end.

Fox let go of me at the end of the dance, told me again to go home and then drifted back into the sea of dinner jackets. I tottered back to Margot and was immediately snaffled by Stark.

'Let's resume our dance,' he said. We were back out on the dance floor in seconds but the mood was gone. He did his damnedest to recapture it, but I was too busy musing over Fox and why he was here and not with his dad. And why he wanted me to leave.

And then we were interrupted again.

'Hi, Red. I think this is our dance.'

Quinn! Had I summoned him up just by thinking of him?

'Oh great. Another one,' said Stark. 'Maybe you shouldn't have worn that dress. It's attracting all the sharks.'

'You'd know,' said Quinn, competently disengaging Leo Stark's hold of me and drawing me into the heat of his own body.

Stark growled a protest.

'This is my partner,' he said.

'Not now,' said Quinn in his trademark grit and raw whisky voice. 'Possession is nine-tenths.'

Stark frowned, snapping his thick brows together, his mouth taking on an ugly line. 'Rock?'

'It's cool,' I said. 'I'll catch you later.'

'I wouldn't bank on it,' said Quinn in my ear as he swung me into the middle of the floor and then proceeded to hold me so close we could have been welded in a furnace.

'Give me a little room to breathe,' I said, straining against him.

He relaxed his hold a smidge. It wasn't enough. I was still having troubles breathing, but that might have been because of who he was, and what he was. Sloppy and shaggy-haired, he was dangerous with a capital D. In a tuxedo with his hair slicked back in a casual ponytail to reveal a black stud in his ear, and with his tanned, craggy face clean-shaven, he was sensational. Whereas Fox was a delicious and delectable dish, his father had the advantage of years. He'd been seasoned by experience and, like an exceptional Indian curry, was full of matured hot spice.

He gave me a long, slow smile that curved his lips and deepened the lines around his eyes. A killer smile that hit the G-spot with a bulls-eye. My mouth went dry and I wished I could gulp down a gallon of champagne to appease the sudden thirst.

'Trying to freeze out my boy?' he said.

'Only since I discovered he was your son.'

'Sins of the fathers…?'

'More than you can guess.'

'Cryptic.'

'It's all you're getting.'

'Really?'

My pulse kicked up. He made the really sound REALLY dangerous.

'Yup, so quit while you can.'

'What are you doing here?' he said, changing tack.

I shivered. 'Your son has just asked me that. Why don't you compare notes?'

'I don't have the time and I need your answer quick.'

What was going on? But I played along.

'Partying,' I said.

'Why?'

'It's Christmas, if you haven't noticed.'

'Who invited you?'

'What is this? The Quinn Inquisition?'

'Answer me, Red.'

There was urgent steel threading his voice. Grief, he wasn't going to start getting proprietary all of a sudden was he? I mean, we might have been lovers once, but that had been a zillion years back. It hardly counted, except where Chastity was concerned and he didn't know about her.

'My neighbour invited me.'

'Point him out.'

'It's a her, not a him. She's the one in the gold over by the bar.'

'The same woman who was wearing the tin foil dress last night?'

'The same.'

'She's into metallic.'

'She's into a lot of things.'

'At least Stark didn't bring you.'

'Why?'

'Just keep away from him. He's a creep.'

'Oh pur-leese! I'm old enough to make my own decisions about whom I can or cannot date.' I sounded as irritated as Chastity had when I'd told her she couldn't snog Fox.

'He's crooked and dangerous.'

'And so are you!'

'Not in the same way.' He gave me another disarming smile, deeper than the ocean, and I resisted it with all my might.

'What happened to messing about on boats tonight?' I grumbled.

'I never said Adam and I were going boating.'

'Come on, I was there. You were talking about launching a boat and setting sail.'

'Your sharp police brain got it wrong. But now you're here, you can make yourself useful.'

'I've already knocked back Maine. I'm turning you down too.'

I tried to extricate myself from his arms, but he held me easily and then said softly in my ear, 'You're probably going to say no...'

'I already did, but you must have missed it. So I'll say it again, NO!'

He chuckled but carried on, 'And I can't see how the answer can be yes with you wearing that dress...'

I glared. He wasn't listening. 'No, again,' I reiterated.

His lips twisted into a faintly sardonic smile and he shook his head.

'Listen,' he said smoothly. 'Do you have your gun with you?'

I strained back and gave him a hard, puzzled look.

'Gun?'

'Ssh, Red. Not so loud.'

'How d'you know about my gun?'

'Just answer me.'

'Well, as a matter-of-fact, I do.'

His chest started to shake. 'You amaze me. But then you always did. Where is it?' He peeked down my cleavage and I thumped him on the arm.

'Under my dress.'

'I saw no telltale bumps when I was watching you earlier.'

He'd been watching me? Spying on me?

I huffed and said, 'Inner thigh.'

'You are one cracking woman.'

'Why do you want to know?'

'You might just need it.'

'Are you going to tell me what's going on?'

'I'm with the feds. There's going to be a shakedown.'

'Tonight? Here? Oh hell, you're undercover.' I shut my eyes for a dizzying moment and recaptured Sodbury's reluctant admission about a drugs' bust, how it was being organised by a larrikin cop who'd been undercover for months. So was it Quinn? Was he the cop? Years ago, on *Wild Thing*'s moonlit deck, we'd babbled on about good versus bad, righting wrongs, being crusaders of truth and justice and all things sacred. And then the next day he'd left me high and dry, literally, and I'd gone on to be a mother and a cop while he'd supposedly messed about on boats...

Quinn pulled me even closer, both hands hot on my bottom and he grazed my neck with his teeth as he whispered, 'Not so loud, Red. Do you want to tip the bad boys off?'

'Tip who off?' I muttered ungraciously into his black-studded ear.

'Can't say.'

'Or won't?'

'Just be careful, Red. No heroics.'

'What?'

'Hush. Let's enjoy the last of the dance. Make up a little for lost time.'

'You're kidding me, right?'

'Would I joke about something like that?'

'Forget it, Quinn.' I pushed away from him and stalked unsteadily on my pins back to where Margot and Stark were standing by one of the fountains. Damn my crippling red spikes, damn Fox and damn Quinn. I was having one helluva night.

And then I thought about what he'd said. If there was going to be trouble then I needed to get my shoes off. No way could I perform professional antics if I was wearing those neck-killers. To clarify, I meant professional police antics... I also had to be ready to pull out my gun. Now that was going to be an interesting little exercise.

I sat down on the edge of the fountain. The moulded concrete felt cool through the thin fabric of the dress. I started to fiddle with the buckle of my shoe.

'What are you doing?' said Margot.

'The shoes are killing me.'

'Babe,' she said. 'This ain't the place to slum it. You can't go barefoot.'

'Just watch me, because I don't care. Vanity, thy name isn't Eve,' I said.

Stark came and plonked himself next to me.

'Let me help you,' he said. 'I'm good at undoing ladies' clothing.'

'Forget it,' I said, slapping away his roving hand that wasn't anywhere near the buckle but half way up my leg. I wasn't quick enough. He hit the hardware. Great.

'You're carrying a gun!' he said, withdrawing his hand at lightning speed and staring at me in total disbelief. I played it cool and tugged down my ridiculously short hem.

'Doesn't everyone?'

'Hell, no!'

'They do in my world.'

He shook his head. 'I have grave doubts about you and the world you inhabit, Rock.'

After my brief conversation with Quinn, I could say the same about Stark.

I carried on fiddling with the strap but wasn't quick enough. Suddenly there were shouts and commands for everyone to stay still and calm. The place swarmed with cops like locusts on crops.

I spotted Ely and Burton and quite a few other familiar faces, including Sodbury. So all the guys from my team were here. How come I hadn't been invited to the shakedown? Obviously I had become cop non-grata. I'd have words about that tomorrow. But for now, there were more pressing things at stake.

Leaving my gun where it was for the moment, I observed the action. People were being hustled into the light of the dance floor. Women were squealing and men blustering. Maine was standing very, very still in the middle of it all, his head held back high and proud as though this was all beneath him. Quinn was by his side looking casual and in control and as powerful as Maine. You had to admire the man. He had presence.

My eyes travelled over the seething mass. Now the sniffer dogs were being brought in and were running, tails wagging, among the guests.

When it was our turn, the dog shoved his snout up my skirt.

'Oh to be that dog,' said the dog handler. His name was Billy Baker and I'd trained with him at the academy.

'Dream on, Billy,' I said. 'I'd prefer your dog any day.'

'You're all heart, Evie baby.' He moved on to Margot and Stark who were both regarding me like I'd caught the plague.

'Relax you two,' I said. 'As long as you're clean, the dog won't bite.'

'That's fine for you to say,' said Stark. 'Because the dog is on your side.'

'If you've got something to say, Stark, say it now to avoid any awkwardness.'

'I have nothing to say. Especially not to you.'

'So speaks a good lawyer.' He glared at me, all good feelings about the Lady in Red gone in a puff.

Billy Baker and his dog left us to hassle some other guests and we sat back down on the fountain edge. My gaze drifted over to the grotto where the party action had been earlier in the evening. The dogs hadn't got that far yet, but they were getting closer and either Santa didn't like dogs or he had something to hide because he was acting as jittery as a jumping bean.

I flashed back to the handing out of gifts. Just what had been in those pretty little gift-wrapped packages? I'd naïvely presumed rum truffles and Turkish delight, but perhaps the goodies had been a smidge more sophisticated.

Santa took a small step backwards. Then another and another until the pools of darkness beyond the fairy lights swallowed him up. The river was behind him. Not good.

In a swift, sure movement, I hiked up my dress and slid out my gun.

'Great,' said Stark. 'She's going to do her Annie Oakley impersonation.'

'Keep a lid on it Stark or I'll shoot you,' I said sweetly and patted him on the cheek. 'I'll catch you guys later.'

As smoothly and efficiently as my stiletto heels would allow I worked my way around the edge of the crowd, hoping to get the attention of Quinn, or Fox, or any of the other lads. I didn't want to take Santa down on my own.

But Maine was causing a fuss and his wife had fainted. Good distraction tactics. But not good enough to put me off my game. I had Santa in my sights. He was running towards the river where a launch was moored. I ran after him, bouncing along on the balls of my feet so the wretched heels wouldn't cripple me. I was hindered by darkness and low-lying shrubs. Now I know why I preferred wearing jeans and sneakers. They were infinitely more practical.

'Freeze!' I yelled. 'Police! I've got you covered.'

Santa slowed down and glanced over his shoulder.

'Get lost, lady,' he said and leapt onward towards the bank.

With a spurt of speed I dived for his legs. He fell hard. So did I. We thrashed about like a couple of eels, me at a total disadvantage in my sausage-skin dress and heels. Santa grappled with his flyaway false beard, pointy hat and heavy black boots. We rolled about on grass lately drenched from sprinklers, getting soaked to the skin. My dress concertinaed so the hem sprang towards my knickers and the top went down to my naval, which momentarily transfixed Santa.

'Wow,' he said and then remembered where he was and what we were doing. He pitched me off to the side. I landed hard on my shoulder and pain jolted the full length of my arm and up to my neck. It was the break he needed. Santa scrambled to his feet.

'Some other time, sister,' he said and raced towards the boat.

Darn it. I'd been so close and now he was getting away. I rolled over on to my tummy, and ignoring the screaming pain in my shoulder, lined him up and fired.

A crack, a scream and he was on the ground, writhing in agony. I'd got him in the leg, just above the shiny Santa boots.

Yanking up my top and tugging down my dress, I jogged over

to Santa. He was trying his best to crawl to the boat. Standing over him, straddling his lower body, I pointed my gun.

'Quit moving or I'll shoot your other leg. You're under arrest.'

As I read him his rights, the cavalry appeared.

'Every man's fantasy, Red' said Quinn as he loped up to my side. He pulled the dress up higher to cover my too-exposed boobs. 'Sex and power. What a combination.'

'Cuff him,' I said, ignoring Quinn's off-colour comments. Adrenaline was whizzing through me, making me feel invincible. I love arresting people!

'Are you going to tell me why you've bagged Santa?' said Quinn.

'Check his sack,' I said, and then told him about the packages and high jinx going on at the grotto. 'And you might want to check out the boat too.'

Billy Baker came up with his dog, whistled appreciatively at my stance, laughed when I gave him the finger and then led his dog to the sack. There was no mistaking the dog's reaction to the contents. Drugs.

I tottered back to the dance floor. The party was over but some people were still drinking and eating. Maine was being led to a police car. He looked at me with disgust. His lip curled and he said, 'I'm disappointed with you Eve. Is this how you repay my hospitality?'

'It ended with a bang. Isn't that what you wanted?' I said and then pushed through the guests to where Margot and Stark were huddled in a threesome with Josie.

'I should have known you'd spoil the party,' said Josie in a tone that dripped sugar-coated arsenic. 'You're trouble.'

'I was just doing my job.'

'I wish you wouldn't,' said Margot. 'It puts a dampener on things.'

'Sorry,' I said, but I didn't mean it. My job came first, always.

'Have you hurt yourself?' she said as I tentatively rolled my shoulder to ease the throb.

'Yeah. The guy wouldn't come quietly.'

'That'll teach you,' said Josie.

'Thanks,' I said. 'I'll try and remember that in future. In the meantime, I have to go back to the station and deal with my arrest. Maybe do him for assault.'

I gave her a sweet smile.

'If ever you need a lawyer,' said Stark. 'Don't call me.'

16

I DID MY STUFF AT THE POLICE HEADQUARTERS AND GOT A TAXI HOME.
Quinn offered to take me, but I didn't want any complications.
My adrenaline high had been replaced by a corresponding low. My
arm, shoulder, neck and head ached like crazy. Bed beckoned. I
wanted to curl up and lick my wounds, and I wanted to do it on my
own, which meant I must have been feeling bad.

The street was as quiet as it ever got. I tripped up the path in a
borrowed pair of sneakers, the red shoes had long been sacrificed
for safety reasons. I wore Quinn's jacket around my shoulders,
more for modesty than warmth, as the night was balmy. I unlocked
the front door and reached for the light switch.

Crack! Flash! Pwff!

I was thrown backwards as my fingers hit live wire and my head
connected with the doorjamb, which caused another starburst and
crackles. What were those Ferraris trying to do? Kill me?

Nursing my hand, with my heart pounding and feeling all jittery
thanks to the electric voltage that had just zapped through me,
I sat down heavily on the step. What a close call. No doubt my
borrowed rubber soles had saved me. I sunk my head between my
knees and breathed deeply. I hurt. And I was rattled.

I stayed there for a good five minutes until my pulse wound
back to a more sedate pace and I didn't feel so light headed. I then
locked the front door, which had been fixed on my insistence by
Dom Ferrari, and negotiated my way in the dark to the kitchen. I
always kept a torch in one of the drawers. I'd lived in enough sub-
standard rental properties to know the power can go off any time.

I just didn't expect it in my own home. I turned the power off at the metre box and then crashed into my bed to sleep off too much champagne, adrenaline, injuries and men.

Friday was my day off. I slept heavily until noon. When I awoke my first panicked thought was that the Ferrari trolls were in the house and I had to face them all before I'd showered and eaten. But I focused on the noises going on outside my bedroom and none of them sounded as if builders were merrily at work – just mundane traffic too far away to worry about.

I poked my head in the bathroom and decided it was uninhabitable. I would go to Saint Immaculata's and enjoy the endless hot water of school showers. Hopefully the heat would ease my aching body. I felt as though I'd just been on the losing end of a rugby scrum.

But it didn't stop me feeling as hungry as a wolf. I headed for the kitchen and was met by a flood. The fridge had defrosted with the lack of power. Great. Just what I needed to start my day. I expected it to be almost empty but there was some solid Italian food sitting sadly on the shelves – salami, pizza, meatballs – obviously left by Ferrari and his boys for snack time. I binned everything, wiped out the fridge and put newspaper on the floor to soak up the drips.

As I laid out the sheets of paper, an article snagged my interest. It was a warning about the dangers of date-rape drugs, putting people on red alert during the festive season. I read it through. It said the usual things about not leaving your drink unattended, watching your drink being prepared by the barman and not accepting drinks from strangers. It explained what the drug gamma hydroxybutyrate was and the effects it had on the nervous system when taken.

As I spread the paper back on to the floor and watched it blot up the moisture, I thought I should warn Chastity. I didn't think Sister Immaculata would have had date rape doping included on the curriculum. Leaving a note on the kitchen table informing Ferrari about the electricity trouble and how dangerous it was leaving live wires for one to find, I scrambled together some clothes and took off for Saint Immaculata's for hot showers and breakfast.

'How did your night go?' Chastity asked as she watched me eat my cheese and bacon croissant. I'd showered and changed into snug clean jeans, and a black cotton top and felt almost human, especially with food inside me.

'It was interesting,' I said around my mouthful.

'Did you dance with anyone?'

'Yes.'

'Who?'

'Men.' Like I was going to tell her.

She rolled her eyes. 'Mum!'

'No one interesting,' I lied. 'And it wasn't easy dancing. Those shoes were not designed for comfort. Nor was the dress.'

I decided to change the subject. 'Do you want to come Christmas shopping this afternoon?'

'Yes, but on one condition.'

'Hit me with it.'

'You don't run after any Santa Clauses.'

I was glad I hadn't told her about last night's collar. She would think I was obsessed with big fat men sporting long white beards.

'Okay.'

'Promise.'

'I'll try not to. Is that good enough?'

'No.'

'Aw, Chastity.'

'I won't come unless you promise.'

'Okay, I promise.'

'And leave your gun behind,' she added.

That girl had fixed ideas on how to shop. I always took my gun. You never knew when it would come in handy. But I indulged her and locked it away in the Iron Nun's safe so it wouldn't fall into the wrong hands.

'Why do you carry a gun?' said my mother. She hovered at my shoulder as I twisted the safe knob.

'I'm a police officer.'

'Not every police officer carries a gun.' She folded her hands primly across her chest, almost in prayer mode. Her eyes held a challenge.

I responded like I always did. Fighting with my mother was what I did best because I'd done it for the longest time. Mind, I didn't always come out top.

'I know not everyone in the force carries firearms. It's personal choice. But I prefer to.'

'I brought you up to love your neighbour.'

'That's fine, Mum. But sometimes the neighbours have to be arrested because they're dangerous. It's my job to protect the public.'

'When did you last have to use it?' Her lips twisted in a superior smile as if she thought I'd never had to use the gun, that I wore it as some sort of feminist protest badge.

'Last night. I shot someone in the leg.'

She gasped and quickly crossed herself. 'You're just saying that to shock,' she said.

'Actually, I'm not.'

'Oh dear,' she said. 'I'll pray for you.'

'Thank you.' I hoped it would help but I doubted it.

Chastity and I shopped until we dropped and I tried really, really hard to ignore the man in red who was following us most of the time. I tried to get a good look at his face, but it wasn't easy, not without alerting Chastity.

I thought about ringing Fox and asking him to come and arrest him. But that wasn't a brilliant idea. I had to keep Fox at a distance. Then I thought of Quinn, but he didn't know I was being stalked by a Santa and it would be too hard trying to explain in a nutshell.

I sighed.

'Chastity,' I said. 'Please can I break my promise?'

'No, or I'm out of here and I won't ever, ever come shopping with you again.'

Fair enough. A deal was a deal.

'Well, then I think it's time we called it a day.'

'But I'm just warming up,' she said. 'I've only purchased half the presents on my list.'

'Forget it. We'll come another day.' Once I'd arrested the stalker.

'But Christmas will soon be here. There's hardly any time.'

'There's plenty of time. Don't argue.'

We went back to Saint Immaculata's. I liberated my gun from the safe and popped it back in my ankle holster, feeling better, feeling whole. I tried to talk my mother and daughter into sharing a curry with me, but they declined. They said they had a prior engagement and, terribly sorry, but I wasn't included.

As if I cared.

I did.

So I went back home with a takeaway meal for one, feeling low. I was on my own on a Friday night, two weeks before Christmas, while the rest of the world celebrated the jolly festive season. In an attempt to make the meal special and to cheer myself up, I found a candle and stuck it in an empty wine bottle. Actually, it was a safer bet than trying the lights again. I didn't need another shock. The candle looked lonely and out of place so I put a lace cloth on the table and tipped my tinfoil-carton meal on to a plate and used a proper knife and fork instead of the plastic ones provided.

It still looked sad.

But it was my chapati and I'd cry if I wanted to.

I had an early night as I couldn't watch television unless I wanted to brave the power. And there was no one to drink with unless I went out. And my shoulder ached like hell. Sleep was the best and only option.

Early next morning, I was hitting the pavements and jogging my heart out hoping the exercise would make me feel better and ease the stiffness in my shoulder. I had another day off and I had no firm plans.

In the harsh light of day, I inspected the progress on the house. There didn't seem to be any, so I rang Dom Ferrari.

'Meeses Rocks,' he said. 'You gonna have to have faith.'

'But nothing's been done since you gutted the bathroom and kitchen. I can't live in the house without decent running water and electricity.'

'The bathroom will be in on Monday, I promise yous.'

'Great. What about the electricity?'

'We haven't touched no electricity.'

'But I nearly killed myself on Thursday night because you'd taken away the light switch and left bare wires.'

'Meeses Rocks, we haven't touched your switches. The sparky is coming next week, after your plumbing is finitoed.'

'So who took away my light switch?' I squeaked.

'Search me, lady. Not me anyhows.'

I put the phone down after more assurances by Ferrari that the work was in hand and not to panic. I nibbled my bottom lip. If Ferrari hadn't tampered with the switch, who had?

And why?

Then I thought of the falling timber narrowly missing my head a few days back.

Was someone trying to kill me? The Stalking Santa perhaps? I shivered. Perhaps it was time to file a report.

There was a tap on the door and Margot called out a greeting.

'Come in,' I said.

'Is it safe?'

'No.'

She laughed and stepped into the kitchen.

'Thought you might like a massage if your shoulder is still hurting,' she said.

'Sounds like heaven.'

'Come round to my place. It's a lot more civilised.' She raised her eyes to the lack of ceiling. 'Safer too.'

'Too right,' and, feeling like Chicken Licken, I told her about the chunk of wood that had almost fallen on my head.

'Lucky escape,' she said and shivered dramatically.

Margot had magic hands. The massage was bliss and I relaxed and all but melted like hot butter over the massage table.

'You know,' she said after a while. 'It makes a change just doing a massage and not being expected to carry it through to the bitter end.'

As a conversation topic, her nugget of information sucked. I did not want to know details, so I changed the subject.

'What did you and Stark do after the raid?' I asked instead, much more in my comfort zone.

'We went off to the Paradise.'

'You go there a lot.'

'It's a nice place,' she said.

It wasn't anywhere close to my definition of nice but I kept silent. I was enjoying the massage too much. I let her hands rhythmically work over my knotted muscles and then I dozed off for an hour or so. When I awoke, I was so relaxed my legs were numb and my brain barely functioning. I slowly pieced myself together, said a thank you to Margot and then went shopping for groceries. I was fed up not having any decent food in the house. It was time to stock up.

Angelina, Chastity's roommate, was on the checkout at my local supermarket.

'Holiday job?' I asked her as she began to scan my purchases.

'Yes. Mum said I had to get one to keep out of trouble during the summer.'

'What a good idea. Perhaps I should get Chastity out into the workforce too.'

'She's already busy.'

That was news to me.

'Doing what?'

'Helping Sister Immaculata.'

'There wouldn't be that much on, with school finished for the summer.'

'Oh there is,' she said. 'You just wouldn't believe the things she has to do.'

'Like?' I was intrigued. Chastity hadn't said anything about her workload.

'Oh.' She suddenly looked flustered. 'I can't say.'

I continued to unpack my trolley and then decided to have a stab in the dark.

'Perhaps you can help me, Angie,' I said. She immediately looked wary and I laughed. 'It's nothing too difficult. I'm just an old fuddy-duddy and I don't know what some initials in text messaging stand for.'

'Okay, cool,' she said dubiously. Good old Angie Airhead. All she needed were shoulder pads to protect her bobbing head.

'CU.'

'Easy. Just as it sounds: See you.'

'GR8?'

'Great.'

'Now why didn't I think of that? Duh. Okay, so what about VV?'

'Virgin Vigilantes,' she said promptly and then bit her bottom lip and muttered, 'Damn.'

I pretended I didn't hear. I gave her a few more initials, got her answers, and packed my groceries into a cardboard box and paid the bill.

'Thanks, Angie. You've been a big help.'

'Glad to be of assistance, Ms Rock.'

So Chastity was involved in the Virgin Vigilantes. But what were they when they were at home? Apart from asking Chastity outright, I would have to do some stealthy digging.

I decided to call Anne Fellows. She answered on the second ring and didn't sound thrilled to hear from me. I went straight to the point.

'Was Bobbie involved with the Virgin Vigilantes?' I asked.

'I thought the investigation had been dropped?' she said.

'Please, answer the question. Mother to mother. It's important to me.' It was a low card to play, but I had a hunch.

'All right, yes. How do you know about them?' she said cautiously. 'Through your daughter?'

As if Chastity would tell me anything.

'What do you know about them?' I said ignoring her question. I didn't want her to know Chastity had been keeping me out in the cold. It might put Anne Fellows off.

'Not a lot, I must admit. It's a sort of select sisterhood. They apparently encourage each other to achieve excellence in their spiritual, moral and academic lives.'

I remembered all the posters and slogans in Chastity's room.

'So it's made up of girls from the school?'

'And former pupils. I don't think there's a cut off point.'

'I see.'

'Do you?' she said doubtfully, obviously worried she'd said too much. 'Please don't interfere, DI Rock. I know Bobbie is fine and that she'll be home by Christmas.'

'How can you be so sure?'

'Because I've been promised.'

'By the Virgin Vigilantes?'

She hung up without giving me an answer.

17

I cruised over to Saint Immaculata's and parked on the forecourt. The place was as subdued as a derelict cemetery and was baking silently in the intense afternoon sun. No one was in the office or the common room. I kept walking down the endless corridors, my sneakers going squeak-squeak-squeak like a clockwork mouse, until I found Chastity and Sister Mercy cleaning out the science lab.

'That's what I like to see,' I said. 'Productive toil. Do you want a hand?'

'No, we're doing just great. Go and sit down, Mum, and take it easy.'

Unless I have a glass of wine in my hand and a steaming Indian meal in front of me, I don't see the point in being slothful. So I grabbed a cloth and grinned at her.

'No. I'll pitch in and then we can get it finished much quicker.'

They both did their damnedest to send me packing, seemed quite agitated about it in fact, but I held my ground and began to clean. I shifted the chemical bottles off the shelves and wiped down all the surfaces. As I scrubbed away in my corner, I began absently reading labels and seeing if I could remember the abbreviations and what each of the chemicals was used for.

I thought I was doing quite well, until I came to a bottle that made me start. Its name was instantly recognisable and I knew all about its properties and what it was used for. I'd read about it this morning, while kneeling in front of my leaking fridge.

So what did the pupils of Saint Immaculata's want with a litre bottle of gamma hydroxybutyrate? Unless they were going to hit the town and drug all the young men in sight, what was the point?

Ah, what was the point indeed?

My hunch was taking shape. I was beginning to get a handle on what had happened to those missing girls and how they were smuggled out of the Paradise Nightclub without any fuss or bother.

Not wanting to draw attention to my discovery, I carried on cleaning for another hour or so and then drifted off with the excuse I needed a cup of tea. Chastity and Sister Mercy were relieved to see me go, I bet. But they would have been wetting themselves if they'd realised where I was heading.

As soon as I was out of earshot, I scampered down the back stairs to the vast basement below. I knew the school intimately. It had been my home for most of my childhood. My guess was the victims were either in the attics or the basement. If the girls had been initially drugged, the basement would be the best bet because they would have been a dead weight to carry. I went through the kitchen, with its array of shiny stainless-steel units, and down the final flight of stairs, passing the storerooms with tins and sacks and goodness knows what that was needed to feed a school this size, and along to the back rooms.

Half way down the cool dim corridor, I spied a slender, familiar figure whose picture I'd had pinned up on my office wall all last week. I smiled. She gasped.

'Hello, Bobbie,' I said. 'We've been looking for you. I'm from the police.'

She slapped the palm of her hand on her forehead.

'That's torn it,' she said.

'I suppose the other girls are here too?'

She nodded and gestured behind her. I followed her down the final leg of the corridor and there, sitting in a cosy cluster of comfortable chairs were Sasha Lucas, Monique Dewson and Ashleigh Johnson. The big room had state of the art computers along one wall, a wide screen TV on another, and a row of neatly made beds.

'We've been rumbled,' said Bobbie and flopped into a vacant armchair.

'Who by?' Sasha twisted around to look and gave me a quick and dismissive once over.

'DI Eve Rock,' I said. 'Pleased to finally meet you. And a relief to find you're all alive and well.'

'It's comforting to know the police can actually solve mysteries,' said Sasha with a cool smile.

There was a scuffling sound behind me. I turned and Sister Immaculata stood in the doorway looking puffed up and cross as a mother bantam protecting her chicks.

'What are you doing in here? Get out!' she said.

'Not so fast, Mum.' I, too, squared up for battle. 'So you had the girls here all the time. I could arrest you for obstructing the police, along with kidnapping and holding people against their will.'

Sister Immaculata puffed up even further. At this rate she'd explode.

'How dare you,' she said. 'I have done nothing wrong. These young women aren't being made to stay here. They are exercising their own free will. They are not prisoners!'

'But you drugged and kidnapped them! How democratic is that? How are you going to explain that to a judge?'

Sister Immaculata's face instantly became a florid mask, her eyes popping in indignation. Spittle flew in all directions.

'You wouldn't dare arrest me!' she declared. 'The charges won't stick. The investigation has been terminated and you are acting outside of your jurisdiction. I shall speak to your superiors.'

Her wrath didn't faze me. I was used to it. I slung my weight on to one hip and stared her down.

'Go ahead,' I said. The silence stretched and her anger abated, but only marginally.

'You're on private property,' she said slightly more mildly. 'You have no right to be here. I suggest you leave.'

It used to be my home. She was my mother. My daughter lived here most of the time. I had every right to be here. But I didn't push it.

'You've been kidnapping women and holding them hostage. How can you justify it?'

'It was for their own good!' A fanatical light strobed wildly in Sister Immaculata's brown eyes. It was the same light that glowed in Chastity when she got fired up about something. I probably demonstrated it too, when arresting someone. It's a worry, these family likenesses. Makes you paranoid about your gene pool.

I sighed. 'How do you work that one out?'

'Learning transcends all. It frees women from the clutches of carnal lusts and raises them above mediocrity.'

I'd heard this all before. I'd been raised on it.

'Yeah, yeah, and so I bet you've clapped up these women down here to help them focus on their studies.'

'Yes! They were getting tempted into the pits of debauchery. We had to stop them and steer them back on to the straight, narrow road of morality. I worked hard to give them a top education. I couldn't stand by and watch them throw it all away on men and the lusts of the flesh, just as you did.'

Hey, that was below the belt.

'You've gone too far,' I said, miffed. She always had done. I reckon it was the only reason I was conceived.

'But Mum!' wailed Chastity, coming out of nowhere and launching herself into my arms. 'You don't understand.'

'I understand all too well. Your grandmother has overstepped the bounds this time.'

'If you interfere, you're going to spoil everything!'

That's me, killjoy mum.

'At least I won't arrest you,' I said. 'That, surely, is an advantage?'

Sister Immaculata said a big 'Hmmph!' and stomped out the room, apparently satisfied her wayward daughter wouldn't upset the status quo by sending her to jail and not passing Go. The other girls stared at me stony-faced and calculating. It did cross my mind they might try and kidnap me and hold me prisoner until Sister Immaculata had finished what she'd set out to do. That would be an interesting scenario. No one knew where I was. And no one would probably care, personally or professionally.

Fleetingly I thought of Fox and Quinn and Margot. Fox was probably annoyed I'd given him the cold shoulder. He wouldn't be bursting any gaskets trying to see me. Quinn wasn't an integral part of my life. And Margot was smack in the middle of the weekend and would be far too busy, flat on her back, to notice where her party-destroying neighbour was.

I could be abducted, imprisoned or murdered even and there wouldn't be a ripple of interest, save from Chastity. And if she was part of the abducting and imprisoning squad, then that was that. My last hope down the gurgler.

Moving confidently among the girls, showing no unease or distrust, especially towards Sasha, I sat down in one of the armchairs. I leaned back and said, 'Okay, so for the record, tell me how you did it.'

'Easy,' said Chastity skipping over and perching on the arm of my chair. 'We found out when they were going to the Paradise and we'd pretend to bump into them there and slip a drug into their drinks. Before they became completely immobilised, we'd walk them out through the main entrance, into a waiting vehicle, and then came back here.'

'And you made the drug?'

'Sister Mercy worked out how to do it. She's brilliant. I helped her. I've learnt heaps about chemistry.'

Which was why Chastity's science grades had been exceptionally high this year. She'd been on a mission. Oh great. Of course, I couldn't blame her. Missions were what made the women of our family tick. And then I thought of Quinn. He'd been one-eyed about hounding the drug trafficking trade, suffering being undercover in the enemy camp for months on end. He was mission-driven too. Hell, Chastity didn't stand a chance. She'd inherited it from both sides of the fence.

'And the whole scheme was devised by the Virgin Vigilantes?' I said.

'You know about the Virgins?' said Chastity, surprised.

'I'm a detective, sweetheart. I know a lot more than you give me credit for.'

'You're cool, Mum,' she said.

Praise indeed.

'What happens now?' said Bobbie.

'Well, I'm not going to do anything. My superiors aren't interested and your parents are happy for you to stay here until you or Sister Immaculata think the time is right for you to leave. I think Christmas is the cut off time.'

'So if the investigation was dropped a while back, why did you keep looking for us?' asked Sasha. She was definitely the leader of the pack. Cool, sophisticated and smart.

'I was worried about you. And I don't like loose ends. Period. But I hope you girls think all this,' I waved my hand around the room, 'is worth it.'

'Absolutely,' said Monique. 'It has realigned us and got us centred on our studies again.'

'That's fine,' I said. 'Academia is okay but do remember people are important too. Your parents went through agonies when you first disappeared. They thought you'd been kidnapped, raped and murdered. We had police officers, some with daughters your age, door knocking and interviewing people and scouring waste land desperately searching for you. We had other parents fearful of their own daughters' safety, believing we had another serial killer in our midst. It hasn't been a pleasant few weeks.'

Bobbie hung her head and I pushed on.

'It's okay to want to excel in your chosen fields, but this is a drastic way of doing it. You shut out the people you love. It's not nice for those left on the outside. You have to get a balance. Learn to compartmentalise so that you can have it all without neglecting an important part of your lives.'

I was a fine one to talk, but then perhaps it was best coming from someone who knew first hand. I smiled, 'End of sermon. Have a good Christmas, girls.'

I left the completely silent room, Chastity close on my heels.

'You were talking about yourself in there and Grandma,' she said. 'She shut you out when she studied like mad and then began the school.'

'Maybe.'

'I didn't realise you felt like that. You always seem so together and capable.'

'Looks can be deceiving.'

Weren't they just. I thought of the Iron Nun in her habit and then in her former days, as a hooker. I thought of Quinn the blond, windswept, sun-kissed lotus-eater, who was actually a hard-bitten undercover cop. And I thought of Fox, the golden sexy angel who would be available if I snapped my fingers but who, in fact, was bad news because, through an accident of birth, he was Chastity's half-brother, family.

Then the image of sleazy Dennis Phipps popped into my head. That sleek, smug snake-oil salesman who'd looked such a loser but had numerous women in his life. Who would have guessed?

'Yeah, looks can be very deceiving,' I said reaching my car and preparing to drive away. Chastity leaned on the open car door and stared intensely at me.

'You're not cross about the kidnappings, are you Mum?'

'Chastity, you broke the law.' I wasn't about to give her instant absolution.

'But it was for a good cause.'

'You could have done it in an easier, less dramatic way that wouldn't have worried people sick to death and tied up police manpower for weeks on end.'

'But the girls wouldn't come voluntarily. We'd already tried the softly, softly approach. But they professed they were having such a good time and to hell with studying. We had to take drastic measures, especially with Sasha. She was heavily into drugs and had to be detoxed.'

Omigod. They'd been doing cold turkey in the basement, and not the Christmas roast variety! I shook my head.

'That was very stupid and dangerous. You have to have a fully qualified doctor in attendance. You were lucky nothing went wrong.' I was chilled to the soul just thinking about it.

'But it was cool. We had a doctor.'

'Who?' I wondered which doctor had been game enough to get involved.

'Sister Mercy.'

Heavens above. I almost crossed myself. I didn't want to hear anymore.

18

IT WAS SUNDAY MORNING AND I HAD A SLEW OF TIME IN LIEU OWED TO me, but that didn't stop me going into headquarters. I'd had more than enough of time off, in limbo. I wanted to get down to some real work. I might have solved the Paradise abductions, but the euphoria I usually experienced when I'd successfully wrapped up a case was missing. It had sort of petered out with the result. No bad guys, I guess, just fanatical females trying to make their world a better place by employing dubious means.

And anyway, I still had Dennis Phipps and Thelma Freeman's murderers to find.

Burton came into the office a little after me. He'd decided to forfeit his Sunday at home so he could avoid the mother-in-law. Sounded like good logic to me. He got me up to speed on what had been happening during my two-day absence.

It seemed the newspapers had been spreading their own particular brand of poison and as a result, irate Phipps' wives and lovers had enjoyed cat spates all over the metropolitan district. Domestics, don't you just love them. As Burton was ticking off the list of who's who in Phipps' sorry, sordid life, the phone rang. It was Sylvia the sex therapist.

'You told Sue about Den and me!' she screamed down the line. 'You promised you wouldn't and now she's trying to kill me!'

'We'll be right over,' I said.

'Hurry! She's breaking down the door.'

'We didn't tell her,' Burton said matter-of-factly. 'But she would have read about it in the Sunday Times. Some journalist uncovered that juicy titbit.'

'We'd better go now,' I said on a sigh. 'Just in case Sue Phipps has completely lost her rag.'

The roads were relatively traffic free. Just mums out in the family four-wheel drive taking their little Johnnies and Jessicas to tee-ball while the devout attended church or golf. We made it to Scarborough in record time. The front door was intact. Sylvia had been exaggerating.

We leaned on the bell but there was no response. Burton cut his eyes to me and we silently went around the side of the house to the back patio where we discovered Sylvia hadn't been exaggerating. The double glass doors had been smashed as if a Boeing had rocketed through it. We crunched over the glass liberally littering the tiled floor.

'Sylvia!' I called. There was no response. We pulled out our guns and did a rapid search of the ground floor rooms and then, our bodies hugging the wall, quietly negotiated the stairs.

As we rounded the corner, we stopped short. Sue sat on the top step, a baseball bat loosely held in her hands. She looked a mess, with unwashed hair and crumpled, soiled clothes. Gone was the neat, blonde bob and chic style of last Sunday. And the door behind her looked rather worse for wear too. It had been hacked half to death.

'Hello, Sue,' I said a couple of metres away from her, just in case she took a swing.

She didn't look up but her hold on the bat tightened, whitening the knuckles. Uh-oh.

'Put the bat down,' I said.

'Why should I?'

'Because it's the sensible thing to do. You've already done enough damage.' I paused and then said tentatively, 'Where's Sylvia?'

'That bitch? She's locked herself in the bathroom.'

'Are you okay, Sylvia?' yelled Burton.

A muffled affirmative came through the wrecked door.

'Give me the bat,' I said again to Sue. She let it drop and it rolled down a couple of steps to my feet. 'Thank you.'

'You're welcome.' Her eyes began to fill with tears. 'Why did he do it? Why cheat with her of all people? She was my friend.'

'He cheated on everyone,' I said.

'I can't believe he did. Wasn't I enough for him?'

I put my arm around her and led her downstairs, leaving Burton to rescue Sylvia.

'Do you want a cuppa?' I said. 'We'll go back to your house and make one.'

Seated back in her now not-so-neat white house, Sue was slightly more composed. By the puffiness of her eyes, though, she'd done a lot of crying this last week. I boiled the kettle and washed up a couple of mugs I'd found soaking in the sink full of scummy water. She was more than a little behind in her housekeeping, but who could blame her?

'So all those newspaper reports are true about Den?' she said.

I dunked the teabags up and down in the hot water and tried to think of a diplomatic way of saying Den was an utter bastard, but I couldn't.

'We did warn you about the other wives,' I said.

'I was on the way out, wasn't I?' she said. 'That old one, Audrey, he'd left her years ago. But that young dancer was new. He was going to leave me for her, wasn't he?'

'I don't know, Sue. If it's any consolation, he always had more than one woman on the go. He may have carried on being married to you and to Lina. He'd managed to juggle the two of you for one year, why not longer?' Maybe that didn't sound too tactful but I couldn't believe she cared if Phipps had considered leaving her or not.

'You really had no idea he was cheating?' I said. I'd asked her this question before but I thought perhaps I'd get a truthful answer this time.

'If I'd have had any idea he was being unfaithful, I would have killed him,' she said and then dissolved into more tears. As she cried, Burton quietly came into the kitchen and motioned for me to see him outside.

'She's done some extensive damage to Sylvia,' he said. 'We need to take her to hospital.'

'Drive Sylvia in her car and I'll follow later in the squad car. I need to get someone in to be with Sue. She's not safe to leave on her own.'

The damage was a broken arm and abrasions to the head. Sylvia was lucky. The result could have been a lot worse. As we waited for her to be x-rayed, I said to Burton, 'I don't think Sue was the killer. She loved him too much.'

'"Hell hath no fury like a woman scorned,"' said Burton.

'How cultured, Burton, I'm impressed. But though scorned women can be ferocious, it doesn't fit Sue's profile. She didn't know she was scorned until Phipps was dead.'

'True. But what about the sex therapist? She knew all about the other women and still became one.'

'Where's the motive?' I said.

'Can't see one, I must admit.'

When Sylvia was in bed and comfortable, we went in to question her. Her eyes were swollen, her head bandaged and her arm plastered. Apart from that she looked fine.

'Have you locked her up?' said Sylvia.

'Who?' said Burton.

'That maniac Sue Phipps. I thought she was going to kill me.'

'You did cheat on her with her husband,' I pointed out. 'She had good reason to be mad at you.'

'But I didn't kill him.'

'Is that what she said? Did she think you had?'

'Yes. Though goodness knows I can't follow her thought processes. I loved him, why would I want to break his neck?'

'You tell me.'

'What's that supposed to mean?'

'Weren't you jealous?'

'I wasn't jealous of Sue.'

'What about the other wife and lovers? He must have talked about his other women,' I said.

'Why must he?'

'Because you were his therapist.'

'We didn't dwell on them.'

'I'm curious. Just what did you dwell on?'

'His need to be loved and how he'd been let down all his life.'

'You can't be serious! He was the one letting everyone down,' said Burton.

'Shut up,' I said under my breath. 'Or she'll clam up.'

I turned back to Sylvia who was glaring at Burton.

'So he didn't mention any of the women in his life.'

'Well, yes. His mother.'

We'd already ascertained she had died in a nursing home a few years back.

'Anyone else?'

'His first wife.'

'Audrey?'

'No, that wasn't her name.' She frowned in concentration.

'He had another wife?'

'Yes, before Audrey.'

Burton and I stared at each other in surprise. We hadn't been aware of a fourth wife. No one had mentioned her existence before.

'Think, Sylvia. What was her name?' I tried to keep my voice neutral but I could feel the sudden ferment of excitement in my belly. This could be the break through we'd been waiting for. Or a figment of Sylvia's imagination to throw us off the scent. Whichever, it would have to be investigated.

'I can't remember and my head hurts. I just want to sleep.'

'As soon as you remember it, call us. It could be very, very important.'

'But she was just another woman in a long line.'

'But one we haven't accounted for.'

'Let's go and visit Audrey Phipps,' I said to Burton as we left the hospital. 'She might know of the other wife.'

'Surely she would have volunteered the information?'

'Probably didn't occur to her. She's no Mensa. She'll answer any questions put to her but she's never volunteered anything extra.'

'Or she's very astute and only tells us what she thinks we want to hear.'

'There is that.' I considered it for a minute, picturing Audrey in her tight-fitting synthetic tracksuit and pink thongs, her stringy grey hair uninspiring and unflattering. She didn't strike me as a shrewd woman.

'Do you think she killed Dennis Phipps?' I said.

'I don't know who killed him.' He sighed. 'I'm keeping an open mind.'

'Whoever it was must have been strong or had a good technique to break his neck. I find I'm always studying people's hands, gauging whether or not they would have the power to snap a spine.'

'Sue Phipps was strong enough to wield a bat.'

'She had anger on her side,' I pointed out.

'Whoever killed Phipps might have been angry too.'

'It was a cold anger,' I said after a pause, again trying to picture the scene, trying to reconstruct what might have happened.

'Sorry?'

'I don't think it was red hot fury that spurned the murderer on. I think it was more calculated.'

'Revenge is best served cold.'

'Exactly.'

'You're not trying to stitch this crime on to the unknown wife?' said Burton, one eyebrow cocked in surprise.

'I don't stitch people, DS Burton,' I said flatly. 'I find out who did the crime and then seek justice.'

Audrey was wearing her black tracksuit again. Did she possess anything else? There was a smell of boiled cabbage in the kitchen and the remains of lunch on the sink draining board. Derek, her son, was sprawled in front of the television watching soccer. He would have been better employed playing it and working off some of his gut.

'We're sorry to bother you, Mrs Phipps,' I said. 'But we need to ask you a few more questions.'

'It's no trouble,' she said. 'I wasn't doing anything special.'

I believed her.

'Is it about Derek?' she said.

'No, Dennis.'

'Oh him. Okay, then.'

'We are trying to find his murderer,' I said gently, trying not to make it sound as if I was talking to a halfwit.

'Yes, of course. I forgot.'

How? It wasn't every day your estranged husband got himself murdered. But hey, perhaps her reality was different from mine. I shouldn't judge.

'Was Dennis married to anyone else when he first met you?'

'No.' She shook her head wonderingly, as if I'd said something amazing but abstract, something that didn't concern her.

'You don't remember there being any other woman?' Burton pushed.

She screwed up her eyes and concentrated hard. We waited. Someone scored a goal and Derek went wild, cheering and singing football chants along with the packed terraces at Old Trafford or goodness knows where. We continued to wait.

'There was someone who used to phone up when we were first married.'

'A woman?' I clarified.

'I think so.'

'Why only think so?'

'Because whoever it was never spoke if I answered the phone. Just lots of breathing and silence. But if Dennis answered, then I would sometimes hear all this high pitch yelling. He would then usually go out.'

'You never asked him who it was?'

'He told me it was no one important.'

'And you believed him?'

'Yes, why wouldn't I?'

'You weren't suspicious he was having an affair or anything?'

'No, we were happy.'

'But he left you.'

'He didn't want me to have a baby, but I did anyway. That's when the rot set in. I had Derek and Dennis left, the bastard.'

We were back to square one.

At the station, we rang the other wives and lovers to see if any of them knew of another wife. They didn't. Were we surprised? No.

'Let's hope Sylvia remembers the name,' I said. 'Or we're stuck.'

19

I HAD A DATE THAT NIGHT WITH MY DAUGHTER. WE WERE GOING TO the carols by candlelight concert in one of the local parks. It was something we had done since Chastity was a toddler and had become something of a Rock tradition. This year, I'd invited Margot along too.

'I don't know about this,' she said when I threw the idea at her. 'I haven't sung carols since seventh grade.'

'Live a little,' I said. 'This could be the turning point of your life.'

'What do I wear?'

'Singing carols in the park is not a fashion statement, Margot. Just wear something comfortable. And take a jumper in case it blows up cold.'

Not that I could see that happening. The heat was unremitting. Cyclones in the northwest of the state were causing high temperatures and humidity in the lower half. You just had to think and you broke out in a sweat.

We were sitting in my bomb-site kitchen, drinking cheap red wine as my power was still disconnected and I couldn't boil the kettle for tea. Well, that's my excuse. It was late afternoon and we had a couple of hours before the carols began. The wine went straight to my head due to lack of food.

'I must eat,' I said to Margot. 'Or I'll just curl up and go to sleep and completely miss the singing.'

Margot waved away the offer of food. She sat at my kitchen table and painted her Fu Manchu false nails while I cobbled together some bread, tomatoes and tinned sardines.

'How's the hunt for Den's murderer going?' she asked, smoothing on a virulent pink polish that would have matched Audrey's thongs beautifully.

'Slowly.'

'No leads?'

'Not really. It's frustrating but par for the course.'

'I was reading the Sunday paper. Den had an awful lot of women in his life.'

'He did.' It amazed me such a jerk could have conned so many women.

Margot topped up my wine, then hers.

'Could it have been one of them?'

'Possibly.'

'So you still think the killer could have been a woman?'

'I'm sure of it.'

'Why?'

'Because we haven't come across any angry ex-husbands or lovers, only a legion of conned women.'

'Were they conned? The ones quoted in the paper all seem to have loved him terribly.'

'True, but they might not be all his women. There could be others lurking out there. As it is, we know there's another wife.'

Margot raised her eyes to me in surprise, her nail polish brush suspended mid air.

'Really? That makes four!'

The wine must have loosened my tongue. I don't usually discuss cases outside of work, but I told Margot about Sue bashing Sylvia and how Sylvia had mentioned a previous wife when we interviewed her in hospital.

'But we don't know who it is yet,' I said.

'Yet?'

'Hopefully it's only a matter of time before Sylvia remembers her name.' Feeling I'd prattled on too much, I let the subject drop and asked Margot about her previous night on the town.

She regaled me with her shocking antics while I ate my snack.

Chastity turned up just as we finished the wine. Margot went home and got changed while I grabbed a plaid rug for us to sit on and a small bottle of lavender oil to keep away the mozzies. When everyone was ready we walked over to the park.

Margot's idea of comfortable clothes was to wear as few as possible. She had a stretchy pink top that showed a lot of neckline and a gold stretchy Alice band that doubled as a skirt.

'You're not going to wear stilettos to the park?' I said dubiously.

'Watch me,' she said with a laugh. 'And be amazed.'

I wasn't the only one amazed. Heads turned as we staked our spot on the grass and made ourselves comfortable on the rug. If she'd had business cards, I reckon she would have clocked up a lot of future clients by the end of the night.

Chastity went and bought the candles and carol sheets from the organisers and then the evening began. We sang many of the old favourites. *Silent Night* and *Come All Ye Faithful* and all that sort of jazz. After a quiet start, Margot got into her stride and was singing as loudly and joyously as the rest of us.

The darkness deepened so the crowd's candles looked like a sea of light, our faces an orange glow reflecting the flames. We were asked by the MC at one point to hold our candles high and wave them to and fro. The result was spectacular and there was a great feeling of charitable togetherness. The Christmas spirit was alive and well. But only temporarily. I had no false perceptions on that one.

Towards the end of the singing, Santa came to see the children. He looked awfully like the one who'd been stalking me, but then, hey, they all looked the same. I didn't get hung up about it. I was feeling too relaxed and mellow and happy. Santa left the stage with a cheery wave and then we all sang Rudolf the Red Nose Reindeer.

And then my hair caught on fire.

At first I was unaware anything was amiss. Then there was this whoosh and heat and smell of burning feathers.

'Fire!' yelled someone behind me. And whoever-it-was engulfed me in their picnic rug.

'Mum!' shrieked Chastity. 'You're burning.'

She helped the man beat me around the head until the fire was put out. I was also beating frantically, don't you worry. Margot sat there open-mouthed.

'I'm so sorry, Eve. I think I must have got carried away and not realised my candle was so close.'

'I'm okay,' I said shakily.

'You should be more careful, lady,' said my rescuer to Margot. 'She could have been really hurt.'

As it was, my scalp was prickling from the heat and the pong of singed hair hung about me. I wondered what the damage would be. How much hair had been ruined?

It was all downhill from there on. Margot kept apologising, Chastity fussed and the mellowness of the wine abruptly wore off. We called it a night. Margot went home and Chastity stayed with me at the house.

'You're right about the house being a mess,' she said coming to kiss me goodnight by torchlight. 'And the shower sucks.'

'Tomorrow we're getting a new bathroom,' I said. 'Mr Ferrari promised. And hopefully the power will be fixed too.'

'Can't wait.'

'It's the simple things in life that make it worth living.'

'I think I believe you.' She grinned and dropped a kiss on my cheek.

The Ferrari crew turned up early. I was up and feeling surprisingly bright and bushy-tailed. The feeling evaporated when Dom Ferrari caught sight of me.

'Gollys, Meeses Rocks,' he said. 'What have yous done to your hair?'

'I had an accident,' I said. 'But hopefully I can find a hairdresser who can minimise the damage.'

'Yous having some bad accidents,' said the troll. 'Yous should be more careful.'

Tell me about it.

Chastity then emerged from her bedroom and the young Ferrari boys fell over themselves to be introduced.

'Yous have a beautiful daughter,' said Ferrari, smacking his lips in appreciation.

'Your sons seem to think so,' I said dryly. 'Come on Chastity, I'll drop you off at Saint Immaculata's on my way to work.'

'I could stay here and supervise,' she said, obviously as taken with the Latin tradesmen as they were with her.

'Good idea,' said one of them and grinned. I didn't trust his gorgeous, baby-seal brown eyes for one moment.

'Bad idea,' I countered. 'I don't think much work would get done.'

At the station, my new hairstyle got a lot of comment.

'We always knew you were fiery, boss,' said jolly joker Ely. 'But now you've proved it good and proper.'

I explained how it happened and my street cred went down a few notches when they heard about the carol singing. What's wrong with carol singing, that's what I wanted to know? I rang around the hair salons to get a serious haircut, but they were all booked up until the next day. I would have to suffer the singed look a while longer, so I wore a black baseball cap to stop the less-than-funny, ha-ha comments.

The lads were working flat out trying to find Phipps' missing wife. During a lull, Fox gestured to my cap and said, 'You should take more care of yourself.'

'It was an accident. Margot got her candle too close. It happens.'

'If I'd been there, I would have protected you.'

'Too complicated. It's never going to happen.'

'Shame.'

'It is. Believe me.'

'Then change your mind.' I looked at him with regret and he sighed. 'Guess not. But I can't understand why.'

'I'll tell you why one day. I'm just not ready to do so now.'

Around lunchtime, while we were all scoffing various takeaway snacks, Quinn wandered into the operations room. He made a beeline for me and stared at my baseball cap.

'Heard you were hot stuff last night,' he said, a slight smile tugging his lips.

'Don't even bother. I've had all the comments I can take.'

'Carols by Candlelight, eh?'

'There's nothing wrong with singing carols.'

'Never said there was, babe. I'm partial to a little singing myself.'

'How nice.'

'You could join me some time and we'll warble together. I find the shower is the best places to sing.'

I rolled my eyes.

'Thanks but I think I'll pass on that one.'

'You don't know what you're missing.'

'You can't tempt me, Quinn.'

'We'll see.'

His arrogance annoyed me and I scowled at him.

'Now you've wrapped up your case, you'll be heading back to your boat and sailing off into the sunset?' Did I sound too hopeful?

'Sorry to disappoint you, Red, but I thought I'd take some time off and hang around old haunts for a while.'

As long as he didn't consider me an old haunt, we'd be okay.

'You could come out to the boat so we could talk about old times.'

So I was considered an old haunt. Hmm.

'Tell me, why would I want to do that?'

'Because you find me irresistible.' He smiled. It wasn't as sweet and dreamy as Fox's smile. It was potent and dangerous. A killer smile.

'Get lost,' I said.

He chuckled and my desk phone rang. He beat me to it, still smiling.

'DI Rock's phone,' he said and then his smile disappeared and his eyes hardened. He handed me the receiver. 'Sylvia McClune is dead.'

My first thought was that she'd died from the baseball bat injuries. But the doctor on the other end of the line said it was more complicated than that. Could I please come to the hospital immediately, he said, and added in a low, thrilling voice that he had sealed the crime scene.

'You think she's been murdered?' I said in surprise.

'No doubt, DI Rock. Her neck was broken.'

Fox and I wasted little time getting there. The nurses were in a state of shock but the doctor was controlled and gave us a concise statement. Sylvia had been in a private room. She'd been given painkillers and a sedative to help her sleep. Someone must have come in while she was napping and killed her because there was no sign of a struggle. The staff had been busy and no one could remember who had gone into her room.

'Killed the same way as Dennis Phipps,' I said to Fox as we looked at the young woman. 'Copycat or the same murderer?'

'Why would they want to kill Sylvia? It doesn't make sense.'

'Perhaps because she knew the name of Dennis Phipps' first wife? I can't think of any other immediate reason.'

'And who else knew she had that information?'

'Quite a few. The other wives and lovers for starters.'

I was exhausted by the time I made it home. I was looking forward to a nice hot shower and an even hotter curry washed down with a rich red wine to make up for my lousy day. Unfortunately, the power was still disconnected and the bathroom untouched. I could have screamed. Instead I went down to my little oasis at the bottom of the garden to have a private contemplation.

I opened the loo door and something shot out between my legs. I glanced down in shock and then…

SCREAMED!

Snakes. There were snakes in my toilet. I yelled again and then sprang back as the snakes poured out of the little brick outhouse. I scrambled up the rickety wooden fence, which – believe me – wasn't designed for such treatment, and dragged out my gun. I let loose with bullets and rude words as I tried to kill them. These tiger snakes weren't acting friendly. One arched up to strike and I shot off its head, then another did the same move and I shot that too. The only problem was, I didn't have enough bullets and I wasn't carrying any spares. So I screamed and yelled and hoped someone would find me.

A couple of small kids that had been playing ball in the back lane ran off. I called after them to get help. Soon I heard the blessed sound of sirens and uniformed officers crowded into my backyard.

'Where's the baddy?' asked one of the guys who was known as a smart aleck.

'If you look carefully, Officer Clark, you'll see him writhing by your feet.'

Clark glanced down and then yelped. Both men backed off.

'We need the wildlife boys here,' said Clark. 'And quick.'

'If you don't deal with them now,' I said through clenched teeth. 'Then you're going to have tiger snakes turning up in people's homes. Children and old people live in this street. Snakes are not an option.'

'We hear you, DI Rock.'

'Then get on with it. My butt's killing me, sitting on this matchstick fence.'

I'd shot four and the officers claimed another three. Not for a minute did I think we'd killed the whole quota. The uniform cops door-knocked to warn the locals while I shovelled up the bits of snake meat and put them in my wheelie bin.

The officers returned from alerting the neighbours to get a statement from me.

'Do you reckon you had a family of snakes living in your toilet?' said Clark.

'Those snakes were big adult bruisers, not Ma and Pa and a handful of babies.' I pointed out. 'To get to that size, I would have been more than aware snakes had been living the high life in my loo all summer.'

'So you think someone put them there?'

'Yes, Clark.' Duh!

'Who?'

Stalking Santa? Or Phipps' killer? Take your pick. Of course, there was also Hugo Maine who didn't feel very charitable and warm and cuddly towards me.

'That's more difficult. I'll give it some thought and give you the list later.'

'List, eh?' said Clark. 'That sounds ominous.' Clark and his partner then checked out my house for stray snakes and assassins.

'All clear, Detective Inspector. Sure you don't want us to hang around, bearing in mind that list and all?'

I'd have loved them too, but I didn't want to appear a wuss and I was pretty confident that whoever had planted those snakes wouldn't be back tonight.

'I'll be fine.'

'Good night. Sleep tight.'

'And I'll shoot any bed bugs that bite. Thank you, boys.'

20

I confess I didn't sleep particularly well. I kept imagining big, black snakes slithering into my bed and sinking their fangs into me before turning into Quinn. Freud would have had a field day.

The next morning I was in no mood to hang around. I did a rapid inspection of the garden as I hot-footed it to the toilet. I pushed open the door with a broom handle while clutching my gun in my other hand. Thankfully there were no snakes. Double relief time.

I collected together some toiletries and fresh clothes, intending to shower at Saint Immaculata's before going to work, and slung them in my car. I jammed the key into the ignition and the car hummed into life.

Then I had a sudden thought.

I'd better warn Dom Ferrari about the snake infestation, just in case one or two wrigglies were still lurking about the house or garden. I didn't want my building team bitten and poisoned. They were far too valuable. My house wouldn't get finished by Christmas if they all died. Did I have my priorities right or what? I hopped out the car and raced back towards the front door.

BOOM! WHOOSH!

The last few metres I completed airborne, flying like Dumbo, but without the feather. I landed on the veranda with a big bump, winded and disorientated. I half turned to look behind me, grappling to gauge what had just happened, and witnessed a fireball.

Which had been my car.

Holy moly and fried little fishes. I'd narrowly missed being blown up. I curled into a foetal ball, shaking uncontrollably, rattled to the core, and watched my car burn. Fiery debris floated in the air and landed in neighbours' gardens. The residents had rushed out on to their front steps and were regarding the blaze in shocked, morbid fascination. The little Scotty dog opposite was going berserk, yapping and running rings around his owner's lawn, peeing as he went. I could empathise. My own waterworks were feeling remarkably dodgy too, as if turned to liquid ice.

Someone must have called the fire department. Soon there were sirens, not that I could hear them clearly with the explosion still ringing in my ears. Then fire trucks and police cars filled the street.

Quinn was suddenly there, his arms around me, holding me in a crushing embrace.

'Hell, Eve, are you okay?'

'I think so,' I said, my voice shaking horribly. I felt like howling my eyes out but years of training prevented me from exercising that little luxury.

'What happened?'

'The car blew up!' I said waspishly.

He gave a dry chuckle. 'I think I'd gathered that much, Red.'

I told him my last few actions and he said, 'The device must have been linked to your ignition. You were damn lucky you weren't in that car.'

Too flipping right I'd been lucky.

'So what's going on?' he said.

'I don't know. But someone wants me dead.' I bit back a sob and, trying to control my trembling, wussy voice, I filled him in about the snakes, the attempted electrocution and flying wood.

'Any ideas who it could be?'

I buried my pride and gave him the list I hadn't given to the uniform cops the night before.

'Maybe you shouldn't stay here until whoever is responsible is banged to rights.'

I'd already come to that conclusion. But where should I go? If

I stayed put, I was endangering Margot and my other neighbours. If I went to Saint Immaculata's, then I'd be putting Chastity and my mother in the firing line. I couldn't afford a hotel and sleeping in my car wasn't an option, given that I didn't have one anymore. But I didn't share this with Quinn. My life was already too complicated.

I was taken to hospital by ambulance and checked over. There was nothing much wrong except temporary hearing loss and bruises where I'd crash-landed. My painful shoulder was even more so, but it wasn't going to stop me from doing what I did best, which was hunting down the villains and making them pay, the bastards.

I was waiting in the foyer for one of the boys to come and collect me from hospital when Fox turned up in his Spitfire. He slammed the driver's door and rapidly strode into the reception area.

His hair was tousled, as if he'd been repeatedly running his fingers through it. His face was a tight mask. He looked as though he was labouring under a lot of stress. When he saw me, his expression lightened.

'Eve,' he said, enveloping me in a huge bear hug. 'I've just heard the news. You're not hurt?'

'I'm fine.'

'Honest? Part of me would have died if you'd been killed.' He kissed my hair, my temple and then sought my lips. I panicked and pushed him away.

'No,' I said. 'Don't go there.'

'Sorry, I didn't mean to freak you out. But it was a bomb, for goodness sake.'

'The bomb isn't the thing freaking me out. It's you. Do *not* hold me. Do *not* kiss me. Do *not* get involved. Is that clear enough for you, Fox?'

'It's too late.'

'It can't happen, Adam.'

'So you keep saying. Why don't you tell me why?'

'Because of Chastity.'

'I don't care if you've got a child. She's a great kid.'

Now came the crunch. I took a deep breath.

'She's your half-sister.'

Well, hah! He hadn't been expecting that little gem. It was like a second bomb had gone off, right under his neat preconceptions, as he processed my information. His arms dropped to his sides and he took a step backwards.

'Oedipus,' he said and his voice croaked. 'So that's what you meant the other day.'

'If your dad and I had done the right thing all those years ago, I would be your step-mother. Believe me, I wish things could have been different.'

He rallied swiftly.

'But there's no blood between us, so it doesn't matter.'

Well, he had a point but I still wasn't comfortable with the knowledge, however tempting.

'It's icky anyway. Too close for comfort.'

'But I don't understand. Dad's never mentioned Chastity.'

I squirmed and scuffed the carpet with my sneakers.

'Eve? Does Dad know?' he challenged.

'Does Dad know what?' and suddenly Quinn was there too. He had a persistent habit of turning up at the oddest and most irritating of moments.

'Where did you spring from?' I demanded.

'That's gratitude. I've come to collect you. And I repeat, does Dad know what?'

'Don't say anything,' I said to Fox.

'He has a right to know.'

'I'm not ready to tell him.' I shot a wary glance at Quinn. Suddenly big, confident Quinn wasn't looking terribly happy. He rammed his hands into his jean pockets and glared at the both of us.

'I can't believe I want to deck my own son. And because of a woman, too,' he said, gruffness giving a hard edge to his voice.

'Excuse me?'

'Dad!' said Fox at the same time.

'It looks like you've bewitched us both, Eve. There's just

something about you that we Fox men can't resist. So you two are going to make a go of it? Is that what you were going to tell me?'

'Actually, no,' I said.

Quinn raised his brows and was immediately a lot more cheerful, the rat.

'Really? I got it wrong? Excellent. But I thought you had the real hots for her, Adam?'

'I do,' said Fox. 'But it's not as simple as that.'

'So we're back to 'does Dad know', is that right?'

'Yes,' said Fox.

'So, is it that Eve finds me more irresistible than you?' He grinned and looked too cocky for words.

'Your arrogance is extremely annoying,' I said. 'You're totally resistible.'

'Eve...'

'Get lost, Quinn.'

His smile widened and he waggled his eyebrows. 'I love a woman who plays hard to get.'

'You'd better tell him,' said Fox, his gaze challenging.

'Why?'

'You owe it to Chastity.'

Cheap shot. I'd spent my whole life not knowing the truth about my father. I'd survived. So would Chastity.

'We're discussing a real person, right? So who is she?' said Quinn.

I glared at Fox and he held my eyes easily with his hard, calm blue ones. It was my turn to shove my hands into my jeans pockets, hunch my shoulders and look cross.

Quinn frowned.

'I think I'm missing something here.'

'You've missed a lot, Dad. Tell him, Eve. Tell him who Chastity is.'

I transferred my belligerent gaze to Quinn.

'Chastity is my daughter.' I paused. 'And yours.'

For once Quinn was lost for words. He stared at me, his eyes a turbulent, crashing sea of emotions.

'Hell,' he said and spun on his heel and went outside. We waited for a minute or five but he didn't come back.

'That went well,' I said to Fox. 'Perhaps you can give me a lift to the station. I don't think my ride is going to happen.'

'Aren't you going to go after him?'

'No. Why should I? He knows where to find me if he wants answers.'

Fox sighed and shook his head.

'Are you sure you want to go back to work? You should take the rest of the day off. No one would blame you. It's been a very stressful morning. For all of us.'

'Don't soft soap me, Fox,' I said. 'I want to bury myself in work. It's far less complicated than my personal life, let me tell you.'

Ely and Burton clucked over me when Fox and I finally made it to the station. Ely even got me a cup of coffee and Burton rustled up a Snickers bar that was warm and soft from being in his pocket. Like Quinn, they wanted to know if I had any idea who'd firebombed my car. I gave them the same list I'd given Quinn and we all scratched our heads over it but got no further.

The city was littered with Santas, so it was hard narrowing that particular suspect down. We had no lead on Phipps, Thelma and Sylvia's murders. And Hugo Maine was still banged up with some of his entourage and facing an assortment of drug dealing and trafficking charges.

'I'm not putting my money on Maine,' I admitted. 'I've only met him once and I wasn't that instrumental in bringing him in. That was Quinn and his team. So I reckon we can cross Maine off the list.'

'Which leaves us the Phipps' murderer or Santa Claus,' said Fox.

I was feeling depressed and frustrated. There was nothing to go on so I read through the statements yet again to see if I'd missed anything. While I was working through the stack, Quinn entered the room. I bit my lower lip and kept my head down, hoping he would ignore me. I wasn't terribly surprised when he didn't.

'I need to speak to you. In private,' he said, his whisky-rough voice subdued and lacking its usual gritty, sunshiny warmth.

'Not now,' I said. 'I'm busy.'

'I can wait.' He sat down next to me and picked up a statement. 'What are we looking for? Anything in particular?'

'Anything, something, that might shed light on why Phipps was murdered. I'm convinced Thelma was killed because she saw something. And Sylvia because she knew the name of the first wife. And I must be getting close, because why would they be trying to kill me?'

'You think the threats on your life are connected to this investigation and not to the stalker?'

'No, I'm not convinced, but I've got nothing on the stalker and plenty on the case. I can't just sit here and do nothing.'

I looked again at the forensics' statement regarding Phipps' car. Blonde strands of hair had been found in the car. There were matches with Sue, Lina and Phipps' mistress Tara Oaks' DNA. And there were other hair strands that didn't match anyone on our suspects list. A broken false fingernail had also been found and again didn't match any of our suspects. But I remembered seeing some bright red nails around that time. But on whom? As I sorted through my memory bank my phone rang.

Quinn, in his usual blunt way, answered it without my permission. He listened to the caller and then said, 'We're on our way.'

'Where are we off to?' I said, immediately rising to my feet, feeling a spurt of adrenaline that perhaps something crucial was going down.

'Your hairdresser. She's been expecting you these past ten minutes.'

Darn. I'd clean forgotten about my appointment and would have gladly cancelled, but Quinn, as if guessing my mood, held me securely by the arm and marched me out to his car.

'I can make my own way,' I said.

'Sure you can, Red. Except that you don't have a car. I have. And this way we get to talk in private.'

I sat in his jeep in rigid expectation, waiting for him to break the deadlock. We drove in utter silence for a good five minutes.

'Speak,' he finally said.

I sighed, feeling more defeated than I had in a long while.

'What do you want to know?'

'First, why didn't you tell me about the baby?'

I counted to ten and then counted backwards to zero, getting my old anger safely back where it belonged, locked and sealed away in a deep recess of my soul where it could only do damage to me and nobody else. I didn't want to shoot the guy. So I did another count to ten and back to make sure. I gave another deep, deep defeated sigh and faced crunch time.

'I went to shore to enrol at the academy. When I got back to the quay, the boat had gone.'

'You could have waited.'

'I had my pride. I thought your sailing off into the proverbial blue yonder was your way of brushing me off and finishing our brief affair.'

'I wouldn't have done that to you.'

'But you did! I was there, remember?'

'It wasn't intentional. I had my reasons, and believe it or not, they were good ones.'

'Well, how was I to know that? You know, Quinn, you weren't there and I didn't want to wait around like some pathetic groupie on the flimsy chance you might come back for me. I had more self-esteem than that.'

'You have to know all the facts,' he said, his voice subdued. 'I was involved in a taskforce that was trying to infiltrate a smuggling ring. It was my first big undercover stint and I didn't want to mess it up. I'd been waiting for the call and unfortunately for you – and me – it came while you were ashore. I had to leave immediately. There was no way I could leave a message without jeopardising the operation. If I could have done so, I would have.'

I shrugged dismissively. It was a long time ago. I'd survived.

He said, 'Every time I sailed back into port, I looked for you. I was sure you'd come back, that I'd see you one day. But, hell, it didn't happen.'

'Actually, I did go back once. I swallowed my pride and returned a few weeks after I discovered I was pregnant. But by then the summer was over, the quay deserted and no one knew a man called Quinn, or his boat *Wild Thing*.'

'You could have tried harder!' There was deep anguish vibrating in his voice and he hit the steering wheel with his open palm.

'Yeah right,' I said with heavy sarcasm. 'You've no idea. That was hard enough!'

My throat was tight with emotion dredged up from that miserable time.

'It was horrible, walking up and down the marina, trying to find you and wondering how you'd react if I did come across you. I wasn't proud of what had happened.'

'What a mess,' said Quinn. 'I'm sorry, Eve.'

'Don't be.' I didn't want his pity. I'd survived, and some. 'Anyway, I ended up with a beautiful daughter.'

'None of this would have happened if I had followed orders. You see, I wasn't meant to have anyone on the boat. I was told to concentrate only on the job. But when I met you at that party, reason went out the window.'

Along with my own. I gave a dry laugh. 'Well, Quinn, you are known as a larrikin cop.'

'And it looks like I've paid for it by missing out on sixteen years with you and Chastity.'

'You can't miss what you've never had.'

Quinn shook his head. 'I did toy with the idea of tracking you down, you know, but too many other people were relying on me. And then, when the op was over, too much time had elapsed and I decided it would be foolish to try and recapture paradise.'

I shrugged, uncomfortable. 'Let it go. It doesn't matter anymore.'

'But it does.' Charged silence filled the hair between us. He cleared his throat and said with abrupt determination, 'Eve, I want to meet Chastity.'

Panic gripped my throat and I had to force out the words, 'I'll think about it.' Did I want him to meet Chastity? Did I want him having a role in our lives?

'Please.' He could obviously feel my reticence. 'I'd like to make it up to the both of you.'

'There's nothing to make up. Chastity and I are a good team. We work well together.'

'Well then, do it for me.'

Oh dear. I didn't have an answer for that one.

He waited in the car while I was in the hair salon. The stylist was shocked by my singed locks and cut the whole kit and caboodle off so my hair was about two inches long all over. I viewed the result with the greatest of suspicion. When my hair had length, the curls were manageable. Short, there was no telling what curly mayhem would happen.

The girl washed and blow-dried it and we found out big time. I came out of the salon looking like an electrocuted orange clown.

'Good look,' said Quinn, ruffling the soft curls and chuckling. He was looking more relaxed and happy now. As though he was back in control. I, on the other hand, was feeling completely wrung out.

'Cut it out or it'll curl even more,' I grumbled.

'Impossible.'

'Don't you believe it.' I then asked Quinn to take me straight home.

'Do you think that's safe?' he said.

'It's my home, Quinn.'

'But –'

'And it's been checked for bombs and booby traps and goodness knows what. And I've got a police officer assigned for round the clock protection. What more could a girl ask for?' Then I saw the look in his eyes and wished I hadn't asked that particular flip question. 'Don't answer that,' I said hurriedly, feeling a flush of heat staining my cheeks.

'I'm more than happy to stay and keep you company, sweetheart.'

'I'm zonked. I don't want company. I want sleep.' But I had my fingers crossed double so I wouldn't be struck down by any passing lightning bolts.

21

FOR THE NEXT COUPLE OF DAYS THINGS RETURNED TO NORMAL. I followed up leads on the Phipps' murder case, ate too many curries and masalas and drunk enough red wine to keep my anti-oxidant level nice and high. The power was reinstalled and my new bathroom was furnished to everyone's satisfaction. In fact, I was so pleased with the shower that I almost kissed Dom Ferrari. But he still had the kitchen to contend with and I didn't want to frighten him off.

By Friday, nothing untoward had happened so I dismissed my cop-protection. The force was shorthanded enough over the festive season without me being babysat by an officer with bum-fluff on his chin who'd be better employed nicking shoplifters and brawlers. There was only one week to go until Christmas and I hadn't made much of a dent in my food or gifts' list. But at least my house was nearing completion.

The evening was hot and I squandered too much time and water in the new shower before pulling on a scrap of a turquoise sundress that barely covered my bottom and boobs. It had been an impulse buy at the Freo markets. Living next-door to Margot must've been rubbing off.

I padded barefoot and damp into the half-finished kitchen to search for food. I didn't fancy my meagre grocery store, but I was tempted to try a slice of a mushroom quiche left behind by one of the Ferraris. I zapped it in the microwave and then added sliced tomato, cucumber and lettuce. Pouring myself a glass of supermarket rough red, I made myself comfortable on the veranda and settled down to eat.

The quiche was unusual but tasty. I toyed with having a second slice but decided against it. Too much cheese and I'd have nightmares. It's the breaks.

A while later, I had the nightmares anyway, and I was still awake. Go figure. Cockroaches the size of dinosaurs were suddenly crawling on the walls, ceiling and floor and flying like ghastly bats, dive-bombing me. I decided to outwit them by flying away.

At least that's what I was told when I eventually awoke in hospital and demanded to know why I was there.

'You've been high as a kite,' said Quinn. He was by my bed and holding my hand, his blue eyes full of concern. Fox was on the other side of my bed, holding my other hand. Stereo Fox. Was I still high?

'You're joking?' I said, confused.

'Someone climbed up on your roof and grabbed you before you jumped,' said Fox.

'Grief, what was I doing on my roof?'

'You were stoned, Red, and yelling about giant cockroaches attacking you.'

'But I only had a glass of wine!' I frowned trying to remember but everything was all a blur. Except for the giant cockroaches. I remembered them vividly. Too vividly. I shuddered and Quinn and Fox held my hands tighter.

'It wasn't alcohol causing your flying delusions, but magic mushrooms,' said Quinn.

'I don't do drugs,' I said flatly. 'I've seen what they do to people and I have never, ever touched them.'

'Well, you did last night.' He regarded me sympathetically and I ground my teeth because he didn't believe me. 'No one's blaming you. You've been under a lot of pressure.'

'Damn you, Quinn, I do not do drugs.'

I glared at him and he had the grace to drop his eyes and look uncomfortable.

'So how do you explain it?' chipped in Fox. He stroked his thumb rhythmically over my knuckles and I tugged both my hands away and shoved them under the covers so neither man could touch me and ruin what little concentration I had.

'I've no idea. I came home, showered and... oh heavens, it was the flan. I ate a piece of Dom Ferrari's quiche. No wonder it's taken them so long to refurbish my house if they're eating magic mushrooms for lunch!' I said indignantly.

'We'll check it out,' said Fox and rang someone on his mobile.

'You shouldn't use those phones in hospital,' I said. 'They muck up people's pacemakers or something.'

'It's an emergency. We want to get to the evidence before somebody else does.'

'I can't believe Dom and the boys are on drugs. They might be a bit slack, but they don't act stoned.'

'Are you sure the quiche was theirs?' said Quinn.

I stared at the ceiling, glad to see there were no nasty cockroaches up there, and then thought about what he said.

'No,' I admitted. 'I just presumed it was as they leave snacks in there sometimes.'

'So it could have been planted there for you to find?'

'Possibly. Probably.' I tried to think back. 'There was a note on the kitchen table saying to help myself. Goodness, what an idiot I am. I didn't even consider someone would try to poison me. I could have killed myself jumping off the roof.'

'I think that was the general idea,' said Quinn matter-of-factly.

'So who saved me? You?'

'Sorry to disappoint you, Red, but no. Some guy who happened to be passing and thought it was odd you shinning up the builders' scaffolding in the middle of the night.'

'Do you know who it was?'

'No, he didn't give his name.'

I sighed.

'I wish all this was over.'

'Amen to that.' Quinn stood and stretched.

'Are you leaving?' I said, suddenly realising I didn't want him too.

'Not if you don't want me to.' He sat down again.

'It's okay, I'll stay,' said Fox.

I glanced from Quinn, to Fox and then back again.

'I don't care who stays or leaves. It's all the same to me.'

Quinn chuckled and crossed his arms, settling in for the duration.

'Liar. By the way, I took the liberty of collecting your shoulder bag from your house last night and locking everything up. I didn't want the house left open for a free for all.'

'Thank you.'

'No sweat, Red.'

The doctor was ready to discharge me after lunch and, after a tussle between the two males, Quinn won the toss to be my personal taxi service.

'Home,' I said when he wanted to know where to take me.

'Not a good idea, Red. Look what happened last time I let you persuade me you'd be okay.'

'This time it's different. This time I'm getting my stuff and I'm booking into a motel.'

Quinn insisted on checking the house before I set a foot in the door. I wasn't happy about it but he obviously had something macho to prove. He told me to sit in the car, took my key and went to insert it. The key was my spare. The other had been attached to my ignition keys. I thought with regret about my little car and I then had a flash of premonition.

'Quinn!' I yelled.

He turned, startled.

'Quick! Hurry!'

He bolted back to the car.

'What? What?'

'Nothing. Sorry. I was suddenly very scared. I was thinking about my car. The explosion…'

'Hell, Red, you had me going for a second there.' He rolled his eyes and patted his heart. 'I thought something awful was happening. This isn't good for my ticker. You've already given it a battering this week.'

'Sorry,' I said again, but this time the word was drowned out, because there was a massive boom, louder than the boom that had destroyed my car.

My house went up in smoke.

Quinn swore and flung me to the ground as flaming rubbish fell all over us, spot burning our skin and clothes.

'Someone really wants you out of the equation, kid,' he said as we crawled along the ground on our hands and knees to cower behind the car and avoid the brunt of flaming debris raining around us, shielding ourselves from the intense heat.

The next moment a burly sandy haired man in a red suit was galloping towards us.

'Eve!' he was shouting. 'Eve, are you all right?'

Quinn tried to shove me behind him and take the force of the attack, but I was fumbling to release Quinn's gun from his shoulder holster and held it straight out in front of me.

'Freeze, or I'll shoot!' I declared.

Santa froze.

'I believe you,' he said. 'But don't shoot, Eve. I just wanted to make sure you were okay, honey.'

'Quit the honey tag. Who are you? Why did you bomb my house?' My voice suddenly broke. My house! The first home I'd ever owned was now burning to the ground, with all my worldly goods inside.

And my new bathroom!

'I didn't bomb your house! I wouldn't ever hurt you.'

Quinn disentangled himself from me, obligingly hitching up my turquoise dress to cover my over-exposed boobs, just like he had with my red dress. He was making a habit of it. Grief, I never had this sort of trouble with my usual t-shirt and jeans. I should give up wearing dresses, period.

By this time most of the street's inhabitants were out of their homes and gawking at the spectacular scene of flames, fire hoses and men in uniform. I was turning into the neighbour from hell. I wouldn't be surprised if the residents' association voted to kick me out of the suburb. I was definitely lowering the tone.

Quinn advanced on Santa and pulled his hands behind him, handcuffing them together.

'What are you doing?' said Santa.

'Arresting you,' said Quinn and read him his rights.

'You can't do that. I haven't done anything wrong.'

'Save it for the interview, buddy.'

Quinn shoved Santa into a police car and then said to me, 'Are you up to interviewing him?'

'You bet. I want to know why this creep has been hounding me.'

'Get back in my jeep then.'

As I buckled the seatbelt, my mobile phone rang from the depths of my shoulder bag. I rummaged around until I found it. The caller was Chastity.

'Mum,' she said. 'Are you busy?'

'Yes.'

'Well, I'll make it quick then. I've been thinking about what you said last Saturday.'

'Yes?' What had I said on Saturday? It was a week ago and so much had happened since then.

'You know, about getting a balance in one's life.'

'Yes?' Were we in for a philosophical discussion? I hoped not. I didn't feel very philosophical with my house burning down in front of my eyes.

'And I agree with you,' Chastity chirruped. 'Too much work and not enough play isn't good for you. So I thought I would take your advice.'

'Chastity, cut to the chase. What do you want?'

'Can I go to a party at Bobbie's house? Gran said it's fine.'

'If it's fine with Grandma, then it's fine with me.'

'And one more thing…?'

'Yes?' I pinched the bridge of my nose, not believing I was having this conversation while my home was erased by fire and there was a Santa stalker to interview.

'Can I borrow your snazzy red shoes?'

I raised my head and stared at my flaming house.

'No,' I said baldly.

'But, Mum! Don't be such a spoilsport. I thought you were just kidding the other day. They aren't too high for me to wear, honest. I'll be very careful and they'll look just great with my new dress.'

'No, Chastity. And stop right there,' I said as she squealed a protest. 'It's not because I don't want you to wear them, but I don't have them anymore.'

'You gave them away? How could you?'

'I didn't. But they've been destroyed.'

'Aw, Mum. You're no fun. Why did you do that?'

'Wasn't my call, sweetie. Someone blew up our house. It's on fire, right now.'

'Very funny!' She sounded sulky, as if I was being personally horrible to her.

'I mean it.'

'Honest?'

'I'm afraid so.'

'Oh, Mum! You're not hurt?' The sulks morphed to concern in a nanosecond. My darling, mercurial daughter.

'No, not a scratch.' Just burn marks. The sundress didn't cover very much.

'Thank goodness. What a terrible thing to happen. I suppose it was caused by that old wiring.'

'Something like that.' Except the wiring had all been replaced just that week.

'Will everything be okay?'

'Yes.' I wasn't going to tell her yet that the house had been annihilated. 'Trust me. I'll keep you posted but I've got to go now. Don't worry and have a good time at the party. And don't be too late.'

'Mum!'

'See you, kid. Love you.'

'Love you too, Mum.'

I ended the call and turned to Quinn.

'Okay, let's roll.'

'Hold it a minute. Is that your tinfoil neighbour running down the street?'

I squinted out the window. Margot was tripping along in the highest of heels and staring at the remains of my house. I opened the jeep door to go to her.

'Omigod!' she said when she saw me. Her face was pale and glassy. 'I thought you'd died! What on earth happened?'

'It's okay, Margot,' I said. 'Calm down. No one was hurt.'

'But the house exploded.'

'We had a lucky escape.'

'We?' She frowned. 'Not Chastity?'

'No, Quinn was with me.'

'Oh.' She didn't sound that thrilled. Probably still held a grudge against Quinn for spoiling Hugo Maine's Christmas party.

'Hopefully there's no damage done to your house.'

'Forget my house. At least you're not hurt. Do you want to stay with me until you can organise something more permanent? I've plenty of room.'

'That's very kind, Margot, but I'd better not. It might put you in danger.'

'You reckon someone is trying to kill you? But surely the house exploded because of a gas leak or something?'

There was nothing gas driven in the house which ruled out that theory but I was too tired to go into specifics.

'I'm not taking any chances.'

'Well you must tell me where you're going to stay. I want to keep in touch.'

'You can reach me on my mobile wherever I am.'

'It's not the same. For my peace of mind I need to know where you are.'

'Then I'll ring you as soon as I know.'

'What did she have to say?' said Quinn as we drove towards headquarters.

'She was worried about me and offered me house room.'

'Too dangerous,' said Quinn.

'That's what I thought.' And I wondered if he thought it was dangerous for the same reason I did.

In the interview room, Santa Claus was looking as red as his suit.

'I'm innocent,' he declared. 'I haven't done anything wrong.'

'You've been stalking Detective Inspector Rock these past two weeks. Do you deny it?' said Quinn who'd pitched in to do the interview with me. I had mixed feelings having him there, but Quinn was adamant. At least he had let me stop off on the way to the station and buy a pair of jeans, t-shirt and sneakers to make me feel more human. I felt ridiculous running about in my skimpy turquoise number.

'Not stalking,' protested Santa.

'You've been spying on me!' I said.

'Watching you, trying to find the courage to speak to you.'

'No way would I date you!'

'No, I didn't want a date.' He spluttered unbecomingly, as if I'd said something repugnant. It wasn't very flattering.

'So what did you want?'

'I wanted to meet with you, speak with you.'

'Why?' He had me puzzled.

'Because, Eve, you're my daughter.'

What? I felt as though someone had hit me hard in the solar plexus.

'I'm sorry?'

'Appears it's a week for confessions,' said Quinn dryly.

'It's true,' said Santa. 'And it was me who stopped you from jumping off the house roof last night. There you were, sitting quietly on the veranda and I thought now was a good time to speak to you. But you began acting all strange and I thought I'd better go away. But then you climbed on the roof and began yelling about flying.'

My mouth opened and shut a few times but no words came out. Santa the stalker was Santa my saviour? And my *father*?

Good grief!

Santa said, 'I knew your mother a long time ago. I wanted to marry her when she fell pregnant but she wasn't interested. She had other ambitions. Being a wife of a lowly artist wasn't one of them.'

'You're an artist?' It was the only thing I could latch on to. Everything else was too scary.

'Not a very good one. That's why I supplement my income every year by being a department store Santa. When I found out by accident where you lived, I decided to see what sort of person you'd grown into. I see you on my way to and from work.'

'My father is Santa Claus.' I gave a rather hysterical laugh.

'Don't knock it,' he said. 'It's good money.'

Santa – whose real name was Henry Talbot – was released without charges. He gave me his phone number and address and expressed a desire for us to get together at the soonest possible moment. I found out he was in contact with my mother and knew about Chastity. He knew a bit about my life too and not all gleaned from the Iron Nun.

He commented that my life seemed rather dangerous, that I drank too much wine, ate too many takeaways and kept dubious company. So tell me something I didn't know, Dad!

'Come back to my place,' said Quinn later. 'I think you need to unwind in peace and safety after your eventful day.'

'I'd prefer a motel,' I said, ignoring the sudden jitterbugging of my pulse.

'Then I'll stay there too.'

'How do you work that one out?'

'I'm not leaving you unprotected, Red. It's either the motel or my boat.'

I accepted Quinn's offer of the boat but with a whole heap of misgiving because I'd got into a heap of trouble last time I was on a boat with him. At least this time I was older and hopefully wiser.

We stopped off to buy some necessary items such as underwear and a toothbrush. He went up in my estimation when he decided we also needed a tandoori takeaway and red wine. We drove down to the wharf where his boat was moored. It was an old tub. Half its paint was peeling like skin after sunburn, the rest was a disgusting grey white. Her name was *Floozy* but she was well past her use-by date and wouldn't flooze anyone anymore. A bit like me, really.

'Needs work,' I commented.

He grinned. 'You think?'

'What happened to *Wild Thing*?'

'She's in dry dock.'

'I see. So this is a bit like that car bumper sticker, which says this isn't my real car, the Porsche is in for a re-spray?'

'Something like that. I needed an old boat for the covert operation. I had to be seen as a bum around the boatyards.'

'Not difficult, I would imagine.'

'Thanks.' He gave a snort. 'You're very kind.'

'You're welcome.'

He helped me on board and then led the way to the galley. By this time I was having very grave reservations about staying the night. The boat was small, the cabin cramped, the bunks tiny. It was going to be awfully cosy.

While he organised our meal, I rang Margot and told her where I was staying.

'I'm so worried about you. I was thinking about what you said – that someone was trying to kill you.'

'Don't fret. It's part of the job.' Though it wasn't every day people tried to blow me up or poison me with a pack of snakes.

'But do you have any idea who it could be?' She pressed.

'Not yet. We're waiting for the forensic guys to give us some clues after sifting through the house debris. But even without their input, I think I'm getting a picture. It's a little blurry at the moment, but give me time and it'll come into focus.'

'Oh Eve. Do take care.' Her concern vibrated down the line.

'I fully intend to.'

'On a more mundane note, how's your shoulder?'

'Sore. Actually, it aches like hell. I must have torn a muscle or something.'

'How about I come over to the boat tomorrow and I'll give you a deep massage. It might help relieve some stress too.'

I thought about it for a moment and then made a decision.

'Sounds good. I'll clear it with Quinn and make sure he'll be scarce during your visit. I don't want him perving.'

He looked at me curiously after she'd rung off.

'So what's with the blurry picture?'

'Ah.'

'I need to know, Red.'

'Trust me on this.'

'Okay, I trust you. But I want more to go on. Tell me what's going on in that pretty little head of yours.'

'Pretty, eh?'

'Very pretty. Now stop fishing for compliments and fill me in.'

'Okay then.' I grinned. And I told him my theory, giving him a couple of leads to following through and explaining my overall plan.

'You're crazy. It's too dangerous,' he declared.

'Please. I reckon we'll get a confession.'

'If we survive this, you'll owe me big time.'

'There's no "if" about it. I'm a survivor and I reckon you are too.'

He shrugged. 'So far so good, but you're a dangerous babe to be around.'

I smiled and he responded with a crooked one of his own.

'So what's the prize if I go along with your plan and we pull this off?' he said.

'I'll let you meet Chastity.'

'I'll hold you to that. But I was hoping for something more.' He waggled his eyebrows suggestively and ran a finger down my arm. I shivered and not because I was cold.

'Dream on,' I said repressively.

'At least you can't stop me dreaming. Just don't get killed, Red.'

'It's not on my list of priorities.'

The next phone call was to my mother. I told her about the house being bombed and she told me my job was totally unsuitable for any daughter of hers.

'We've been there before, Mum. Forget it.'

'So where are you staying? Do you want to come here?'

'No. It's too dangerous. I don't want you and Chastity at risk.'

'There's safety in numbers.'

I was touched that she would put herself on the line for me.

'Thanks, Mum. I appreciate it. I'll be staying with a cop. There's safety in guns.'

Which reminded me, I had to locate another gun before tomorrow morning. I felt naked without my Smith and Wesson. Even more naked than I did in the turquoise dress, and that was saying something.

'Keep a close eye on Chastity for me, Mum.'

The Iron Nun read the subtext correctly.

'I always do. Always will. Whatever happens, don't worry, Eve. But be very, very careful.'

'I will. And by the way, I met Henry Talbot today.' I could imagine her shifting mental gears, frantically crossing herself and muttering a rapid prayer. 'And I've invited him for Christmas lunch.'

I hung up and grinned at Quinn.

'Not everyone gets to have Santa Claus as a Christmas guest.'

'He's also your father.'

'And my mother is a hooker-turned-nun. What a combination.'

'So if we see you speeding to crime scenes in a red habit and riding a reindeer, we'll know you're reverting to type.'

I slung a cushion at him.

'The day I take to wearing a habit is the day I die. No oath of celibacy for me.'

'Is that right, now?' His eyes glinted with dangerous heat and we were back to where we were a moment ago, with me shivering seismic waves.

'Forget it, Quinn. If you want to endear yourself to me, you can find me a gun.'

There was a pregnant pause and then he said, 'Other women want chocolates and flowers.'

'I'm not other women.'

'No, you're not. You're in a league of your own. You're one very special lady.'

The way he was looking at me made my insides go mushy. I fought my response and said, 'So, can you get me a gun?'

'No problem, Red.' He rose to his feet and began unscrewing one of the polished wooden side panels in the cabin. It swung open to reveal a small but impressive armoury.

'Nice one,' I said. 'I like a well-endowed man.'

22

There was something about waking up on a boat. It was the slap of waves against the hull, the rattle of rigging against masts, the smell of diesel mingled with saltwater and cooked breakfast.

Cooked breakfast?

I sat up and Quinn grinned at me.

'Sleeping Beauty finally awakes.'

As modestly as Quinn's t-shirt would allow, I scuttled across the cabin and locked myself in the tiny bathroom. I then had the nastiest of shocks. So much for Sleeping Beauty. This was more like something out of a seventies horror movie. The mirror was small but it was filled with orange mayhem. The clown look was way out of control. It was a bushy halo and I no longer owned a brush to attempt to tame it. A brush went on my mental shopping list of must-haves.

I sluiced myself with water and used my fingers to try and sculpt my hair into a semblance of respectability. Gel was going on the list too. Or wax. Or a buzz cut.

In jeans and yesterday's t-shirt, I sat with Quinn on Floozy's deck and ate bacon, sausages, mushrooms, eggs and tomatoes until I was bursting.

'I'd forgotten what a brilliant breakfast you could cook,' I said between mouthfuls.

'I wonder what else you've forgotten of my brilliance?' He raised one wicked, blond brow and winked. I battened down a surge of longing. It wouldn't be a good idea to go skipping down that path.

Or would it?

Hmm. I'd have to think about that one.

Quinn was relaxed and in his element. He wore an ancient pair of shorts and a sleeveless, faded denim shirt. It revealed impressive biceps of someone used to flexing his muscles in hard outdoor work. His long hair was ruffled and bleached by years of sun and sea, his eyes the chameleon colour of the ocean. He was craggy and sexy and I wanted him like hell.

'You're staring,' he said.

I shrugged, fighting the embarrassment of being caught out.

'Adam is very much like you when you were younger.'

'That's probably why you were attracted to him.'

'You are so arrogant.'

'It's why you love me.'

'You've got tickets on yourself, Quinn. It'll never happen.'

He smiled. 'We could work on it.'

He then reached over and cupped my cheek with his hand, the sudden gesture making my heart lurch. He searched my eyes and seemed satisfied with what he saw. Slowly, surely he leaned towards me so his lips brushed mine.

It was a tentative kiss as kisses go, soft and as gentle as sea spray. And unfortunately it was over before it even got started.

'What time is your tinfoil girl coming?' he said huskily.

'Ten.' I had to cough to clear my throat.

His smile was slightly crooked and he sighed. 'Okay. I'll wash up the dishes and then get out of your hair.'

'I'll do the dishes. And don't mention the hair.'

He laughed.

'It's not that bad.'

'You're a liar, Quinn. You'd best get going.'

He didn't argue. But then I've never met a man yet who would argue over the washing up. Just before he left, he pulled me against his chest and gave me a short, hard kiss.

'Be careful, Red.'

And he was gone.

Margot was late. When she did appear on the wharf she was looking decidedly nautical in plain white shorts, pale blue top and white sandals. There was nothing outrageous about her get-up. The only flash of colour was her lipstick. It matched her scarlet painted nails.

'You blend in with the scenery,' I said gesturing to her understated clothes. I'd never seen her look so normal.

'This is my boating attire. I thought you'd approve.' She glanced over at the boat. 'I hope the cop has gone.'

'Why? Don't you like Quinn?'

'Nah. He's not my sort at all.'

'I didn't know you had a sort. I thought you just liked men in general. All of them.'

'Well, you were wrong, girl.'

'Sorry. Now where do you want to do this massage?' I said deciding I'd better change the subject as she was obviously feeling a little cranky this morning. Maybe she'd spent the night working.

Or worrying.

'On deck?' I said.

'No, too open.'

'Okay, the cabin.'

'It's a bit cramped,' she said when she'd followed me down the handful of steps. She was staring around the tight confines. 'I think it'll have to be on deck after all. I hadn't realised the boat would be so small.'

'It's no Hugo Maine luxury launch,' I said with a laugh.

'No. Now that is some yacht. What a baby!'

'Do you go on it often?' I stripped off to my underwear, which was of the black sports variety, boring and unimaginative but comfortable and bought in haste the day before. I lay down on one of Quinn's towels, hoping Margot wouldn't take too long because the sun was already hot enough to bite. I didn't want to burn to a cinder.

'Yeah, a fair bit. Usually when Hugo has a party or needs some R and R.' She opened her large patchwork bag and rifled around for her oils, placing the bottles on the deck in a neat line.

'So pretty often then. Are you on his pay roll?'

'Why? Do you want to join too?'

'No. I'm just curious.'

She shrugged.

'He wouldn't employ you anyway. Not after the other night's debacle.'

'The drugs' bust was nothing to do with me. I didn't know it was going down. I was just in the wrong place at the right time.' Or was that the other way round?

'And you reckon Maine would believe that? You had your gun with you, for goodness sake.' She slicked on some oil from one of the bottles and began kneading my sore, knotted muscles. The smell of almonds filled the air and mingled with the salty tang of the sea.

'I always carry my gun. It's a habit.' A bit like my mum's. So maybe we weren't that different after all, Mum and me.

'Do you have it now?'

'No. It got destroyed in my house.' My poor old house. I sighed. 'You know, Dom Ferrari had just finished my bathroom. Can you believe that? And I only got to use the new shower a couple of times.'

She laughed.

'Hard luck.' Her hands were strong and sure and under her fingers my muscles, in theory, should have begun to relax. They didn't. 'Hey girl, you're as tense as a virgin. Whip off your bra so I can really work on your shoulder muscles.'

I dutifully complied, flinging my bra to one side and lying back on the towel.

'That's better. I can get more purchase.' she said after a few minutes hard kneading. 'So, when's the cop due back?'

'Ouch. Not for ages. Did I tell you that he's Chastity's father?'

Her hands stopped their rhythmic movements.

'What? He's turned up after all this time?'

'Sixteen years. Yep, I was sure surprised. Caught me completely unawares. It's not nice when someone from your past suddenly walks slap bang back into your life without any prior warning.'

'No, it's not,' she agreed with feeling and began rubbing again, rather more rigorously and deeply this time so that it hurt more than it soothed.

'Ouch,' I said. 'Is that what happened when Den turned up at the Hit and Miss?'

Again her hands stopped their slide across my back.

'Excuse me?'

'How long ago were you married to him? Eighteen? Twenty years?'

'You're talking nonsense, Eve. I've never been married. You must have landed on your head yesterday. You must be suffering from concussion.' She poured more oil on to my back and smoothed it over the shoulders and up towards my neck where my muscles were so taut you could have played them like a fiddle. Pungent lavender and tea tree scents joined the other aromas humming around my body and drowned out any whiff of fear.

'You told me a little while ago that your ex-husband didn't want kids and as a result you'd always felt cheated.'

'That wasn't me,' she said emphatically. 'You must have got me muddled up with someone else.'

'I don't think so, Margot. You must have really hated him to kill him so cold bloodedly.'

The silence stretched between us, punctuated by the rigging clattering in the stiff sea breeze and the raucous noise of seagulls, probably fighting over fish guts thrown into the water by some fishermen further along the quay.

'There was nothing cold blooded about it,' she said, her voice suddenly shrill and vicious. 'It was red hot fury!'

She slammed the heel of her hand into the muscle below the shoulder blade and I winced. Her fingers pulled and kneaded at the bunched tissue. I gritted my teeth, not even letting an 'ouch' slip out.

'That bastard stitched me up,' she said.

'How so?' I raised and turned my head to try and see her expression. But she was having none of it and shoved my head back down hard on to the rough towel.

'I was modelling when I met Den. He swept me off my feet and we were married within a month.'

Yes, that tallied with his modus operandi.

'I immediately got clucky. I was already knocking thirty and my clock had been ticking loudly for a decade. I love kids with a passion. But Den persuaded me to keep modelling. I loved him so much I even got sterilised so that we wouldn't have an accident. He told me it was for the best, and I believed him, fool that I was.'

'And?' I lifted my head again and she slammed it back down with more force than necessary so my face bounced this time on the towel, making my nose smart as it impacted on the towel-covered deck.

'Then he ditched me for that fat tart Audrey because she was pregnant with his baby.'

'I'm sorry,' I mumbled, not daring to raise my head this time.

'Well, darl, so was I. I nearly killed him then and there, but I was too soft in those days.' Her hands were working feverishly away on my back. Every time they reached upwards to my neck I had visions of her snapping it, just like she had with Dennis and Sylvia.

In spite of the heat, a cold, metallic fear washed through me. My veins felt as though they were being flooded with mercury. It robbed me of the natural instinct of flight or fight. I felt impotent.

'Do you intend to turn me in?' she said conversationally.

I wondered if this was a joke or if she was testing me. If I gave the wrong answer then – crack – and that'd be the end of Eve Rock. I tried to sit up and face her, but again she shoved me down, so my face was buried back in that wretched scratchy towel. I'd have to have a word with Quinn about fabric softeners if ever I made it out of here alive. She leaned over me, her breath hot on my cheek.

'Well, Eve? Would you turn in your old friend?'

'Margot, you've murdered two people. How can I not arrest you?' I said, though my voice was muffled. Of course, I wasn't in a position to arrest anyone. And I was having serious doubts I was going to survive this encounter, despite my earlier bravado with Quinn.

Margot knelt up and resumed massaging my shoulders and neck. The feel of her strong fingers failed to soothe. I kept thinking of Phipps and Sylvia. Their necks clean broken. It was all to do with technique…

'I didn't want to hurt you,' she said in a businesslike manner as her hands smoothed up and down, up and down. 'But you persisted in digging for details. You were getting too close.'

'You propped up that piece of wood in the roof to fall on me.'

'That was a juvenile prank, nothing more. I would have been lucky if it had killed you.'

I shivered. Luck for whom?

'And you frayed the wires.'

'My dad was a sparky. I knew what to do. Both accidents could have been blamed on the builders.'

'What about the snakes?'

'Ah. Easy.'

'You can't tell me you went to the local pet shop and bought them?'

'No. I asked one of Hugo's security team to organise them for me. They're good at these sorts of things. Top class.'

'And it was Hugo's boys who organised the car and house bombs too?'

'They couldn't believe how hard it was to kill you. Usually it only takes one hit. Since then they've regarded you as something of a challenge.'

Great. They ought to film us for a reality show. It would go down big on commercial TV.

'They nearly succeeded with the magic mushrooms,' I said.

'That wasn't the boys. That was me. I cooked up a supreme dish, one of my best, but even then there was someone hanging around to rescue you. How unlucky was that?'

'Depends where you're viewing it from.' Her hands were on my neck again and I was sweating buckets. I had to distract her long enough to try and wriggle free.

I played the gossip card. 'You know, that rescuer was the stalking Santa.'

'Figures. He was hanging around enough.'

'That was because he was my long-lost dad and was plucking up the courage to talk to me.'

'Really?' Her hands lifted for a split second and I swung on to my back, hands up ready to fend her off. She lunged back at me, but I tried to roll away. She pursued me like a demented tigress, grabbing at my arms but failing to get a hold because her hands and my flesh were too slippery from the oil. But we didn't let it stop us. We grappled about on the deck like a couple of mud wrestlers. Margot got me in a pincer hold around both my legs as I scrambled to get some distance between us. I writhed from her grip, twisting round and landing a heel in her chest. As she fell backwards, I tried to stand but the oil-slick boards offered no purchase. I flipped, going down hard on my backside, jarring every bone in my body.

Margot took advantage and snagged one of my legs in her powerful hands. I kicked out with my other foot. Margot swore and held on grimly. I kicked again and got her cheekbone. Her grip loosened and I took advantage by scrabbling to my knees, my hands up, ready to defend myself.

Margot flipped Quinn's towel and slung it at my face, momentarily blinding me. I tried dragging it away but not before she sprang at me, her momentum tipping me over so I landed flat on my back. Instinctively, I kicked up and out with both feet and sent her tumbling away. I untangled and threw the towel to one side. I jack-knifed into a sitting position, scooting backwards on my bottom. Margot, her eyes flashing, lunged towards me again, raking me across the face and chest with her Fu Manchu-long nails.

I swung a wide arc with one hand and smacked her across the skull. The impact sent a sharp pain up my arm. Margot dodged a second blow and scuttled backwards. She snagged up her oversized bag and rapidly rummaged through it. She then dragged out a gun.

My gun!

'I see you recognise it,' she said, breathing heavily from our spat. 'I took the liberty of lifting this from your house before Hugo's men laid the bomb.'

It worried me I hadn't realised how dangerous Margot was until this moment. This was the woman who had shared my confidences and my curries for the past few weeks and I hadn't had an inkling that all the while she'd been trying to kill me. I remembered thinking that every girl needed a friendly neighbour. Now I wasn't convinced.

'Before you blow me to kingdom come,' I said, my chest heaving like Margot's. 'You should know that Dennis treated Audrey badly too. He left her when the baby was little.'

'You expect me to feel sorry for her?' She shook her head and laughed. It was hard and mirthless. 'I don't. She got a kid and I didn't. That's the bottom line.'

I had to keep her talking until I could figure my way out of this.

'Dennis didn't seem to have much time for children,' I said. Okay, it sounded lame. Tough, it was all I could think of under stress.

Margot glanced at her watch and then leaned back against the deck rail, still with the gun on a level with my heart, and said, 'He had two with that prissy Sue. Maybe it was just me he didn't want kids with.'

'Perhaps you should have some counselling to help you find closure on this issue,' I said, worriedly regarding the stubby blue-nosed gun barrel.

'No. This is perfect closure for me, honey.'

Omigod. She was serious!

Margot lowered the gun and checked her watch again. Perhaps she was worried Quinn would soon arrive. I certainly hoped he would because I didn't know if I'd be agile or quick enough to spring towards her and grab the gun while she was preoccupied.

'So you hadn't seen Den for years?'

'The Hit and Miss was the first time in two decades.'

'Quite a shock, then.'

'He told me that night his wife didn't understand him. Can you believe he would have spun that corny old line? And to me! At first, I presumed he meant Audrey and then he began talking about Sue and the kids and, darl, I saw red.'

I'm sure she did.

'So how did you get him out of the nightclub?' I had a pretty good idea, but I wanted to hear her say it. I also wanted to string out her confession as long as possible. Maybe then Quinn would be back to help.

'Dusty was with him in one of the top rooms. After she left, I slipped in there and suggested we went to the park for old time's sake. The silly fool was up for it. Once on the grass, I was giving him a rub and just, snap! That was it.'

'But you were seen.' I decided to go all out with the details. I might not get a second chance.

'Yeah. The girl on the bike. She thought Den had collapsed and came over to see if I needed a hand. Said she knew CPR and all that crap. She was only a little thing. Easy to deal with.'

'You drowned her.'

'Pure necessity.'

I shivered again, even though my skin was blistering from a combination of the salty wind, hot sun and massage oil.

'And then you murdered Sylvia in case she remembered your name.'

'You can take the blame for her. You were the one who told me she knew of a fourth wife.' Margot was impatient now. She checked her watch and tapped her foot.

'Don't worry, Margot, I blame myself for that every single minute.' I'd sealed Sylvia's fate by talking shop outside of work. I'd broken the rules and someone had died because of it. It was a dark lesson to learn.

'Relax, Eve. I'll relieve you of your guilty burden. We can both have closure.' She raised the gun.

It was now or never. I sprung up and slung myself over the side of the boat just as a shot rang out. Pain sliced through my arm as I hit the water and tumbled under. The sea was freezing after being in the midday heat and I lost my breath with the shock of it. But I ploughed through the water, hoping no more bullets would find their mark.

Bang! I suddenly hit the base of the boat with my head and I almost choked out the little air I had left in my lungs. I determinedly pushed on and came up on the other side of *Floozy*. I hugged the side of her hull, sucking in huge gulps of air, trying to steady myself. I peered upwards. Margot was racing from one side of the boat to the other, leaning over the rails, trying to locate me.

My head hurt from hitting the hull and blood was trickling down my arm. I hoped there were no stray sharks around to get tempted by the blood. I quietly swam towards the rope ladder Quinn had left dangling and climbed up, slithering and slipping on to the deck. It was hard when my arm burned from the bullet, but I managed it without alerting Margot. I reached under the life-ring and found the gun I'd hidden there earlier. It was one of several I'd planted around the boat as a precaution. I cocked it ready to fire and stealthily tiptoed towards Margot, water and blood sluicing off me all the way.

'Hold it there, Margot. Drop the gun.'

'I underestimated you,' she said as she slowly began to raise her – my – gun instead of dropping it.

'I'll shoot,' I said.

'Go ahead, darl. So will I.' She suddenly swung the gun upwards. I fired as another shot rang out. The impact knocked her backwards into the sea.

I ran over to the rail. She raised her gun again at me and fired as she went under. At the same moment a body smashed into me and sent me flying on to the deck.

Quinn!

He landed heavily on top of me and I gasped for breath. I glanced down and saw blood streaking across my bare breasts.

'Well, it crossed my mind we might exchange body fluids,' said Quinn with an ironic gleam in his eyes as he too stared at the blood. 'But I hadn't expected it to be that sort. Are you okay?'

'I will be when you get off me.'

He grunted as he rolled off me and I realised that it wasn't only my blood smeared all over me but his too. Margot's bullet had hit him in the shoulder as he'd pushed me down.

'You've been shot.'

'So have you, sweetheart.'

'You'll make a good detective one day,' I said.

'You too.' He grinned but it was more of a grimace.

I wiggled out from underneath him and grabbed the almond oil-soaked towel, padding it up and holding it hard to stem the blood flow from his wound. My own arm was red, but I wasn't bleeding as copiously as Quinn.

I left him to look over the rail at the water. Margot's body floated just under the surface of the water, her bare arms and legs a ghoulish green with red staining the surface. She was staring up at the sky, like a giant starfish. I doubt if she could see anything.

Police and ambulance were already amassing on the wharf. Emergency officers were running towards us. I waved and yelled at them to keep back.

'We've got to get off this boat,' I said to Quinn.

'What's the rush?'

'I think Margot's planted a bomb. Get moving.'

'You go.' Quinn began fossicking behind one of his many panels in the side of the boat, cursing that his injured arm wouldn't work properly. Blood was dripping at his feet. I had a similar red pool at mine.

'Quinn, what the hell are you doing? We haven't got time!'

'I'm with you, Red.' He wrenched out a small electronic box with wires sprouting from it in all directions and pushed me towards the gangplank.

'You were taping us?'

'Evidence.'

'When did you organise that?'

'The whole boat was taped for the drugs' operation. I activated it before I left.'

We jumped on to the wharf and I was suddenly horribly aware of my unfettered, bouncing breasts as we ran towards the emergency services and the curious eyes of too many of my male colleagues.

'Damn, I should have grabbed my shirt!'

'Not on my account,' chuckled Quinn. 'But you can have mine.'

As we ran, he unbuttoned the blood-soaked garment and clumsily slung it around my shoulders. Between us we only had one pair of arms that worked.

We were maybe a hundred metres or so from the boat when there was an almighty boom. *Floozy* exploded and rained fire and debris all over us.

'Has anyone ever told you that you're an exciting woman to be around, Red?' said Quinn, hauling me into relative safety behind an ambulance.

'Not recently.'

He yanked together the unbuttoned sides of his shirt over my blood-smeared breasts and planted a swift sure kiss on my lips.

'Well, I'm telling you now.'

It was the third kiss of the morning and, like the others, it was far too brief and chaste. I lifted my one good arm to snake around his neck and hauled him towards me so I could demonstrate what a proper kiss was really like. There were more explosions, but this time they were in my belly. Heat streaked through my entire body. I finally unstuck my lips.

'Remember in future,' I said. 'When you kiss me, kiss me properly.'

Quinn's eyes were the colour of turbulent deep sea so I knew I'd stirred him up good and proper.

'Yeah, DI Rock, I'll try and remember,' he said and we both grinned.

23

WE WERE CHECKED OVER AND PATCHED UP IN HOSPITAL AND THEN discharged ourselves against doctor's orders.

'Now where?' said Quinn. 'You've blown up your car, your house and my boat. What would you like to have a go at next?'

'Now that's a loaded question.' I batted my lashes at him and he gave a dirty chuckle.

'So?'

'Forget it. I need to buy some clothes first.' I'd had to borrow a dress from one of the nurses. 'I don't think floral pastel hues are my scene.'

'I don't know. You look kind of cute in that gear.'

'Suddenly I wish I had my gun.'

'I'm glad you haven't.' He ruffled my short curls and dropped a kiss on my nose, then mouth, which sort of led to full scale, mind-blowing lip synchronisation of the hottest kind.

'We've got to get out of here,' I said trying to control my sudden spurt of lust.

'What? More bombs?'

'Very funny. You know what I mean.'

'So what do you suggest? We've no home to go to and no credit cards or money to hire a room. Between you and your crazy friend, you've destroyed all our worldly goods.'

Damn. He had a point.

'Of course, we could find an empty private room somewhere in this hospital,' he said.

Now there was a thought. I grinned, 'Good thinking.'

'Except I can see DS Ely bearing down on us.'

I shut my eyes in frustration.

Quinn laughed and gave me a hug.

'It can wait.'

For him, maybe, but I'd had a roller coaster three weeks and I could do with some major stress relief.

Ely was carrying a bottle of red wine.

'You look sweet, DI Rock. You should wear flowery frocks more often.'

'Careful, Ely. She's already threatened to shoot me for saying something similar.'

Ely grinned and held out the bottle.

'You won the bet,' he said. 'Murder, not suicide. I bow to your superior knowledge.'

'Thank you, Ely. We'll go and crack it with the others. But first I need to shop.'

'Typical woman,' said Ely.

'First item on my list is a .38 Smith and Wesson, and I'll use it on you if you don't watch that mouth.'

'I apologise, DI Rock.'

'Well, it'll cost you another bottle of wine. And I need some cash.'

We shopped for clothes and essentials for both Quinn and myself and then headed for headquarters where we celebrated the wrap up of the case. I pushed myself to join in the high spirits but the truth of it was I was sad and disappointed Margot had been our murderer. I'd lost a friend and confidant, as well as a good neighbour.

And then I glanced over to where Quinn was leaning against the doorjamb, a little out of the proceedings but watchful and alert. His eyes cut to mine and his lips lifted in the slightest of smiles, warm and intimate, and I thought perhaps I'd scored a new friend, a lover even, instead.

The week flew by as the paperwork was dealt with and Hugo Maine's hard boys were arrested and charged with attempted murder and arson. Margot's funeral was organised. My personal paperwork – ordering new credit cards, driver's license and filing insurance for my car and house – went cheek by jowl with my mad Christmas shopping frenzy.

There wasn't much time to see Quinn. He was working on getting *Wild Thing* out of dry dock and putting back together his life after I'd destroyed it.

I moved into Saint Immaculata's. It was the only logical place for me to go until I could work out what I was going to do about my lack of housing. Dom Ferrari was all for building me a new one. I had my reservations.

Chastity press-ganged me into making mince pies and sticking together loads of colourful streamers to decorate the common room. I couldn't do much, because my arm was in a sling but she was content to have me there so she could chat to me endlessly.

'This is going to be the best Christmas ever,' she said hanging baubles and tinsel on the tree. 'I'm so happy. You, Gran and I will have a real family Christmas for once.'

'Actually, we're going to have a couple of guests,' I said. 'Didn't Gran tell you?'

'No, who?' She eyed me suspiciously.

Where to start?

'You know the man who saved me from jumping off the roof?'

'Santa?'

'Well, it turns out he's my father,' I said in a rush. It took a bit of explaining but Chastity was okay about it. Concerned and curious, but reasonably okay.

That was the first hurdle.

'Anybody else?' she said.

'I haven't told Gran yet, but I've invited Adam Fox…'

'That cute cop? Oh, thanks, Mum.'

'I didn't do it for you,' I said sternly. 'I need to explain something very, very important to you.'

'What? You want him for yourself?'

'No, Chastity. I do not. Adam is coming with his dad because –'

'Father Fox,' she said happily. 'How nice.'

'Who's Father Fox?' asked the Iron Nun coming into the common room at that exact moment. 'Is he Catholic or Anglican?'

'I don't know,' said Chastity. 'He's a friend of Mum's and he's coming to have Christmas with us.'

'That's nice. And if he's dating your mother, he must be Anglican. Or at least I hope he is.' She raised her brows questioningly.

She wasn't asking on purely religious grounds, but practical. An Anglican priest hadn't made a vow of celibacy. She was hoping there was a slim chance I would finally get married.

'Actually, Mum, I don't know what religion he is.' Call me chicken, but it was the truth. I just failed to deliver the crucial information that he wasn't a fully paid up member of the dog-collar fraternity.

'Are you dating him? Is he as hunky as Adam? Do you like him?' Chastity asked in her typical rapid questioning technique.

'What is this? Immaculata Mastermind? Get on with decorating the tree or I'm out of here.' I'd lost the window of opportunity to come clean. The coward in me rejoiced, but I knew I was on borrowed time.

By the end of the week I was becoming increasingly worried about the looming Christmas lunch and it wasn't just because I wanted to have the turkey and trimmings done to a turn. I still hadn't had a chance to tell Chastity and the Iron Nun about Quinn.

Actually, I'd had plenty of time, but my nerve kept failing me. What a wuss.

All too soon it was the big day and our guests turned up bearing gifts. Henry Talbot was first. He was shy and diffident, but Chastity made him feel instantly welcome, bless her cotton socks, even if the Iron Nun wasn't quite so forthcoming.

I hadn't had much chance to talk to Henry over the past few days, but I hoped we would get to know each other well. It was a New Year resolution.

Then Quinn and Fox arrived – two blond hunks in crisp cotton shirts and pressed jeans. They made a striking duo. Fox had a bunch of red and white carnations. He gave them to me and kissed me on the cheek.

'To my favourite lady,' he murmured.

I admit to a deep pang in my heart for what couldn't – well, *shouldn't* – be. Not if I was a good girl. I just had to get my relationship with Adam Fox into perspective. I'd decided to look at it this way: I fancied Brad Pitt, right? But that didn't mean I was going to do anything about it. Foxy was in the same sort of category.

But then Quinn stepped forward into the limelight and the pang was forgotten. The same sort of rules did not apply with Quinn. He was in a class of his own and the possibilities were endless.

His arm, like mine, was still immobilised in a sling. He smiled deep into my eyes and for a wild moment I thought he was going to drag me to him and kiss me senseless. The daydream passed as Sister Immaculata rushed towards Quinn, her hands outstretched.

'Father Fox,' she said, 'it is so good to meet you. I'm so happy that my daughter has finally brought a nice man into the family.'

Quinn's brows rose so high they were almost lost in his thick blond hair.

'There must be some mistake. I'm no priest, ma'am,' he said in his trademark blunt way.

'Not a priest?'

'I'm a cop.'

'Oh.'

The world iced over with that one word.

'I think you have some explaining to do, Eve,' she said frostily.

Too right. But now? No way!

I did rapid introductions and then filled glasses with wine and handed them around.

'Here's to family reunions,' said Quinn, clinking his glass against mine. The puzzled faces of my mother and daughter confirmed his suspicions. He shook his head and tut-tutted. 'You haven't told them yet, have you, Red?'

'Told us what,' said Sister Immaculata.

It was about now that I could have done with something exploding. The Christmas turkey, perhaps? Or the pudding. Either would do the trick. I felt a sudden surge of sympathy for that Dutch kid who'd held a finger over the hole in the dyke to keep back the flood. When I opened my mouth, all hell would be let loose. And there'd be no going back.

I took a deep breath.

'It's complicated,' I said with great understatement and Quinn chuckled. He clinked my glass again.

'Amen to that,' he said.

ABOUT THE AUTHOR

Sarah Evans, an English ex-pat journalist and former home-schooling mum, is the author of a lifestyle/recipe book *Seasons and Seasonings in a Teapot*, romance and crime novels, novellas, short stories and poetry.

She gives author talks and teaches memoir, creative writing, poetry and song-writing. She lives on a 20-acre hobby farm in rural Western Australia with her family and a menagerie of fur and feather and has added granny duties to her repertoire.

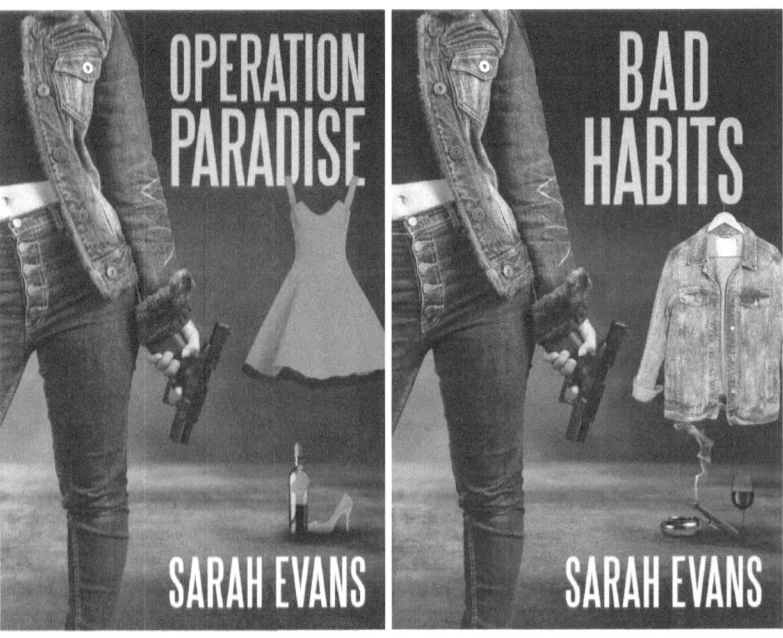